ONE SORCERER AND A SACRIFICE

CAIT AMBROSE

I

My living room looked like the chick from the Exorcist had gone full "fuck me, father" on the moth-eaten sofa. The coffee table was an inexplicable clutter of items I didn't care to identify, the carpeting scarred from cigarette burns and stained with fluid that I hoped was tomato juice and vodka but might've been blood.

In short, exactly the type of mess I didn't want to return to after a twelve-hour shift serving skeezebags at the Devil's Share—a back street bar in the Lower Ninth Ward that was my place, but not choice, of work.

And that's a Tuesday night, folks.

I inhaled through my nose, trying to bring myself back from the brink of rage, and instantly regretted it.

The place didn't just *look good*. Scents clung to the humid New Orleans air trapped in the building—a thin layer of filth that clogged the nostrils.

"Debbie!" I yelled.

My roommate had to be home. When I'd left this afternoon, the apartment had been in its usual, desexed state of chaos. Nothing like this.

A groan emanated from behind the sofa.

I strode around it, grimacing at the occasional squelch of blood-slash-tomato-juice underfoot.

Debbie lay face down, wearing nothing but an oversized shirt, her cheek pressed into the carpeting, her eyelids fluttering, bushy brown hair tangled into a bird's nest. Her pale fingers scraped along the ground seeking something.

Probably a cigarette or another drink.

If I hadn't had to live with this woman for the past year, I would've called 911.

Instead, I bumped her with the toe of my boot. "Get up," I said. "Get up and start cleaning, right now."

Another groan.

"It's 5:00 a.m. Billy's coming in two hours." It was inspection day.

Last month we'd barely managed to make rent—Debbie had scraped together her half through means I didn't question. And her continuous partying, the unearthly noises at all hours of the night, the music that kept the entire apartment building up hadn't done us any favors. We were on our last leg with our landlord, and if he found the apartment in this state, we were officially doneso.

While Debbie probably had an equally greasy friend's apartment to sleep at, I didn't. I had nothing, and no one, and only enough money in my account to cover a coffee and a granola bar.

The folks at the Devil's Share didn't tip well, and the bar didn't offer commission.

"—I don't want to go to church," Debbie mumbled, her bloodshot eyes drifting open and shut.

"As if they'd take you. The entire place would burst into flames the minute you stepped over the threshold."

This wasn't how life was meant to be for a regular twenty-one-year-old. Most girls my age had started college or taken up cute preppy jobs at their father's firm or were waiting tables because it helped pay for their education.

Most of them had parents, though, to be fair.

I extracted a hair tie from the pocket of my leather jacket and used it to pull my purple locks into a messy bun.

"Don't make me do this, Debbie."

"—Santa Claus," she squeaked.

I bent and grabbed her by the shirt sleeve, grimacing at the unseen cooties undoubtedly plastered all over it. I tugged her over onto her back, legs flopping with two tremendous thumps. Her head rolled, and she sniffled.

"Everybody wants a piece of me," Debbie whimpered, temporarily lucid. Or was it a bizarrely accurate fever dream?

"OK, Britney. I want to sympathize with you, but I'm guessing the whole orgy thing was your idea." I charged through to our tiny kitchenette and filled a glass with water. I returned and doused her in it. "Up!"

"What are you, crazy?" she whined, pushing sodden hair from her forehead—or trying to. Her hand missed and rammed into her nose instead. "Trying to get some sleep here."

"Get up," I repeated.

Her bloodshot eyes met mine, bleary but full of the heat of a drunkard scorned. "What is your problem?"

"You," I said. "I've made that pretty obvious."

"No, you know what your problem is?" The word problem came out as 'prolim.' "You don't get spanked enough. I told you, you should come to one of our parties. Try living life instead of chasing it, y'know."

"Surprisingly eloquent for someone in a half-corpse state," I replied, anger tunneling through my gut. I forced myself to take deep breaths. "Billy is coming."

"Oh yeah?"

"Yeah."

"How do you know that?" Debbie asked. "Just because he's a man don't mean he's up at all hours of the morning choking the monkey."

I considered getting another glass of water to wash the nastiness from my roommate, but that was like spritzing water into the mouth of an open volcano and expecting it to freeze over. She was too far gone.

To Debbie, subtlety was a town in Texas, and chastity was a friend from the strip club.

For the millionth time, I questioned how I'd wound up in this situation.

The scrape of keys penetrating our apartment door's lock cut through my melancholy.

It was already too late.

Billy, destroyer of hopes and dreams, hater of renters who couldn't pay their keep, eater of jelly donuts, twenty millionth of his name, had come early. Of course, he was early. And of course, he'd let himself in. He loved catching people off guard.

Mrs. Hicklebaum down the hall had told me she'd woken to him standing over her bed one morning holding a dead rat. Long story.

"Debbie, you—"

The door crashed open, and Billy entered our living room, Naruto Shippuden t-shirt stained with blueberry jelly. Good taste in shirt, bad taste in jelly. Our landlord paused, swinging a ring of keys from his chubby index finger, beady eyes narrowed at the dildo collection on the coffee table.

"Looks like I missed the party," he wheezed.

"Billy," I started. "I can explain."

"Oh yeah?" Billy waddled over to me then spotted Debbie supine on the floor. He froze, going pale. "What the hell is this? Some kind of sexual incident?"

"Look, it's early," I said. "And I've had a really long night. Can you just cut us a little slack?"

"What happened to her?" Billy asked.

"I haven't brought myself to ask the details."

"Is she dead? Did you do this to her?"

"That would be a no, and a hell no," I replied, trying to place myself between him and my grumbling roommate.

"So she doesn't need medical assistance."

"Possibly," I said. "I'm sure she appreciates you asking."

Debbie had sunk back into a stupor now that she didn't have to argue the pros and cons of participating in mass sexual acts. "I want to be a fairy princess," she called, her voice sounding disembodied.

Don't we all. "This isn't a good time for an inspection, Billy," I said. "I think I need to take Debbie here to a hospital. Could you come back later, please?"

Billy wriggled his nose and looked around. "Naw. You're out."

"What?" My insides clenched. "Hold up. Wait a second. Look, you can see that obviously something bad happened here, right? I wasn't around for it, but if I had been, I would've stopped it. Could you just… Look, I have nowhere else to go. Could you give me a couple hours to get things worked out here? I guarantee by the time you come back, I'll have the place spotless."

"Doubt it." Billy sniffed. "That's tomato juice. Bitch to get out the carpet. Your security deposit's already depleted. So, no, honey, I ain't gonna do that. I've gotten thirty-five complaints about this particular apartment over the last two weeks alone. Y'all are done."

"Wait, wait, wait." I squelched over to him, made a grab for his forearm then thought better of it. His arms were hidden beneath a mat of thick black hair, tangled with sweat. "Just wait for a second," I said. "We can work this out." I reached into the front pocket of my jeans and took out the measly twenty dollars I'd earned in tips. "Look, I'll pay you to give us another chance, OK?"

Billy stopped, wriggling his lips from side-to-side, his thin wisp of a mustache dancing. "You think twenty bucks is going to make up for months of bullshit from you two? I'll give you your notice this afternoon, and you'll have three days to get out."

"Three days! That's… how am I supposed to find another place to stay in three days?"

"Not my problem." Billy shrugged. "Three days' notice is the law, honey. You get out within three days or I file an eviction lawsuit." He gave a faux tip of an invisible fedora then high-tailed it to the door. It shut behind him.

Debbie let out another moan from behind the ruined sofa and followed it up with a retching noise.

I stood there, frozen, breathing hard.

What the hell was I supposed to do now?

2

That night...

"SO WHAT ARE you going to do?" Julia asked as she poured a beer for a customer.

The Devil's Share reeked of stale alcohol and lost dreams. I fit right in, unfortunately. Regardless, the bar was the last place I wanted to be right now, but without another source of income, I didn't have a choice.

"What am I going to do," I said, tying my bright purple hair into a high ponytail. Tonight's outfit was standard bar wear—a white tank top, faded blue jeans, and a pair of skull-stomping high heel boots that elevated me above the sticky stained floors. "What am I going to do? That's a great question."

"You don't know." Julia, a mom of two with problems of her own, raised an eyebrow. She was protective of me, but there was nothing she could do to help. Not that I'd let her.

"I don't know," I said. "I have no fucking idea. Debbie's really screwed the pooch this time, and I've got to magic an apartment out of thin air. With no money."

"I'd offer you the couch—"

"Don't even say that, Julia." I cut her off before she got going. "You've got your own shit to deal with."

"True. But what about your parents?"

I shook my head. I hadn't discussed my past with Julia or anyone else. How was she supposed to know that *it* had happened.

"Sorry, honey. I wish I could help you." Julia swept off to deliver the beer to her customer, offering me a sympathetic look on her way.

I scanned the interior of the bar, my gaze lingering on the darkened table in the corner. Every time I came to the bar, I got the feeling that something was missing there. Like, if I turned and looked again there'd be a... a something. Or someone?

That's great, Evie. That's great. Go crazy. That'll make everything better.

By 9:00 p.m., the bar had grown marginally busy. The regulars were here, including Gordon, who frequently fell asleep on the bar and forgot to pay his tab. He let out a rough snore once in a while, barely audible over the music pumping from the jukebox in the corner.

I moved from table to table, taking orders, cleaning messes, delivering refills. Nights like these, where it was quiet, were my favorite—in the loosest sense of the word. When it was just regulars, I was less likely to be hit on or have my ass grabbed, and, subsequently less likely to break a guy's finger.

And I couldn't afford to get on my boss's bad side again. I

was on my last warning for accosting the customers. Was it really me accosting them when I was the one having my cheeks squeezed?

Regardless, this gig was the only one I had left, and I didn't have a lot of references. Most of my jobs had lasted all of three months. The longest, here, had gone on for six.

I'd been cursed with bad luck from the day I was born.

It'd started with my name.

Guinevere Crowley.

Who the hell named their kid Guinevere? A sicko, that was who, and the Crowley part? Yeah, the only Crowley I knew of, thanks to a quick internet browse during a coffee-fueled anxiety attack, was a famed occultist with a thousand-yard-stare and a seriously shitty hairstyle.

Going by the nickname Evie hadn't changed my luck.

Weird things happened around me, and I'd slowly come to accept that. Stoves setting themselves on fire, mannequins moving when I wasn't looking, windows shattering of their own accord. I was like the less cool, less PG version of Harry Potter. Except I didn't live with muggles. I'd have taken Petunia Dursley over Debbie the drunkard any day.

But this? Being kicked out of my apartment when I was flat broke? This shit took the cake, man.

Gordon stirred from his slumber and stuck a finger in the air.

"What's up, Gordon?" I asked.

He grumbled something indistinct from beneath his beard hairs. If I was the less PG Harry Potter, then this guy was the incredibly drunk, unfortunate-looking, short Hagrid. He stared at me through bleary eyes.

"Gordon?"

"Beer."

I chewed on the corner of my lip, glancing back at my boss's closed door. Joel was here today, probably drunk or high or some combination of the two. Substances did nothing to soothe his temper.

"Gordon, you haven't paid for your tab, and even without that, I wouldn't give you another beer. You've had enough." He couldn't talk properly or even see me. His gaze was focused over my left shoulder. I wasn't about to let the guy get alcohol poisoning.

"You cutting me off?"

"I'm going to have to," I said. "For your own good." Even though Joel had a rule about not cutting off anyone's tab, no matter how much they drank or owed. He liked people in debt to him.

"You can't do that." And, of course, Gordon knew the rules in the Devil's Share. Namely, there were none. Joel was willing to allow the occasional bar fight in aid of keeping up the bar's sleazy aesthetic.

What are you doing, Evie? It doesn't matter what you do. It's not going to stop him from drinking.

But the truth was, I'd grown increasingly concerned about Gordon's drinking habits. And working in a bar was damn depressing when it came to that. I was hired to fulfill Gordon's prescription, basically.

"No, I can't do that," I sighed. "But I'm going to."

"Don't do it," Julia hissed as she moved past me. "You know that's going to cause trouble."

Maybe it was because of what had happened with Debbie, maybe because I was tired of being a part of the problem, whatever that meant, or maybe I just had a friggin' death wish. "I'm cutting you off," I said firmly.

Gordon growled and lurched from his chair. "You can't do that!" he roared.

The office door slammed open. Joel emerged, all six feet somethin' of him, and he bore down on us. "What the fuck is all that noise?"

"She's trying to cut me off," Gordon said, the words slurring together. "She's trying to cut me off from having a drink."

"Yeah, I think he gets it," I whispered.

"She can't do that." Gordon grunted.

Joel turned on me. "Get out."

I swallowed. "Come on, Joel, you know I'm doing the right thing here. He can barely stand."

"Out. You're done."

"Please.

"Now," my boss yelled, cheeks red. "Before I call the cops on your deadbeat ass."

I would've been mad at the insult, but he wasn't wrong. I'd managed to throw away this job right after losing the apartment. Like an idiot.

I grabbed my stuff from behind the bar, feeling rather than seeing Julia's sympathetic gaze, and made my way out. One look back showed me Gordon resuming his seat and being given a beer. I let myself out into the humid night air, cursing my idiocy.

Was I trying to self-destruct?

3

Three days later...

I SAT on the bottom step of the building, my phone in my hand, and my backpack next to me. It contained all my earthly possessions: underwear, three spare tank tops, white, black, and black, a pair of jeans, a swiss army knife, a tin of cat food, a battle worn copy of *The Complete Gods and Goddesses of Ancient Egypt* by Richard H. Wilkinson, and a solitary tarot card with a guy's number on the back. I had no idea where it'd come from, but I kept it anyway.

I scrolled through the contacts on my phone, pausing on a few of them, thumb hovering over the dial button.

But I didn't hit it—none of the folks I knew needed a freeloader sleeping on their sofa for the next couple of months. And apartments within my price range were non-existent at the moment.

Sweat beaded on the back of my neck in the Louisiana sunshine. I couldn't just sit here. I had to *do* something.

Think. Think. Think.

A meow from the alleyway between the apartment building and the tattoo place next-door drew my attention. My heart turned over.

It was the momma alley cat I'd been feeding since I'd started living here. I'd named her Bastet and watched her care for her kittens, even though I couldn't officially take her under my wing. No animals allowed in the apartments.

"Hey," I said and offered her a smile.

Bastet wandered over and twined between my legs, purring. She was skinny, but not too skinny. I'd spotted her scavenging in the dumpster and feeding herself, so I was pretty sure she'd be OK without my help. Hopefully.

But still, I'd miss her.

"I'm leaving," I said. "I think. Heck, I might join you in the alley if I can't find another place to stay."

Bastet meowed in what I liked to assume was encouragement and rammed her black furry forehead into the palm of my hand.

"I've got something for you." I brought out the tin of cat food I'd stuck in my backpack and opened it with my swiss army knife. A woman's best friend. I ensured the edges of the tin weren't sharp, then set it down for Bastet.

She ate greedily, purring.

"Maybe I'll come back once in a while. Once I get another job and can afford cat food. It's not cheap. Not that I'm blaming you or anything."

And now, I'm having a full-on conversation with a cat.

I shut my eyes for a second, seeking relief from the searing sun and my hopeless state.

A sharp *pop* sounded.

I opened my eyes. "What the—?" The street was empty, and the noise had been more of a crack than the pop of a gunshot.. Bastet streaked toward the alleyway.

Something flopped onto my head and slid off it. I reached up, trying to grab whatever it was, but it fell into my lap before I got the chance.

A thick, cream envelope rested against my thighs. My name was written across the front of it in stark black lettering. Handwritten in thick slashes, like the writer had been angry about having to pen it.

I blinked.

Had this... No. There was no way this letter had just dropped out of nowhere, right?

I looked up at the clear blue sky, then turned to glare at the windows up the side of the building. It was two stories high, and a few of those windows were open. Maybe it was one of the tenants, throwing out one last reprimand before I left?

Has to be.

I considered the letter.

Guinevere Crowley.

The only person in this building who knew my full name was the landlord, and I highly doubted Billy was much of a writer. Besides, there were no jelly stains on the envelope.

Intrigue built in my chest.

I cleared my throat, inhaled, grimaced at the influx of heat, then flipped the envelope over, hiding my name and revealing the rounded lip on its back.

A golden image was stamped across it—a man seated

between two pillars, wearing an Egyptian headdress. Two children knelt either side of his feet.

My skin prickled.

What the hell?

I traced the image with my fingers and felt nothing but the smoothness of the paper envelope beneath it. It was almost a shame to wreck it, but I tugged on the loose lip of paper, slipped my finger underneath, and ripped it open.

I reached inside and withdrew a thick, cream page folded into a narrow slip.

"OK?"

I unfolded the page and a card fell into my lap. A tarot card. I lifted and flipped it. The same image that had been printed on the envelope stared up at me in shades of gold, orange, and red. The Egyptian priest, seated on a chair, two children kneeling either side of him. Words were printed on the gold border of the card.

The Hierophant.

"What the hell?" A second mystery tarot card. I flipped it over, but the patterned back—black with golden hiero-glyphics—held no further information.

I set the card on my lap then turned to the letter that'd come with it.

You are cordially invited to attend court at the Hierophant Society.

Dress code: Black tie only.

You are required to bring your tarot card enclosed herewith to the address that follows, at 9:00 p.m. sharp, June 25th.

Punctuality is paramount.

Court will begin promptly at 9:30 p.m.

And beneath it, an address listed on St. Charles Avenue,

which happened to be one of the richest streets in New Orleans, lined with mansions, filled with people who'd barely notice my existence if I strolled by their equally fancy cars in the street.

There was no signature at the bottom of the letter. I turned it over, but the back was empty of text.

"What the fuck? Am I unironically Harry Potter now?"

I snorted.

A black tie event. Me?

But what the hell else did I have to do tonight? And the tarot card being styled with hieroglyphics and Egyptian figures intrigued me. At worst, I'd encounter a couple cult weirdos—tarot and all that jazz—and at best, I'd find a fancy garden shed or particularly comfortable flower bed to sleep in for the night.

A feeling I associated with all the unexplainable events I'd encountered over the course of my life rose inside me.

I turned the tarot card over and stared at the image on the front, the hair on my arms rising.

THE EVENING SETTLED AGAINST MY SKIN LIKE A WARM, unwelcome coat. It was silky and hot, my sweat trapped by the humidity. It was the kind of night where you could shower, towel dry, and wind up wetter than you'd been under the faucet.

I hovered near an old live oak tree, its leaves clustering overhead, shading me from the light of the ornate lampposts that lined St. Charles Avenue. Streetcar tracks ran through the center of the avenue, but the line was quiet for now. In a few minutes, though, a car would whine down the track, ferrying tourists past the mansions.

I loved this part of the city. For a couple of minutes, I was young again, wide-eyed, unaware that life was about to kick me in the teeth and giggle like a psychopath when I got up again for another round.

I turned my gaze to the mansion, my hand moving to the pocket of my jeans where the tarot card and invitation waited.

Was I really going to do this?

It had taken me an hour of walking and hitchhiking to get out here—buses were out of the question, given that I had a total of forty dollars to my name.

So, it was find out more about the card or nothin'. And man, I was tired of nothing.

Was it ridiculous to be out here on a whim? Yeah. But I was impulsive like that, at least when it came to my curiosity.

I checked the time on my phone.

8:59 p.m.

Fuck. OK. Let's do this. Let's Harry Potter this shit.

The mansion itself was a gorgeous triple story home with two castle-like towers. White columns on the porch sat either side of a grand door that was shut tight. The decorative window above it displayed a glimmer of the opulence within —a crystal chandelier, delicately lit and sparkling.

A garden, overgrown but in the well-cared for, purposeful way, separated the front of the house from the wrought iron gates and stone columns. An intercom sat against the rough stone, but it wouldn't be needed tonight.

A beast of a guy wearing a silk suit stood behind those gates. He didn't have any weapons that I could see, but I'd learned not to take people at face value. Where I came from, everybody had an angle, agenda, and a weapon.

I stopped in front of the gates.

The beastly guy looked me up and down, narrowing one eye. Light from the house glinted over his bald head. "This is a private party," he said.

"Invitation only, right?" I dug the tarot card out of my pocket and held it up between two fingers, showing off the front image. "Yeah, I got that."

The bouncer smirked. "Where you find the card, girl?"

"Does it matter?" I asked. "I got it, don't I?"

"Oh, you gone get it, all right," he replied, still grinning, showing off a gap between his two front teeth. "Well come on in, sweetheart." He opened one of the gates and held it for me. "Welcome to the Hierophant Society."

No complaints about my lack of black-tie attire. That was good and also alarming.

The bouncer pressed a finger to his ear. "Miss Braddock. I got a guest down here for you. She, uh, she a little different, if you catch my drift."

I hadn't crossed the threshold yet, and I teetered.

What are you going to do? Turn around?

I sucked in a breath, feeling as if I was on the brink of something great? Ominous? Finally, I entered the grounds. The gate clanged shut behind me.

The bouncer studied me with no small amount of cynicism. "Like I said, sweetheart, you go on up to the house. Miss Braddock will be right down to deal with you."

"Nobody deals with me," I replied, then walked down the garden path, my boot heels tapping on the brick paving.

I reached the porch just as the front door flung outward

and a leggy woman with dark skin and bright red hair emerged onto the porch. She wore a black velvet dress that clung to her curves, a long slit up its side revealing the lace pantyhose underneath.

She folded her arms, her long silk gloves up to her elbows, and studied me, full lips pursed and crimson red.

"Who are you?" she asked, waspishly, her accent tinged British.

"I was invited." I lifted the tarot card again.

"Give me that." She snatched it from my fingers and turned it over, checking the back. Seemingly satisfied, she thrust it toward me again. "This is a private party. No normies allowed."

"Normie? What are you, a music snob? I received an invitation." I lifted my chin.

"You're not dressed for court."

None of this made sense, but I wasn't about to tell this chick that I didn't know why I'd been invited, or what the Hierophant Society was.

I'd always felt a part of me was missing, a piece of history that didn't quite make sense or gel with the rest. Or maybe it was that fervent hope that I could change who my parents were or what they'd done. That I could disconnect from this life and find another.

Being at this unknown, dangerous house, with nothing to lose, with no ties to any of the people here, was better than slogging through another day or sleeping on a park bench.

The woman, Miss Braddock, I assumed, studied me, weighing and measuring, her eyes so keen they might as well have been probes. "What is your name?" she asked, after a long silence.

"Evie."

"Your full name."

Fuck that. "Evie Crowley."

"Let me see your invitation."

I considered flipping her off and making the long walk back to the Lower Ninth Ward. There was nothing for me there, but it was better than dealing with these uppity Garden District assholes. Probably didn't think they had a New Orleans accent.

Anything's better than what you've got. Anything's better than this life.

The thoughts came out of nowhere, and I nearly paled at the strangeness of them. I ripped the note I'd received this morning out of my pocket and thrust it toward the woman.

She took it, flicked it open and read it. "Guinevere Crowley." A sharkish grin parted those full lips. "Well, why didn't you say so?"

"I did."

"Right this way." She folded the letter again, drawing perfectly manicured nails over the edges of the page. Miss Braddock turned on her designer heels and entered the mansion.

4

THE INTERIOR of the mansion was exactly what I'd expected.

Opulence, chandelier light, teal walls, dark wood, and the distant chatter and music of a party in full swing down the hall. Miss Braddock didn't lead me toward the party but swayed her hips up a set of stairs instead. She paused only briefly, waiting impatiently for me to catch up before moving off again.

We wound deeper into the mansion, the sounds of revelry dying behind us. Though we headed upward via a hidden twisty staircase, a narrow hallway, and yet another staircase, I got the distinct impression that we were moving into the belly of the beast.

"Where are you taking me?" I asked, not expecting an answer.

"To see Mr. Sword," my escort replied. "As I do with every irregularity in the society."

"Irregularity!" I took offense to that. I mean, I *was* irregular to her, maybe, and sure, I hadn't worn a fucking cocktail dress, but this was a good faux leather jacket. The best very little money could buy.

After years of being rejected by just about everyone I'd met, I wasn't about to take that 'irregularity' comment lying down. Hell, the only reason I was here was because I had nothing better to do.

Irregularity my ass. I'm not the one sending people tarot cards.

By the sixth flight of stairs, it hit me. We'd gone up way higher than three stories, but when we passed the windows, now sparsely situated along walls lit by the occasional sconce, they showed the garden far below, the bouncer in his silk suit a small speck. Too far down.

What the fuck?

"Here," Miss Braddock said, pausing in front of a thick wooden door with an ornate golden handle. She knocked once and waited.

"Come." The voice sent a shiver through the center of my chest. It was deep, masculine, powerful.

And apparently, I haven't gotten any action in a while.

Braddock opened the door and entered, holding it open.

I walked in after her and met the gaze of what I could only describe as the jock movie villain in every angsty teenaged rom com ever produced.

Crystal blue eyes, pale skin, blond hair coiffed just so, a jawline that could crack a rock, and a black suit with a black buttoned shirt beneath it. He was probably a couple years older than me. Pushing twenty-five?

"Zoey," he said, his gaze cutting toward Miss Braddock. "What on earth have you brought me?" His accent was American, the gentle tinge of Louisiana twisting his words.

She strutted forward and placed my invitation on the desk in front of him. She tapped it once.

"Ah. I see. Thank you. I'll summon you if I need you to take care of her."

"What the hell does that mean?" I asked.

Zoey cringed openly and shot me a look that was pure acid. "Of course, Mr. Sword." She left the room and shut the door with a soft click.

Mr. Sword interlaced his fingers and balanced his chin atop them. He scrutinized me, from my purple hair to my fake leather jacket, to the tips of my stained boots.

"Mr. Sword?" I arched an eyebrow. "Is that a metaphor for something? Or are you overcompensating?"

He inhaled through his nose, expression impassive. "Guinevere Crowley."

"I take it it's your turn to mock my name. Lay it on me."

"My name is Nathan Sword."

"Oh shit, that's your real last name? And I thought I was screwed." I grimaced.

The room—a study—was furnished in antiques. A massive desk, a bookcase groaning under the weight of gold, black, brown, and red-backed tomes. Ornate stiff-backed chairs waited in the corners, looking about as appetizing to sit on as a pin cushion. The floor was polished to perfection too.

A lair. That's what it was.

"You're here by mistake," he said, tapping the invitation. "Did you receive a card with this letter?"

"I did."

"May I see it, please?"

"Sure." I took it out of my pocket, thrown off guard by his

politeness. He was super hot, but I preferred men who had a little edge to them. Grit.

I placed the card on the desk.

Nathan peered at it but didn't pick it up. "I see what's happened here," he said. "We've made a clerical error."

"Oh yeah?"

"You weren't meant to be invited," he said.

"I highly doubt there's another Guinevere Crowley in the Lower Ninth Ward," I replied, my impatience growing by the second.

This whole place had thrown me off my game, from the ominous comments the bouncer had made, to Miss Bitch in the heels, and the ten too many staircases in the triple story mansion. The obstinate part of me—one of the largest parts, granted—wanted to know what the hell was going on.

"The Lower Ninth Ward." Nathan's sneer was one I'd seen plenty throughout my life. "I see. Unfortunately, we don't accept just anyone into the Hierophant Society. And certainly not your type."

"My type?" I cracked my knuckles. "Oh, forgive me, you mean someone who wasn't born smoking a silver spoon?"

"I'm sorry," Nathan said, primly, folding the letter then placing the tarot card on top of it. "But I'm afraid I'm going to have to ask you to leave."

I clenched my jaw.

He was rejecting *me* after inviting me here? Making me follow High Heels Hannah up twenty million inexplicable staircases? I don't think so. "You're lying," I said.

Nathan's expression darkened, and there was that edge I'd been looking for. It somehow turned his 'Chad' look into a much more attractive, gritty 'Troy.'

"Look," I said, sauntering forward and placing a hand atop his rich-boy desk, "I know you're probably a pro-manure salesman, but I've spent a lifetime shoveling shit, and I'm not buying what you're selling. Furthermore, I didn't hoof it up twenty million stairs only to find out you want me to walk all the way back down again for no reason. I've met my cardio quota for the week, so how about you cut the crap and tell me why you invited me to this party. Failing that, how you managed to make a 'clerical error' like this."

Nathan surveyed me like a bug to be squashed under his designer heel. "Errors occur frequently," he said. "They're a natural part of human existence, unfortunately. I assure you, the person who invited you will be dealt with swiftly."

Why did that make my hair stand on end? "What is this place?" I asked.

"It's a society," Nathan said. "As you know. And an exclusive one. I'm afraid I can't offer you more information than that unless you're a part of the society."

"And how do I join?"

"By invitation."

"I have an invitation."

"An irregular one," he replied, lifting the card and studying it. "Most irregular."

No shit. It wasn't every day that a letter dropped out of mid-air into one's lap. I was still trying to figure that part out —not that I'd tried very hard. It made my skin crawl thinking about it.

Nathan got out of his seat and circled the desk. He towered over me, smelling of spicy cologne, his blue-eyed gaze connecting with mine.

Heat flushed my chest, crawled up my neck toward my cheeks. *Pull yourself together.* He's just a hot, rich guy.

He ran a thumb over his jaw, considering me. "If you'd like to join the society," he said, "there are other ways to get in."

I didn't like his tone. "Good, this should be fun," I said, glaring up at him. "I haven't punched someone in the stomach in a while."

Nathan smirked. "No need for that." He moistened his lips with the tip of his tongue. "I'm looking for an assistant. One who will do everything I say, when I say it. Society members are privy to certain secrets, and the person who becomes my assistant will need to ensure those secrets are kept, no matter the cost."

"And you're just offering me this job because what? You feel sorry for me?"

"You've got fire," he said, laughing. "I like fire."

That same hair-raising sensation I'd had when I'd first received the letter rose inside me again. A certainty that if I said 'yes' to this offer, my life would change, and not necessarily for the better.

Nathan stared me down, waiting for my answer.

"Rather the devil you know," I said. "Thanks, but no thanks." I resigned myself to having wasted my time by coming here, and the fact that I had one helluva a walk back to the Lower Ninth Ward ahead of me.

Nathan caught my arm, and a second wave of heat passed through me. An unnatural crimson burn that started from the point of contact, just below my elbow, and rose quickly toward my shoulder. "Are you sure?"

First, he'd rejected my presence, now he wanted me to stay on as his assistant? He knew my name and nothing else. Other than the fact that I had a poor attitude. I pulled myself out of his grasp, the heat vanishing so quickly I reeled—had I imagined it?

I walked from the room, leaving the tarot card and invitation on the desk, my heart pattering like a rabbit chased by a dog.

Get out before it's too late. It was an irrational thought, but I followed my gut instinct and hurried down the long hall, the door to Nathan's study clicking shut behind me.

5

Storming off had felt cool for approximately one minute and thirty seconds. That was how long the anger and leftover creepiness had lasted before I realized that I was now trapped in a triple-story building going on skyscraper with no way out. There were too many corners and passages and so many staircases that my head swam.

Don't panic. You're fine. This is just some kind of architectural illusion. No biggie.

The wallpaper was that jacquard style shit that only rich people put up, and the red carpeting that ran down the center of the hallway never ended. Whichever way I turned led me down another of those cursed red carpets. I was trapped in the mansion version of *Groundhog Day*, and I'd become increasingly convinced that this fucking red carpet was out to get me. Somehow imbued with Nathan Sword's ill intent.

I figured the best way to get out of this place was heading down, so I hunted out flights of stairs and took them wherever I could. The hallways were narrow then broad, with doorways arching off them, or windows that showed the garden below—no more bouncer or gate.

Panic threatened, but I forced it down.

I'd been in bad situations before. Being lost in some rich asshole's mansion was practically a vacation from regular life.

Errant thoughts dogged my every step.

Invited to a society. Tarot cards. And another tarot card I'd found weeks ago in my pocket—a guy's name and number on the back. Ari. That was the name. When I called the number there, was no answer.

I reached another flight of stairs and made my way down. The hum of people talking nearby told me I was on the right track, but I stumbled, catching myself on the polished balustrade and swaying on the spot.

"What the hell?" I placed a hand to my forehead. I was covered in sweat, hot as a fucking oven. What was this?

Something about this house isn't right.

I steadied myself on the balustrade then walked down the stairs. I stepped into a hall, the fresh breeze from an open window nearby drew my attention. A view of the grassy yard outside. Fuck it, if I couldn't find the front door, I'd climb out here and—

"—and gentlemen," a voice spoke from a set of doors, only slightly ajar, to my right. "It's time we proceed with the night's festivities." It was a male voice, stiff and accented with rich Louisiana. "I'm very excited to announce that we'll be inducting a total of three members to the society this evening. You know all three by now, many of them are your charges. You have watched as they've grown under the tutelage of the fine sorcerers, witches, and teachers at the academy."

I froze.

I heard that wrong.

No. I hadn't.

These society people were on another level of crazy.

I glanced toward the window to my left, the scent of night air drifting in—sweet olive trees and jasmine.

"It's an honor to have watched these applicants grow in strength and in loyalty to the Hierophant Society," the man continued. "I call them forward now to undertake the bonding ritual."

Ritual. OK, now this I've gotta see.

I crept toward the doors and peered through the gap.

Beyond it, groups of people sat at circular tables covered in white tablecloths. The place was decorated beautifully, with lanterns on the tables, their flames flickering low. A polished bar ran the length of the wall, the bartender behind it leaning on it and watching the speaker at the front.

He was tall and blond, just like Nathan, but his eyes were gray, hard as steel. They swept over the gathered people, weighing each of them as he spoke. Whoever this dude was, he emanated power in a way that Mr. Sword upstairs hadn't, even though he was probably the same age or maybe a couple of years older.

"Join me."

Three figures rose from a table at the front. Each one wore a black robe decorated in gold hieroglyphs.

"Remove your robes," the man said.

Dutifully, each of the three figures stripped themselves of robes. They were bare-assed as the day they'd been born. Each paid the speaker rapt attention.

I was starting to get seriously culty vibes from this place. Like, worse than when I'd first received the tarot card.

"Present your cards."

Speak of the devil.

Each of the 'applicants,' as the speaker had called them, withdrew a card. I didn't have to see them to know they would bear the same image as the one on the card I'd received.

The Hierophant.

A quick internet search of the card while I'd made my way over here had told me that it was meant to represent tradition and convention.

"Repeat after me," the speaker said, eyeing each of them.

My dizziness rebounded, and I leaned against the doorjamb.

"I pledge myself to the Hierophant society," the speaker said.

The three applicants repeated his words.

"I pledge my soul. I pledge my magic. I pledge my eternal loyalty with no expectation beyond power, knowledge, and death."

A headache started between my eyes, and I bit down on the inside of my cheek. My vision doubled then returned to normal.

I massaged my temples.

Get out of here. Get the fuck out. This is…

"—forward," the speaker said, gesturing to the man at the start of the line.

He faced the crowd of onlookers, his expression elated, his eyes unfocused.

The speaker's smile was soft, and a scream caught in my

throat. Run! Don't let him touch you. But the words wouldn't come, and there was no meaning to them. Why run? Why?

Bile crawled up the back of my throat. I swallowed.

The speaker took the Hierophant card and placed it against the applicant's skin, right over his heart. And then a swell of something intangible, a sweeping of wind around my body that didn't disturb my clothing or hair.

Brilliant, blue light sparked from the ends of the speaker's fingertips. The card crumbled to dust underneath his touch, and the imprint of the Egyptian Hierophant, the two children kneeling either side of his seat, burned bright blue into the applicant's chest. Swirls of lights surrounded him, emanating from the point of contact between the speaker and the man's skin, and that rush of air intensified.

The applicant cried out and clenched his fists, eyes burning that same actinic blue. Finally, he settled back on his heels, a triumphant smile on his face.

"Welcome, brother," the speaker said.

The wind disappeared, and I slumped against the door, sweat dripping from the end of my nose, my eyes watering, my ears burning.

Magic.

Every fiber of my being wanted to deny that it was real. The stuff of legends. Bullshit. Had to be a trick of the light or the… but no, my gut knew the truth.

I had just witnessed something unnatural. Something that wasn't meant to exist in the real world.

Run.

Panic that had been held at bay by the headache, the dizziness, the weirdness of what I'd witnessed, slammed into my chest. I turned to flee and ran straight into a brawny, suited chest.

Arms surrounded me, an iron encirclement I couldn't escape.

Bright blue eyes looked down into mine. "It looks like you're going to have to be my assistant after all, Miss Crowley," Nathan said.

6

I BALLED up a fist and punched Nathan in the solar plexus with all my might. It was like fisting a brick wall, but his grip on me loosened—incrementally. I wrenched free, my survival instincts kicking in like crazy. Running away was my strong suit.

I pushed past Nathan, my stomach lurching at the sudden movement and sprinted for the open window opposite. I hit it with my palms and launched myself through it, tumbling into the flowerbed below.

The sweet, sticky night embraced me like a drunk lover. My throat clogged with fear, the wild thoughts driving me forward.

Over grass.

Magic. It was magic. His eyes were glowing!

Toward the exit. But where? Where was the exit? I didn't stop to turn and get my bearings. They would be after me. The finality of Nathan's words had drilled that point home.

"It looks like you're going to have to be my assistant after all, Miss Crowley."

Did he think he was going to keep me here?

He had another fucking think coming. I hadn't spent the last twenty-one years on the streets without learning a thing or two.

You can't do anything against magic, dipshit.

It couldn't have been magic. It had to be a trick of the light. But the lies didn't sit well with me.

I pumped my arms back and forth, heading toward the far wall, a stone facade covered in weeping vines. But the wall didn't grow any closer. The stickiness of the night closed in on me, and the distant echo of laughter chased me, followed by a haunting, faded scream.

The dizziness was back, swelling in my head, tipping the grass to the left and then to the right. I stumbled, putting out my hands.

"No!"

I forced myself forward, my feet slipping, blood rushing in my ears. The wall was distant. More distant than it had been before I'd escaped the window. I glanced over my shoulder and found the house behind me, feet away.

Impossible.

I ran another couple of steps, but the ground tipped upward. I fell on all fours, slamming my palms into the moist grass. Pain jarred up my arms and into my shoulders.

Get up! You have to keep moving.

But this couldn't be happening. I had to be sick. Or going mad. Or anything but what was happening—not that I even knew what *that* was.

I lifted my head and promptly fell back onto my ass, shaking all over. I took deep breaths, trying to calm myself, but every inhalation brought more warmth and humidity, clogging my throat and lungs until I was certain I would choke on it. Choke to death.

Light spilled out of the darkness in front of me—a thin blue seam that had come from nowhere. Not a lantern or a flashlight. It simply existed.

That seam widened, and a polished black dress shoe emerged from within it, followed by the leg of a perfectly tailored pair of pants. Nathan Sword stepped out of the light, clasping the placket of his coat, shaking his head at me, smiling softly.

"Now, now," he said, "was there truly a need to punch me in the stomach, Miss Crowley?"

"Fuck you," I managed. "Freak! Get away from me."

"You're a nuisance." He dusted off his coat sleeves, the seam of light popping out of existence as fast as it'd appeared. "But you're impressive at least. Not passing out or screaming like the usual witless girl."

Witless girl? If I hadn't been on the verge of tossing my cookies all over his fancy shoes, I would've decked him.

"You'll have to stay here now."

"I'll call the cops," I managed the empty threat with a straight face, though I swayed to one side. The ground was tipping again.

"That's adorable," Nathan said. "Darling, the cops can't help you here. No one can." He bent down, bringing his devilish blue eyes to my level. "You belong to the Hierophant Society now, the House of Swords. Welcome."

I lifted a hand and took a mad swipe at his face. But my arm wouldn't work properly. It flopped back down to my side, impotently. Well, shit.

"Listen, you can come with me or—"

That final burst of energy from lifting my arm had drained me. I tipped over sideways and hit the grass, his voice fading from my ears. I stared directly ahead at the wall, distant, mocking. My vision faded.

———

STONE COLUMNS EITHER SIDE OF THE ROOM. ROUGHNESS UNDER my bare feet.

I stood in the shadows, breath catching in my throat. The room was unfamiliar. No. That was wrong. It was perfectly familiar. A drifting impression of a sweet and sticky night, a tang of fear, an intangible memory drifted across the surface of my mind then out of it again.

Something about this wasn't right.

The chamber was never this empty. Where were Horus' priests? The guards?

I turned my head, my long, dark hair swishing, the beads woven into it clicking softly. Wait. Dark hair? My hair is—

Another strange thought that faded.

Could I do this? The priests would surely return. They would find me here and eject me before I could do what I had sworn I would do, and then all would be for naught. But the suspicion that had awoken within me nearly three Inundations prior niggled at the back of my mind.

They would try to use the book for their own purposes.

What use were the priestesses of Ma'at if they did that? I touched a hand to the golden feather symbol at the end of my necklace.

I took a breath, steeling myself for what might come of this mission, undertaken in secrecy, and stole forward.

My bare feet whispered across the stone. I had left my sandals outside the palace, praying for silence for the swiftness of my feet as the swiftness of Ma'at's justice would be delivered to those in the Hall of Judgment.

A pedestal dominated the center of the chamber, the torches along the walls casting flickering light that caught the sharp edges and facets etched into the stone. Atop that pedestal.

The book.

A golden cover, a serpent twisting around a man bearing an eagle's head. Apep and Atum. Chaos and creation.

My fingers itched toward the cover.

Take it and flee.

And then what? Would I never know what they had been keeping from us all this time? What they had decided was too sacred to be shared with justice keepers?

A jealousy rose within me. A certainty that they had enough. They had magic and respect. They were the Pharaoh's advisors, in a constant position of power. And what had we been given?

My fingers itched toward the edge of the book's cover, papyrus poking from it. I took a breath and opened it.

Gold light spilled from inside and joy burst from within, a humming that filled my ears, dulling everything but the sound itself. A hum that would not cease. That drilled. That pained. That burrowed into my consciousness.

Wetness trickled down my cheeks. I touched my fingers to the moisture and they came away red, coated in blood. My jaw dropped, and I released a scream that I could no longer hear, backing away, grasping at my ears, pulling with power that was quickly waning.

I fell, and the columns, the golden light, the beauty and terror, burned to blackness.

7

I OPENED my eyes to darkness. Flashes of the dream lingered for a couple of seconds then faded from my mind, replaced by another series of images.

Nathan Sword, handsome, blond-haired and with those sharp blue eyes stepping out of thin air. Smirking at me. Promising me that I would never leave. That I was forever trapped in this place.

I sucked in a breath and forced myself upright, fisting handfuls of silken sheets. The soft scent of New Orleans' night air, accompanied by a distant burst of laughter, the warm notes of jazz, invaded my senses swiftly.

Breathe. It's bullshit. This is not real.

The Hierophant Society.

The tarot card with Hieroglyphics. And the sweeping dizziness that had confronted me directly after witnessing that... what the hell had it been? A ritual. A magical ritual.

Whatever it was, I wasn't about to hang around and sip on the Kool-Aid. I had to get out.

I lurched off the bed, finding that I was barefoot and

feeling violated for it, and stumbled my way through the room. It was huge. The shapes of an armoire, a dressing table, maybe, stood out to me. I moved past them, and what might've been an armchair, toward the rectangular outline of light rimming the bedroom door.

Get a grip, girl.

Kind of difficult to do when a man had full-on Houdini'd himself out of thin air in front of me. It had to be a cheap parlor trick, right?

Sure. That explains the changing eye color. The dizziness. The way I couldn't reach the edge of the yard and the fucking wall. How the air turned to molasses.

I would've blamed voodoo, but I happened to know Mama Michelle, the new voodoo queen out in the French Quarter, and this smacked nothing of that. No markings on the ground, no spitting booze over the arm or welcoming spirits into our presence.

"You're only as bad as you feel, dawlin'."

The door handle was cold against my skin. I tried it, panic crawling up my throat.

Locked.

OK. I'd break it down. Or climb out of a fucking window.

I took a step back, braced myself, then rammed my shoulder into the door. It was like running into a slab of stone. The hinges didn't so much as creak.

"It won't open." The soft accented voice, male, came from the opposite end of the room.

My heart did a gymnastic flip that would've secured a gold medal.

I turned and found *him* sitting there. Well, not technically *him*. I couldn't tell if it was Nathan or not, yet. The guy, it was definitely a guy, sat on the window sill at the far end of the room in silhouette. The shutters were closed, and the tiniest inkling of light from outside showed he was there.

"Don't bother trying again," he said, and this time, I was sure it was him. That voice would haunt my nightmares for years to come.

Assuming I didn't die in his sex dungeon downstairs within the next couple of days.

I took a breath. "My guy," I said, breaking the silence with my voice—making the tone loud and obtrusive, if only to give myself comfort, "you had better let me out of here before I start tearing this room apart."

"That won't be necessary," Nathan replied. His voice had the same timbre as the ritualist from downstairs. A relation, perhaps? "Or possible."

I scrambled for an appropriate response, but if there was one, I couldn't find it. "Is this your thing?" I asked, not daring to walk toward him but pressing my back to the door instead. Maybe it would help stiffen my spine. "Sitting in the dark watching women sleep?"

"It's too dark for you? I'd hoped the lack of light would relax your symptoms."

"Symptoms?"

"Dizzy, weren't you?" Nathan asked, quietly. "Dizzy and sick. Headache?"

"How did—?" No. I wouldn't give him the satisfaction. "Don't change the subject. You were creeping on me in the dark." It was easier to fixate on that rather than the, uh, magic portion of this evening's proceedings. Oh, and, you know, the fact that I was locked in a room with this psychopath.

Nathan snapped his fingers and flickering light spread

through the room. He held a single finger aloft, a pure blue flame hovering a half an inch above it. He smiled at me, those blue eyes sparkling. "Is that better?"

Breath left my body.

"You're confused, of course. They're always confused."

I forced air into my lungs. "Who? Your victims?"

"People who wind up where they don't belong. Humans."

"Humans. Humans? Humans."

"Say it again," he said, passing the flame from one fingertip to the next, trickling it up and down every digit along his right hand and back again. "Maybe it will register the fourth time."

"What do you mean by that? Humans."

"I mean homo sapiens. Have you taken a biology class?" His gaze swept over my clothing, my leather jacket, white tank, and jeans. "I'm guessing no."

"Really?" I asked, my mouth dry. "Now you're going to be classist? In this moment?"

"By humans," Nathan said, rising from his easy lean on the window sill, "I mean people like you. People who can't do what I do." He strode toward me, and I pressed my back against the door, the handle jutting into my lower back. "People who couldn't imagine what *we* are capable of."

"Don't come any closer," I said, but my voice cracked.

He stopped a foot away from me, the light casting a cold quality over his face. He was older than me, a few lines on his face, and much taller. His every movement was precise, leaking an undeterrable power.

"Closer?" Nathan breathed. "Why would I do that? I have you exactly where I want you."

"Can you stop being creepy for a second?" I couldn't look

at the flame. Not because it was bright, but because I didn't want to believe it was real.

Now, I'd seen my fair share of creepy in NOLA. I had a friend at work whose cousin had performed a ritual to commune with her ancestors, and there were plenty of haunted houses around the city, but this was… This defied reality.

This wasn't bumps in the night or spooky spirits. This wasn't drunk tourists on a ghost tour through the French Quarter.

The man was playing with fire that disobeyed the laws of physics.

"Look at me, Miss Crowley."

I hated that name. It reminded me of *her*.

"Look at me."

I met his gaze, only because I wanted to do it defiantly.

"Your world is about to change forever. Had you been any other girl, I would've let you go. Sure, I would've had to deal with your memory of this evening appropriately, but there's something about you." He paused, bringing the flame closer to my face, so that I flinched back again. It was cold rather than hot. "I believe that you received an invitation to this society by accident, or perhaps, it was an intervention of sorts." He tipped his head back, exposing his Adam's apple as he looked toward the ceiling. "From *them*. Regardless." Nathan took me in with his gaze again. "You will be staying here with me. As my assistant."

"No."

"You wanted to be a part of the society, did you not?"

"I wanted to know why I got an invitation." And now, I

wanted to know why he could do that thing with the fire. Like magic. Magic. Was I twelve?

"And you don't want to know why anymore?" he asked.

A tense silence parted us. The scent of his cologne warped my perception, and I turned my head again, refusing to face the flame above his fingers or the ones reflected in his eyes.

Nathan grasped my upper arm and marched me away from the door. The sudden change in his demeanor sent a thrill of fear through me, and I tried to tug free. He was too strong.

He let me go, and I fell backward onto the bed.

"You'll get your wish. You will find out why you were invited, and so will I. I can't let you leave now, Miss Crowley, not even if I wanted to. Not after that show earlier. Not after your symptoms." Nathan walked to the door and paused, looking back over one broad shoulder at me. "If you run, the council will take over. Even I won't be able to save you then."

"What council?" I barked, trying desperately to get him to stay. He was the guy with all the answers.

"Try to get some sleep," Nathan replied. "Tomorrow's going to be a big day." He shut the door and locked it, plunging me into darkness.

8

"WELL, that was like masturbation without the payoff," I said into the quiet of the room. The joke didn't land, even for me, let alone what else might be watching me from the corners. Who knew in this place?

I swallowed, my eyes slowly adjusting to the dark after Nathan's departure. Nathan and his flame fingers. I wonder what that's like in the bedroom?

"Get real." I rolled my eyes at myself.

My default setting was ridiculous humor, particularly when I was mid-panic, but it wasn't serving me in this case.

"OK," I whispered, rising from the bed, my hands slick with sweat. "What would our Lord and Savior Cthulhu do in this situation?" I felt around in the darkness until I found the bedside table, and, thankfully, a light.

I switched it on and the bedroom was bathed in buttery yellow light. I held back a gasp.

I'd been imaging a room full of torture devices or broken glass or something evil and ominous. But this space was gorgeous, cream jacquard wallpaper, a bed with matching cream silk sheets, dark wood paneling and floors. There were winged armchairs, a living area, bedroom area, a massive armoire, dressing table, and a doorway that led into what I hoped was an en suite bathroom.

A bookcase dominated the spot where a TV would've gone in another home, and I was happy about that.

Well, about as happy as a woman who'd been abducted by a fire-wielding Aryan-wonderboy could be.

At least I'd have something to read while I waited for my impending doom. Books had been my only friends during my years at the orphanage and in foster care.

I forced myself to start exploring. There had to be a way out, right? I wasn't really going to hang around here waiting for Nathan to come back and burn me to crispy bacon.

With magic. Actual magic. Sans the wands.

The mysterious door did, indeed, lead to a not so mysterious bathroom. It was huge with a clawfoot tub and zero windows.

I marched over to the sill where Nathan had been sitting and pulled back the thick, cream curtains. The window was shut, looking out on grass that was impossibly far below. Too far to be real in a mansion that should've only been three stories high.

"Did I trip and hit my head or something?"

I grasped the bars on the window and tugged on them fruitlessly then marched to the living room and tried lifting one of the armchairs. I nearly threw out my back. At twenty-one.

"What the hell?"

Upon closer inspection, the armchairs were nailed to the floor. A quick trip around the room told me that *everything* was nailed to the floor. Everything. The dressing table, armoire, bookcase, bed—a queen-sized. The only things that weren't nailed down were the books, and, forgive me, but I wasn't about to throw them at the bars on the window.

First, it wouldn't work, and second? They were books. Sacrilege.

I plopped down on the bed and scrubbed my eyes with my palms. Why was this happening? Why now?

Thought I hated to admit it, it wasn't the first time something strange had happened to me or around me. I had a knack for having dumbass accidents or causing trouble without even trying. I'd figured it was just my lot in life, but this?

My exploration of the bedroom had provided me with no answers, so I moved over to the bookcase and pulled books from the shelf, checking each title. Many of them were unfamiliar to me, and that was saying something.

The Duality: An Exploration of the Creative Force that Binds Us

So, a spiritual book? I flipped through it, inhaling the comforting scent of the pages, then replaced it, carefully.

The shimmering spine of the hardcover beside it drew my gaze.

An Exploration of Magical Races: A Purpose-Driven Guide

I backed up until the backs of my legs hit the bed and sat down. The sides of the book's pages were painted golden, and as I parted them, I half-expected a puff of glitter. But no, the pages were a plain cream, the print black.

Was I really going to do this? Just sit here and read while peril and magic swirled around me?

What else do I have to do?

My best chance at escape would come tomorrow morning when Nathan returned. I'd lure him into the room then make a run for it. Beyond that, I wasn't sure what else I could do. It wasn't as if anyone would be looking for me.

There would be no search parties. No questions asked. Besides, I wasn't the type of girl who needed a knight on a horse. I'd save myself.

I opened the book to the first chapter.

Chapter 1—The Duality

According to ancient lore, passed down from word of mouth, and the recent discoveries tied to the Tome Immaculate, the founding of all races began with the slow separation of Atum and Apep.

"What the—?" I sucked in a breath.

OK. This was weird. I happened to know who Atum and Apep were, and not in that "my cousin's brother works with him" NOLA kind of way.

Atum and Apep were Gods in Ancient Egyptian Mythology—a topic that was a passion of mine.

While I don't see a necessity to recant the ancient founding lore here, it is important to note that the basis of most of the modern magical races we know today is focused on one of the two "forces" from the duality. Chaos and order. Apep and Atum.

The concept that either is purely evil or good is a modern, societal view that has no bearing on how the races themselves were formed, operate, or the powers they possess.

While some may view a race as purely bad or having a basis in chaos, as is the case for The Sons of Sekhmet, for example, there is very little truth to this viewpoint.

The Duality is meant to create balance—a concept that has been largely lost to magical society for the past several centuries.

It is important to note this so that we may view the origin of the newest race as a necessity rather than a risk to our magical world and how it functions.

Though, the Societies may view this as heresy. Facts are facts. Magic is born from necessity delivered by the Duality.

"A Duality." I traced my fingers over the word on the page. I turned it and found a picture opposite it.

A gold embossed image of an ancient Egyptian man, facing off to the right, carrying a staff and holding an ankh. A golden snake twined around his body, its mouth open, fangs extended, as it leered down into the man's face.

The image was captioned. *The Duality, Apep, the snake, and Atum, the first of the Gods, locked in eternal battle.*

I looked up from the book, blinking, my eyes suddenly scratchy. Was I crazy, or was this image super familiar?

I settled back against the cushions, propping my bare feet on the folded comforter at the end of the bed, and started reading. If there was an explanation—albeit a supernatural one—for what had occurred this evening, I wanted to find it.

9

THE SHARP SCRAPE of curtains being drawn woke me. Light penetrated the darkness, and everything came back in one foul deluge.

I gasped, eyelids snapping open, and forced myself upright. The book I'd been reading flopped off my chest and thumped against my thighs.

Nathan Sword, douchebag supreme, stood near the windows, his arms folded over an creaseless white button shirt studying me, one eyebrow arched, a smirk on his lips. "Did you enjoy your bedtime story?"

I glanced at the bedroom door. Shut and locked. Damn. Why had my dumbass fallen asleep? I'd intended on staying up all night. Discovering the secrets of whatever the hell cult I'd wound up in. I wanted to believe that there was a reasonable explanation for everything that had happened so far, a rational, scientific one, but even I wasn't that stubborn.

Especially with the books in here. There were different types of "magical races" each one with different strengths and weaknesses, and pictures that should've given me nightmares.

"Get up," Nathan said. "We've got work to do."

I glared at him and considered posting up in bed with these magical books for the rest of the day, but they wouldn't get me anywhere closer to getting the hell out of the "society."

"Look," I said at last, "I don't know what kind of, uh, creature you are, maybe you feed on rat blood or something vile, but us normal people need to eat. Breakfast."

Nathan pursed his lips, exuding that cocky boy vibe that should've melted my underwear, if I hadn't been equal parts starving and annoyed. "Fine. Come."

"At least buy me breakfast first."

Nathan ignored the jibe, beckoning as he walked for the door. I lurched off the bed, hating him and this situation—and myself for being intrigued.

Magic.

Real magic.

I'd always wanted an escape from my life. A place where I belonged. But being imprisoned by a hot dickhead was the opposite of an escape. Wasn't it?

"Why do you want me here?" I asked, as we descended the red carpeted stairs, passing jacquard wallpaper and paintings of people in that frilly old-timey attire. "What did you mean last night?"

Nathan didn't answer, just stared directly ahead, his blue eyes focused, jaw clenched, a muscle hopping in his cheek.

"Hey. I'm talking to you." I grasped his arm.

Nathan turned on me and grabbed me by the chin. He walked me back into the wall, pressing me against it, the gilt frame beside my head rattling at the slight bump. "Don't tempt me," he said, in a low growl, the words sending a mixture of fear and arousal thrumming through my core. "Do not tempt me."

I raised my chin. "Or what?" I asked. "Do you think I'm afraid of you?" Because I am. But I'll never let you see that. Never let you—

"You should be," he said, his fingers tightening. "You should do as I say if you want to live."

"Tell me what's going on. You can't keep me here. You can't force me to do what you want."

"I can, and I will. For your own good."

"This doesn't feel like for my own good," I said, meeting him stare for stare, even though his eyes glowed as they had last night during the "magic" portion of the evening's festivities. I considered head-butting him and trying to make a break for it, but I wasn't into another run across the ever-expanding back yard right now.

"You misunderstand what's happening here." His breath was hot against my skin.

"Yeah, because you haven't told me a damn thing that makes sense. You're holding me captive then telling me to follow you and expecting, what? Obedience?"

"If you do as I say, if you follow every word of my advice, I will give you everything you've ever dreamed of," he said, leaning closer, his hand sliding down my throat and coming to a rest on my collar bone. He pressed the full weight of his body against mine. "Everything you've ever wanted. Your wildest fantasies. Your darkest desires. Deepest cravings." His tone dropped with every word.

My pulse raced, but I kept my expression impassive. I wouldn't react to this. It didn't matter that images of his lips against mine filtered through my mind. This guy was a fucking psychopath. Sure, I had terrible taste in men, but this was a step too far.

"I will give you a home. A purpose," Nathan continued, his lips right beside my ear, sending goosebumps down my neck and side. "All you have to do is everything I say. Exactly as I say it. Tell me you can do that, and I will give you what you want."

"I want answers," I managed.

"That depends on the questions you ask."

"Why am I here?"

He dragged his nose against my cheek.

My nipples hardened, and I rolled my eyes at them. Really, girls? This is what gets you going?

"You're going to help me find what I'm looking for," he said. "You were invited, were you not?"

"You said it was a mistake."

"Maybe it was, maybe it wasn't, but I need you now."

Was he putting a spell on me? My body ached for more of those cheek nuzzles, for his breath on my skin, and I *hated* that.

"Let go of—"

A throat cleared in the hall, and Nathan finally released me, stepping back and straightening his shirt.

The red-haired bitchy girl from last night stood in the hall, wearing a pair of leather pants, a lacy black bustier, and a seriously unimpressed expression.

"Miss Braddock," Nathan said, "just the woman I wanted to see."

Her eyebrow lifted incrementally.

"Kindly take Miss Crowley for a quick breakfast and her initiation," Nathan said. "I have business to attend to."

"By business, he means a cold shower," I put in, forcing a smile.

Nathan ignored the quip and strode back the way we'd come, opening a section of wall and disappearing deeper into the house. Because, of course, there were trap doors and secret passages in this upside down pineapple cake of a doom house.

"You shouldn't speak to him like that," Braddock said in that British accent then started walking.

I followed her. Maybe, I'd find my opportunity for escape along the way? "Why?" I asked. "Let me guess, he'll throw fire-balls at me. Breathe fire? Fart it at me?"

"Because he's the most powerful man in New Orleans," she replied. "Maybe even the country. He can make your life better than it's ever been." Braddock paused. "Or he can destroy you."

I swallowed, staring after her.

"Follow."

And I did. Damn her and this entire place, but I did.

IO

Miss Braddock led me down five flights of stairs and into a tiny room with a square table and single chair, both ornamental, polished and probably worth more than all the money I'd made in my entire life. A plate had been set out, a single piece of toast with a sunny side up egg on top of it, a bowl of fruit and yogurt next to that.

"Hurry up and eat," Braddock said. "Mr. Sword wants you initiated as quickly as possible."

I opened my mouth to argue, but she'd already left the room, shutting the door behind her. The key turned in the lock.

I strode to the curtains and drew them back, but found more of that annoying cream wallpaper instead of windows. What the hell was this place? First the backyard, now this? No windows. And when there were windows, they were barred like a prison.

No escape yet.

I eyed the meal that had been laid out for me, cautiously.

Should I trust it? Probably not, but I figured that if they planned on killing me, they would've done it already.

"What, no dietary requirements taken into consideration?" I muttered, then sat down and started eating. I'd underestimated how hungry last night had made me. My stomach growled even as I practically inhaled the food. It tasted good. Maybe a little too good. Just like the air in this room wasn't humid.

In fact, apart from last night when I'd come over with that weird sickness and been out in the yard, I hadn't felt uncomfortable, not temperature-wise at least.

Don't fall into his trap. Whatever it is. No matter what he offers you.

I might not have had anywhere else to be, but I didn't want to wind up evil. Like *her*.

And Sword and his friends smacked of evil. Abduction was near the top of the list of really crappy, evil things to do.

I finished my meal, took a sip of water, and, right on cue, the door opened. Braddock stepped inside. "Let's go."

I didn't bother asking how she'd known I was done. I got up and followed her out into the hall and down another flight of stairs. We took several turns, left and right, left, left again, and more of them until I was thoroughly turned around.

"How the hell is this possible?" I whispered.

"Sacred ground, old rituals," Braddock replied, pushing back her cherry red hair. "The Hierophant Society provides for us in many ways."

I hadn't expected an answer from her, not that I'd technically received one. What she'd said was so cryptic she might as well have maintained her silence.

The floor underfoot went from carpeted to limestone, and

the sense of claustrophobia I'd had about being trapped in this mansion tripled. "Where are you taking me?"

"For your initiation."

If she thought I was going to bare my ass cheeks and let some dude magic a tarot card against my naked titties, she had another think coming.

"It's non-intrusive," she said stiffly, sensing my hesitation somehow.

"Somebody's got to explain what's going on at some point."

"That point is now." Braddock stepped into a hallway lit by torches in brackets along the limestone walls and led me toward a door at the end of it.

"What's with the medieval firelight?" I asked.

"Electricity and magic don't mix that well."

I sucked in a breath. Magic. Get over it. "It didn't seem to be a problem for Nathan last night."

"Mr. Sword only used a small amount of magic," she replied. "Even simple rituals and performances take little enough magic that it doesn't interfere with the electrical grid. But down here, it's different."

"Why?" Because there's some extra magical shit down here. But what?

Braddock ignored me and stopped in front of the door. It was ornate, made of wood, with carving etched into it. With a shock, the realization came to me: it was the same image of the Egyptian priest, two children kneeling either side of him. The Hierophant.

My "hostess" knocked once on the door then waited.

"Enter." The voice was croaky.

Braddock opened the door and held it for me.

No turning back now. No escape.

I stepped inside, saw what was in the room and bit back a scream. Another wave of nausea beset me, but the dizziness didn't come this time. I blinked repeatedly. What is that thing?

It was a humanoid. Sure. Human enough. With two arms and two legs, a torso, sitting behind a desk that bore hieroglyphics and an image of Apep and Atum in an embrace. Gold and blue. But screw the desk, the creature behind it was far more interesting. And terrifying.

Glowing red eyes, twisted red skin, all sinew, interlaced with black pulsing veins. He wore a cotton shift that exposed those sinuous arms. His fingers ended in blackened claws.

Braddock closed the door, locked it, then waited, her hands at her sides, relaxed but alert.

"A new addition to the academy?" the thing asked, and now I got why his voice was so croaky. He was all fleshy and raw. "What have you brought me this morning, Miss Braddock? It has been some time since I have witnessed anything other than one of your acolytes as you call them."

"A temporary addition, Scholar Harwa," Braddock answered smoothly. "She's not one of our acolytes."

"An exception to the rule." The thing. It wasn't a person, but for lack of a better word, the person turned those fiery red eyes on me. "How fascinating." The movement of raw red lips exposed fangs beneath. Two elongated canines.

Vampire?

"Yes," Harwa said. "Vampire. Not thing. Though, a vampire is a rough estimation of what I am in human terms. Unfortunately, your vocabulary is and always has been limited."

He had read my mind.

Harwa smiled, showing more of his fangs. "Most children are easy to read, especially those of the human persuasion.

But you are different, are you not? Is she not, Miss Braddock?"

"Mr. Sword would prefer she has a *brief* education, Scholar Harwa. Discretion is highly advisable."

"I have no control over that portion of her education. Mr. Sword will have to speak with the council about that. You understand, of course, the importance."

"I'm sure that has already been arranged," Braddock said, irritably.

She had cojones, I'd give her that. To talk to this vampire in that tone.

"I agree with you, child." Harwa smirked at me, but didn't share my thoughts with Braddock. "The Academy provides protection, you see. I couldn't pierce her throat and drink that sweet, sanguine nectar no matter how much I desired it."

Well, fuck. OK.

"The same goes for you," Harwa said then turned to Braddock. "Will you endure?"

"I'll be outside. Brief education, books, and a timetable. Mr. Sword needs her trained in base combat, understanding classes and abilities, introduction to magic and that's it. No history beyond the basics."

"More's the pity." Harwa sighed. "We need more students."

"She's human. She's no use to the Academy or magical society. Give her the briefest of it. The briefest."

"I might be old, Miss Braddock, but I do have ears. Ones that function quite well, thank you." He tapped the pointed raw-red ears on the side of his head.

Braddock gave the barest of nods then exited the room. She shut the door and locked it again.

Great. Trapped in a room with a crispy-looking vampire. Exactly how I'd planned on starting my week.

"Crispy vampire?" Harwa asked. "Polite, aren't you, child?"

"Tell you what, you stop calling me a child and I won't call you crispy."

Harwa gave a dry chuckle. "Negotiation from a human? What was it you thought? Cojones?"

Even his laugh was creepy.

Harwa ignored that particular comment, if he heard it. He rose from the desk, achingly slow, then beckoned for me to follow him to the wall opposite. I'd barely taken in the room thanks to his presence, but I did now.

It was stone, like the rest of the "basement" of the house had proven to be so far, with that dark wood Egyptian-desk with golden and blue carvings. An image had been etched into the wall, not the Hierophant, but the coiled scales of a snake, golden and glowing, curled around a man in an Egyptian headdress.

"Everything's Egyptian," I said. "Ancient Egyptian." I wasn't complaining. I'd been obsessed with ancient Egypt since as far back as I'd been able to read.

"Where did you think magic came from?" the vampire asked, and to his credit, he didn't call me "child" this time.

"I didn't know it existed until last night," I replied, keeping my distance from him, but drawn to etching on the wall. There was more to it than just the central picture. And all of this, the aesthetic, the pictures, seemed ridiculously familiar. Had I dreamed of this? No. This was just weird-ass déjà vu.

Harwa turned glowing red eyes toward me. "You don't know," he said. "My, that complicates things, but no matter. Let me see. Where to start? There is a duality."

"Apep and Atum."

"I thought you said you didn't know about these things," Harwa growled. "I prefer no interruptions."

"I know about Apep and Atum."

"The dual energies of chaos and order. The snake and the god, both powerful, opposites of the whole from which all magical races sprang forth." Harwa traced his black claws down the drawing toward several images that had been etched underneath. There were six of them. "Six main magical races. Beneath those, another six forms of magic. Beneath that, the twelve societies."

I frowned at those societies. "Those are tarot cards, aren't they? The societies? That image is the same as the picture on the card I received."

Harwa didn't growl at the interruption this time. "Correct. There were twenty-two houses before the Changing. But that's a lesson for another time. What you need to know is that you are currently on the grounds of the Hierophant Society. This room is what connects that society to the Academy of Scribes, where all magically attuned beings receive their education. From vampires, as you called me, to shifters, to the fae, to sorcerers and so on. Each society has a room of admission, much like this one. Each state in this country has its own mirroring society and academy, though they all answer to the heads of their society. The Academy of Scribes educates acolytes and members, even those who are loosely affiliated with the societies under the edicts of Horus' Council."

"And that is?" It was a lot of information to process at once, especially coming from a cr— from a vampire.

A small smile showing white fangs. "Horus' Council is the governing body of all magic. They ensure that our societies are protected, that we can trade, co-exist and remain undis-covered."

"Undiscovered."

"By humankind, of course."

But I was human.

"Yes," he said.

And that meant…

"You will not leave magical society without supervision, memory evisceration, or death."

"Well, isn't that fun," I said.

"We're just getting started, my dear."

II

"THERE HAVE BEEN other humans here before?" I asked.

"Once every other millennia," Harwa replied, and walked back to the desk, leaving me with the etchings. "And they've met one of the three fates I've mentioned. Mostly, they die. It's most unfortunate that we meet under these circumstances, though I suppose, they could be worse for you. If we had met on one of my nightly strolls in the city, you would have met a worse fate. As it stands, you're protected by virtue of your affiliation with the Hierophant Society."

I swallowed again. "Now what?"

"Now, I give you your books, your map of the Academy of Scribes, and your key. After that, well, I believe that is up to Miss Braddock and her master."

"Mr. Sword is her master? Kinky."

Harwa shook his head. "What is it with young ones and sex? Humans, shifters, fae. What is the obsession?"

"What about vampires and blood?" I countered. "Is that a thing?" I couldn't be sure how much of the fairytales and nightmares were true. I couldn't be sure of anything anymore.

If I'd wanted an escape, a reality check, my world blown apart, well it was safe to say I'd gotten it.

"Yes, indeed. But, as I mentioned, we are not technically vampires." Harwa shuffled to a door at the opposite end of the room. "I shall return shortly. Feel free to take a seat while you wait."

I doubted I'd ever sleep again, let alone sit.

Harwa exited the room through the door behind his desk, and I caught a glimpse of what was beyond it. A massive atrium full of sound and light, not flickering but steady, and the scent of something spicy, roses and—

The door shut.

What the hell is going on?

Harwa wasn't gone for long. He returned carrying an armful of thick hardback books. "You know," he said, as he set them down on the desk. "This is most unusual. We haven't educated humans in an eon. Of course, there are certain connections and alliances between our world and yours, but to actually educate one on our premises? Interesting. But then, as I said you are... but no, Miss Braddock requested discretion, yes? Yes."

"Discretion about what?"

"If I told you, it wouldn't be very discrete, now would it, Miss Crowley."

I bit back a retort.

So far, in my quest for answers, I'd gotten nothing but confusion. Sure, there was this entire new world to deal with, one that was a lot more interesting than my normal "human" world, but I was still in the dark.

I needed a minute to take a breath. Work out what the hell was going on here.

"You're in luck." He pointed to the books he'd stacked on his desk. "There is much thinking and studying to be done. These are yours. Consider them a loan from the Council of Scholars. I've only to—"

The door that led back up the stairs and into the New Orleans mansion clapped open, and Nathan strode into the room, his blue eyes flashing. He crooked a finger at me.

"Come."

I raised an eyebrow. I was in no position to be sassy, but it came to me naturally. "I'm in the middle of something here."

Nathan's gaze swept toward Harwa.

The vampire stiffened, his red-raw lips peeling back over his fangs. "Mr. Sword," he said. "I was about to give your charge her timetable for the—"

"She's not my charge. Books and schedules can wait. There are urgent matters to attend to." Nathan didn't thank Harwa or acknowledge the vampire's reaction to his presence. He beckoned again then opened the door and held it for me.

"Sorry." I cast that back at Harwa, then exited into the hall beyond. What was I supposed to do? I was effectively Nathan's prisoner. Resisting wouldn't get me the information I wanted. About why I was here. Why I was different.

You're not evil.

The thought rose, unbidden.

You're not like her.

Nathan took the lead, marching up the steps two at a time. "Don't apologize on my behalf again," he snapped. "Especially not to a vampire."

"He's not a vampire," I said, ever the smart ass when given the opportunity.

"If he'd been free of the Academy's bonds and met you

outside of this house, he would've drained you of every drop of your blood." Nathan's focus remained a head, and he talked mechanically. "No one in this world is your friend or confidant. No one will treat you with respect until you've earned it."

"I didn't think he was my friend," I replied, heat creeping up my throat.

Nathan didn't reply but picked up the pace.

"Where are we going?"

No answer.

"Hey, you were the one who wanted me initiated or whatever," I continued. "You've effectively plunged me into this world, and you owe me—"

"You turned up on my doorstep. You requested entry. You showed the card."

"So, we're victim-blaming now?" I asked. "Last time I checked, you were the one who abducted me, you psycho."

Nathan fell silent, and no amount of cajoling or teasing or bullshitting could get him to talk again. The rest of the ascent took ten minutes, and we dipped down side passages underground that I hadn't known existed.

The hair on the back of my neck rose. The space beneath the mansion was effectively riddled with tunnels. Catacombs, if what I'd seen last night was anything to go by. I half-expected us to walk into a room full of skull torches or a torture chamber or—

"Here." Nathan opened an underground doorway, and we entered a room illuminated by flickering light. A group of people stood within. Zoey Braddock, now wearing black leather from neck to toe, including gloves, and three others—a guy with dark circles under his eyes who kind of looked like a weasel, another woman who was stocky and held a cigarette between her teeth, a shock of pink hair atop her head, and a teenaged boy, probably around eighteen was my guess, who leaned against the wall, dark hair shielding the side of his face.

All in leather.

The teenager rolled a silver coin over the backs of his knuckles. "I wasn't aware we were taking strays with us." He spoke confidently, like he was the one in charge of the group.

"Quiet, Sylvian," Braddock replied.

"He's right," the weaselly looking guy said in a strange accent. South African, maybe? Or British? "We've been preparing for this kak for months. I'm not gonna have a new asshole ripped for me because—"

"Shut up." The pink-haired woman's voice was deep, and the other silenced instantly. She turned to Nathan. "What's going on?"

Nathan's teeth ground together so hard they squeaked audibly. "I'll be accompanying you today, as will my new assistant."

"Jou naai, man," the weasel said. "I didn't spend months in fucking Waset, busting my ass only for you to—"

Another glance from the pink-haired woman.

Despite the situation, whatever the hell it was, I couldn't help being intrigued. I wanted to absorb the information in front of me. I kept my ears and eyes open, and my mouth shut.

This was a task team of some kind, was my guess. And they were on a mission? For what? And why?

"You are here on my brother's orders," Nathan said, after a weighty silence. "And by extension, my orders."

The weasel's lips curled over his teeth momentarily, and then he squirreled the disdainful expression away.

Was Nathan not as powerful in the Hierophant Society as he was making himself out to be? His brother's orders?

"If I choose to accompany you, then you will accept," Nathan said. "The same goes for my assistant."

"Assistant." Sylvian, the teenager, didn't look at me. "A human assistant?"

"Human." The weasel started. "Well, fuck that. I'm not going anywhere with a human. Fuckin' clumsy. Fuckin,' fuckin,' you trying to get us killed? You realize this can go tits up at a moment's notice."

I stared at the teenager. How had he known I was human? Was I giving off a smell or something? A vibe? Or was there a type of magical class that could detect what people were?

"It doesn't matter what she is," Nathan said. "She's coming. And so am I."

"Kak," the weasel rumbled, one last time.

"Get it together, J.P., before I get it together for you," Pink-hair said.

"Don't make promises you can't keep, hey?" J.P., the weaselly guy, winked at her.

She flipped him off.

This is a lot.

"We're leaving now," Nathan said.

"Mr. Sword," Braddock replied, "we were in the middle of our debriefing. I assumed you'd want your assistant to go over the basics before she accompanies you on important missions. That's why I left her with Harwa to—"

"Continue your debriefing."

"What? In front of her?" J.P. asked. "In front of the human?"

"I have a name," I said.

"Oh, fuck me. She's got a name. What's it? Homo? Surname Sapiens?" J.P. smirked.

I opened my mouth to snap back, but Nathan laid a hand on my forearm. "Continue the debriefing."

The group of leathered up individuals shared uncomfortable looks.

"Now," Nathan said.

12

Quiet greeted Nathan's insistence, and for a millisecond, I felt sorry for him. Then I remembered he'd basically abducted me and the sympathy vanished.

Finally, the pink-haired woman cleared her throat. "Our mark is located in the French Quarter. Name is Fredrick Dorgoste."

"Weird name," Sylvian said, still rolling that coin over the backs of his fingers.

J.P. snorted at him. "OK, *Sylvian*."

"And he knows where the book is?" Nathan asked.

All four leather-clad people turned to stare at him.

"No," Zoey said at last. "Mr. Sword, I did inform you that finding the book will be complicated. More complicated than one reconnaissance mission."

"Then who's Fredrick?" Nathan asked.

Finally, I'm not the only one who's lost.

"I thought you'd never ask," J.P. said. "Can I talk now or what?" He directed that toward the pink-haired leader.

She nodded. The three other team members, including Braddock, relaxed visibly.

"OK, so this ou, Fredrick, he's one shady type. Hangs out with a lot of vamps, but if we want to get to the book, we gotta go through him." J.P. relished the attention it seemed. He strutted back and forth, drawing back his skinny shoulders. "He's the last contact who was in touch with Kasha Ramone."

"And Kasha is?" Nathan asked irritably.

"Kasha Ramone is supposed to have a part of one of the decks. You know, a Pharaonic Deck. The cards that will get you to the book. Kasha's a Teller."

"What, like a bank teller?" It came out before I could stop it.

"Please stop the human from talking, man, this is just fuckin' unprofessional," J.P. said.

Braddock took a deep breath. "A fortune teller has the ability to see glimpses of the future, but only with a deck of cards. You're sure," she continued, talking to J.P., "that this Ramone woman is the correct Teller? She has one of the decks?"

"Last time anybody heard from her was after the Sokar Festival incident two years ago. Remember that shit? Nearly blew up half the French Quarter? Rumors been going around that the incident was a cover-up so she could get away with the cards. There's nobody who knows where she is because she killed her whole fuckin' family and the previous owner of the deck. Except for Fredrick because Fredrick's got a lekker habit. Hooked on the good stuff. Rhine addiction. Poor fuck. The vamps don't want to touch the stuff, and he's got to be getting it somewhere. It's got to be from her. The two go way back. Like… Academy."

"So, we get to Fredrick, we get to Kasha Ramone and the deck," Pink-hair said.

"Ja. But it's not so simple as that." J.P. cracked his knuckles.

"Of course, it isn't," Braddock sighed. "What's the complication?"

"Fredrick's hanging out in the Upside Down Club."

Everyone in the room, except for me, inhaled sharply.

"So, you see," J.P. continued, "we don't really need a human tagging along on this mission. Unless you want to use her to throw the vamps off our scent. You take her there, you are offering them like, fuckin', meals on wheels."

"It won't help for stealth," Braddock agreed, passing her fingers through her glossy red hair.

"Who cares about stealth?" Sylvian tossed his coin up into the air and caught it. "We'll be fine."

"Ja nee fok, maar hy's slim, nê?" J.P. guffawed.

"Stop doing that," Sylvian said. "Nobody understands you."

"I think, genius, that's the fuckin' point," J.P. replied. "The problem with your little plan is that we need to get the mark outta there so we can squeeze him for information. This is not a guns blazing type of mission."

"Then why am I here?" Sylvian rolled his eyes.

"I ask myself that question daily."

"Enough," Pink-hair said, and both instantly shut up.

Whatever leadership skills she held, they were enough to quiet everyone in the room with a word. What was that about? The more I watched the four interact, the more I noticed the shifts in behavior. I was so out of my depth here. This was like layers of culture and society I'd never encountered before, and I reeled to keep up.

"Mr. Sword," Pink-hair said, "I suggest that if you insist on accompanying us, you leave the girl behind."

"Girl?" I'd had enough of these *people* talking about me like I wasn't here.

"She's coming with us," Nathan insisted.

"But why?" J.P. asked. "What's so special about her?"

Nathan turned to Zoey. "Miss Braddock, kindly help Miss Crowley into the appropriate gear for the mission." Then to the pink-haired woman. "Vera, please assign one of your people to ensuring that Miss Crowley is kept safe."

Vera grimaced and looked at Sylvian.

He raised his hands. "Alpha, if you tell me to look after her, I'll do it, but you're going to need my help on this. I'm the only one who's properly combat trained."

Vera turned her head toward J.P.

"Listen, I'm the one who can sneak you in there in the first place. I'm not gonna have a human tied to my belt like kippie the cunt. Come on, please, man. Please."

Vera sighed. "Zoey, I'm placing you in charge of the human."

Braddock stiffened. "Yes, Alpha."

"Get her ready, and we meet at Exit 15 in twenty minutes. Stealth will be our highest priority during this mission. I will have comms at all times unless stated otherwise."

"Yes, Alpha." That came from Sylvian, Braddock, and J.P.

"Move out."

"Let's fuckin' do this!" J.P. let out a whoop and dashed from the room.

13

If I'd have a chance to escape, tonight would be it. And if what J.P. had said was correct, it was probably a good idea to make a break for it before the vampires in this "Upside Down Club" got their claws on me.

Even though the evening air was muggy, I shuddered at that thought. The thump of jazz music in the distance did little to dampen the scent of urine tainting the night. Oh yeah, we were in the French Quarter, all right, and in a street where there were plenty of bars and drunk tourists sauntering down the sidewalk.

It'll be easy to get lost here. Slip away.

Braddock turned her head and stared at me, as if she'd read my thoughts. "Don't do anything stupid, Crowley," she whispered, her British accent pronounced. "If you try to run, Nathan will find you. You'll do as you're told."

I didn't respond. I'd learned that it paid to shut up on occasion, if only to save your sassy retorts for a more opportune time.

And I needed to think.

J.P. led the group, slinking along the sidewalk in his leather jacket and black tank top, occasionally casting a glance down a side street. He was tailed by the pink-haired Vera, then by Sylvian, who strode straight-backed, staring straight ahead. Nathan walked alongside him. Everyone wore variations of leather or the black stretchy material they'd forced me into. It stuck to my skin, but was breathable and light.

I frowned. "Nobody cares."

"What?" Braddock asked.

"Nobody cares that we look like we're on our way to a leather convention. I get that everyone's drunk, but we stand out, and we haven't gotten one weird look."

Braddock sighed.

"It's clear that your master wants me to learn more about all of this stuff, so you might as well fill me in on a few details."

"For the last time," Braddock said. "Mr. Sword is not my master."

"Then what is he?"

"He's the son of the Master of the Hierophant Society," she replied. "And he runs the society's in-house affairs."

"So, he's not the boss." Interesting.

"Not in quite the usual sense," Braddock said. "But he's high up in the society. The Steward."

As I'd suspected. Nathan was a rich dude with power because his daddy had given it to him.

We rounded a corner, and the tourists on the street parted around our group like water around a rock. "Are you going to tell me why that's happening? Every time I look at someone on the street, they look away."

The more I knew, the easier it would be to escape.

And then what? Where will you go? The alley with the cats? Back to your normal, crappy life where there's nothing and no one?

I exhaled roughly.

"J.P. is an illusionist," Braddock said. "Infantry groups for societies usually consist of four members. The Alpha like Vera, a shifter who controls the show and ensures everyone obeys orders, the illusionist or tactical specialist."

"Wait, what do you mean a shifter?"

Braddock shook her head. "I'm not going to explain magical races to you right now. J.P. is our illusionist. After him, there's the offense specialist like Sylvian, usually a destruction or malleation sorcerer. The final member is an associate from within the society."

"An associate?"

"It's a high up position within the society's hierarchy. I'm responsible for ensuring that the orders the Alpha gives are in-line with the society's interests," Braddock said, without emotion. "Associates usually have defensive abilities. Physical."

"What do you mean by that? Physical?"

"All magical abilities are split into either physical or mental classes. I am a physical defense specialist, meaning that I can protect you from physical attacks. But if a vampire who specializes in mental malleation attacks you, I won't be able to help."

"Oh." Because what else could I say? This was a lot to process.

"This will be covered in your classes," Braddock said,

sounding irritated at herself for having explained any of it. "Assuming you survive the night."

Nathan's head turned, and he caught us with some bright blue side-eye. "You'll make sure she survives, Miss Braddock."

I barely had time to process his sexy smolder before we turned a corner, walking under the iron eaves of creole town-houses. The jazz music had grown distant, and the air down here was clearer, the sidewalk empty of tourists.

J.P. entered an alleyway then raised a hand and brought us to a halt. "There," he said, nodding toward a darkened house opposite.

"I thought you said this was a club," I whispered.

Everyone ignored me.

J.P. met Vera's gaze. The Alpha nodded.

"I'll be back now now," J.P. said.

"What does that mean?" Sylvian asked. "Now now?"

"Like now now." J.P. shrugged. "Not just now. Now now."

"Huh?"

J.P. crossed the street without answering and disappeared. Literally. One second he was there, the next he was gone.

"What's he doing?" I whispered.

"Quiet," Vera snapped.

A ripple of something that had come from her hit me in the chest, and my teeth jammed together. It wasn't that I couldn't talk, it was that I no longer wanted to. This was her power? To shut people up?

"I don't like this," Sylvian said softly. "Too quiet."

I expected a snarky response from one of the other team members, but they appeared to agree. All eyes were trained on the house opposite.

I studied the faces of my captors, Nathan's in particular.

His jaw was set, a muscle twitching in his cheek, his fists balled up. He looked surprisingly good in the tight fitting black fabric, not that it mattered right now.

Why had he insisted I come? Why was any of this happening?

All I'd wanted for years, for as long as I could remember, was to belong somewhere. And now, it seemed Nathan was trying to force me to belong here, in this strange world, with people who didn't want me around. And that made me mistrust him even more.

What kind of sorcerer was he? What magical ability had he used to make me ill last night when I'd tried to run?

That last question was surreal.

The watching continued. None of the "soldiers" moved a muscle. The atmosphere hung humid, growing heavier by the second.

A wave of nausea assaulted me, and my eyes crossed. I stumbled and reached out, grabbing for something to brace myself on. Chills broke out on my skin, and I gagged, bringing my hand to my mouth.

"Help her," Nathan said urgently.

"She's sick?" Sylvian asked.

"Not quite."

Braddock's face swam into view, free of concern, laden with duty. "Can you hear me?" she asked softly. "Can you breathe?"

I nodded.

"Hold on to this." She placed one of my hands on a dumpster, and I caught a whiff of the rotting contents. Did wonders for the nausea, of course.

I retched again and swallowed. What was this? Had I picked up a new illness? What the hell?

"She's not— What is this?" Vera asked. "Mr. Sword?"

"You don't need to worry about that."

"You said she was human."

"I did," Sword replied. "Something's coming."

I blinked, clearing tears from my eyes.

A figure materialized out of nowhere and fell onto their knees on the stained concrete. J.P., his leather jacket ripped, his face bleeding. He groaned, forcing himself upright. "They know. They're coming now."

"Not now now?" Sylvian asked, removing his coin from his pocket.

"Now you decide to grow a brain? Really?"

I retched again and shut my eyes, swaying from side-to-side.

"Formation," Vera said, and another ripple pulsed through my chest. I opened my eyes and sucked in a gasp. The world swayed around me, hazing in and out of vision. Snapshots of reality. Tableaus of horror in utter silence.

The five armored party members stood in a semi-circle in front of me. Sylvian held his coin aloft between two fingers, Nathan pulsed light, Vera grasped a massive fuck-off sword, Braddock stood calmly, hands at her sides, and J.P. crouched, grasping his bleeding cheek.

In front of them, an approaching line of people, some wearing cloaks, others just in regular clothing, jeans and shirts, both men and women. All with glowing red eyes.

The entire scene was frozen before me. I couldn't move, couldn't think, barely breathe.

I blinked.

Is this really happening?

Noises roaring around me, the rush of air. The wet sound of something. I didn't know what. A scream. A grunt.

"Braddock!" Nathan's roar. "Braddock!"

Blink.

Another freeze-frame and quiet.

The people were gone, replaced by monsters with red-raw twisted skin, long black claws, sharpened fangs. Vampires like Harwa. One had Vera by the head, fangs digging into her flesh, drawing blood. Braddock stood behind a pillar of light, pressing a hand toward it. Nathan was caught, standing between me and Vera, anger peeling his lips backward.

There were so many of them. Creatures on the roof, others hanging from the balcony, caught dropping in from the sky, arms crossed in front of their chests.

Sylvian stood nearby, a finger pointed toward a vampire's chest. His silver coin appeared to have burst through it, leaving a hole where the heart had been, blood droplets spraying outward in perfect concentric circles.

I'm going to be sick. I'm going to be sick.

I blinked.

Resumption of sound.

"I've got her," Nathan said, close to my ear. "I've got her."

"What are you doing?" Braddock screeched. "Are you insane? Vera!"

"Vera can look after herself. She's more important."

"More important?"

A horrible wet squelching, followed by a bellowing shriek, and then Braddock's command to retreat.

I opened my eyes to a final freeze frame.

Nathan's face above mine, half in shadow, his blue eyes roving over my face, lines creasing the skin at the corners of his eyes and forehead.

Darkness fringed my vision and reality vanished.

14

"You chose her... team member... Do you realize how that will reflect...?"

"I understand my choices. You don't understand the importance of..."

"Then help me understand, Nathan."

"... wanted to do this. This is above your station."

"I've been following your orders dutifully, doing what you asked and... explain this to them?"

"Leave that to me."

"You owe me..."

"... a damn thing, Braddock."

The snippets of conversation broke through blackness. My eyelids fluttered open, and I sucked in a breath at the swell of pain in my forehead. A migraine from hell.

I didn't move to probe myself for injury, opting, instead, to take in my surroundings. We were somewhere in the city, not the French Quarter, judging by the houses. Maybe on my turf? The Lower Ninth Ward? It was dark, the buildings either side of us quiet. Warehouses maybe?

Braddock and Nathan were a few feet away, engaged in a tense stand-off. Sylvian stood at the far end of the alleyway, peering down the street. J.P. and Vera were absent.

I turned my head slowly, wincing at the resulting pain. The other end of the alley was open.

Now. If you want to run, you can do it now.

It would hurt like hell, but I could do it. I could get out.

But where would I go? This alley was as good as any, right? I didn't have a home. I didn't even have friends at the moment, apart from a momma cat in a darkened alley somewhere.

I hated to admit it, but Nathan was right. That kidnapping, psycho son of a bitch was right. I'd seen too much.

How was I meant to go back to a normal life now? The life where I didn't fit in, where I would always be the freak with the purple hair? No family. No life. No future.

With these assholes, at least there was the chance of something great, right?

I tensed.

You should run. Now. Before it's too late.

But I couldn't bring myself to move.

Nathan had saved me. He had saved me.

"Your chickie is awake." J.P.'s voice came from my right where there'd been nothing but a brick wall seconds ago.

Nathan and Braddock immediately broke off their conversation and came over. Sylvian stayed where he was. Did I really see him use his coin to—? What was the word for it? Eviscerate, probably.

"How are you feeling?" Nathan asked, crouching beside me.

I took a breath. "Like I just discovered magic was real, I guess? What happened?"

"We were attacked," Nathan said slowly. "You passed out and fell. Hit your head."

"Mr. Sword," Braddock cut in, maintaining decorum now that I was awake, it appeared. These two were up to something. I just wasn't sure what. "Mr. Sword, we should start moving. We're lucky they chose not to follow us."

"Ja, well, that's what happens when you leave them a fuckin' food parcel, isn't it? Hey? What did I tell you about this mission? I told you it was not guns blazing. I told you that this bitch here would be meals on fuckin' wheels, and you didn't listen to me." J.P.'s tone was acidic. "Now, what? We going back to the society with our tails between our legs like *dogs* because you couldn't understand that this wasn't for you. This was *our* mission."

"Stop it," Braddock said stiffly. "Remember whom you're speaking to."

"I don't give a flying fuck," J.P. spat, his long teeth amplifying his weaselly features. "If you didn't bring the human with us, Vera would still be alive."

"Vera's dead?" I croaked.

The vampires. There had been that flash. A snapshot of real time before I'd passed out. Vampire claws digging into Vera's cheeks.

"Ja, sweetie. Vera's dead. Vera's probably fuckin' drained dry and stripped for parts by now thanks to you."

"Enough," Braddock said.

But without the Alpha, or so it seemed, there was nothing keeping J.P. from saying his piece. He dropped down beside me, his face drawing close, breath reeking of cigarette smoke.

"They chose to save you over her. You, a waste of flesh. A waste of time. And they left Vera to die for what? What's the reason? Huh?" He grabbed a fistful of my hair. "What's so special about you?"

I lifted a hand to grasp his wrist, but my fingers closed on air.

J.P. was no longer next to me.

Nathan had him by the throat, feet off the ground. "You don't touch her, ever. You don't talk to her without permission. And you do as I say, do you understand me?" His eyes glowed blue.

J.P. kicked and tugged on Nathan's strong forearms. "Fuck you," he choked out. "You're not my General."

"I'm as good as your Alpha for the rest of tonight. Do as I say or I'll make it my special mission to ensure your General *does* hear about this."

J.P. paled at that.

"Are we good?" Nathan asked.

J.P. didn't reply, but Nathan dropped him regardless.

"She's gonna bring you down," he said, retreating toward the other end of the alley, rubbing his throat. "She's gonna be the end of you. Humans don't belong in our world."

His words stung, even though he was probably right.

I swallowed and tried to get up, pressing my palms against the cracked concrete.

"Stop," Nathan said, beside me again. "Don't move yet."

"Is Vera really dead?" I asked, a strange hollowness developing in my chest. I hadn't known her well, not for more than a couple of hours, but I was still sad. Guilty.

"She's dead," Braddock said. "She took down several

vampires before she died and gave us the opportunity to escape with our lives."

"She'll be honored once we get back to the society."

Braddock looked away to hide her expression, but I caught the glimmer of anger before she did.

"What about the guy?" I asked, the pain in my head so severe I could barely keep my eyes open. "The guy you were after? The mark."

"Gone," Braddock said.

"We'll get to him another time." Nathan brushed hair from my forehead carefully, looking deep into my eyes. "Our main priority is getting you back to the society. I'll ensure that you're taken care of. Don't worry, Guinevere, you're safe with me."

Why was it that I found comfort in his words? Apart from him using my full name, of course. Something was so off here, and it wasn't just my concussion.

First, he'd abducted me, then he'd brought me on this mission and endangered others' lives because of it, and now he wanted me safe back at the mansion?

"Close your eyes and rest," Nathan said, brushing his fingers down my cheek. "We'll be home soon."

15

NATHAN AND THE YOUNG "NURSE" who'd come to attend to me stood just outside my room—or prison cell, as I'd thought of it yesterday—talking in hushed tones. The nurse was a magical healer of sorts. At least, I figured she was, since she'd banished my headache with a touch and a smile.

I lay on the bed, my arms folded, my booted feet on the comforter. If I'd had the energy, I would've stripped and showered, then returned to curl up into the fetal position and try to sleep.

I got the feeling that my dreams would be haunted by the memories of the past two days.

How was I meant to process all of this? From the ritual last night to the vampires this evening? It was too much.

You wanted to fit in. Where better than here?

Until they found out who I really was. What I really was inside.

The door clipped shut and Nathan came over. He switched on the bedside lamp.

"I thought electricity doesn't work around magic," I murmured.

"Small amounts of magic don't affect the power grid," Nathan said. "Still, we can't wear microphones or hi-tech equipment when we plan on using our power or going anywhere we'll encounter a lot of magic."

I nodded, but my head wouldn't move. Too exhausted.

"Vera's really dead," I said.

"Yes. She's dead. And she will be honored." Nathan brushed his hand through the air.

"You can't do that."

"Do what?"

"Brush it aside like it's nothing. She was a person," I said.

"She was a shifter," he said.

"So why didn't she change into whatever she was? That's what it means, right? A shifter? They turn into werewolves?"

"She was a dragon shifter, and, uh, she neglected to inform me that she was unable to shift tonight. Perhaps, she thought she wouldn't need to. Vera's death is not your responsibility."

"But it's yours, right?" I asked.

Nathan sat on the edge of the bed, his hip pressing against my thigh. He stared down at me, that haughty rich boy vibe taking over again. "Are you presuming to judge my actions when you have no understanding of how anything in the society or this world works?"

"I know that a leader takes responsibility for their people," I replied. "You did the wrong thing. J.P. was right. I shouldn't have come with you on that mission."

"You don't even know the importance of what tonight was," Nathan snapped. "If twenty soldiers had died and we'd gotten what we needed, it would've been worth it. For the greater good."

I tried to recoil and failed. "I won't be a part of something like that, whatever it is. The greater good? So many atrocities have been committed in the name of the greater good. Screw that. You can kill me instead."

"That's very noble of you, Guinevere, but you don't have much of a choice."

"It's Evie!"

Nathan got up and walked to the end of the bed. "The healer says you need rest, but that you'll be fine tomorrow. Which is good because you'll be starting introductory classes at the Academy in the morning."

"Why?" I asked.

Nathan cleared his throat and started removing my boots. I couldn't fight him off.

"Answer me," I said. "Why do you want me here? Why do I get sick whenever magic happens? What is that about?"

"I don't know yet," Nathan said. "But it's important, and I'm going to make sure that you're prepared for whatever comes. Fate delivered you to the society, and I won't let you go. It's too dangerous for you out there."

"I don't understand."

He dropped my boots beside the bed and removed my socks. I kind of relished the fact that he had to deal with my stinky feet. Consider it a minor punishment for what he'd done to me thus far.

"Neither do I." Nathan came to my bedside again, carefully sat me upright, and unzipped the back of the black skin-tight suit I'd been given.

"What are you doing?" I gasped at the cool influx of air.

"I'm caring for you," he replied, his jaw clenched. "I'm making sure that you're safe and protected. Despite what you might think, everything that I've done has been for your own good. You, Evie, are... you're going to help me make things right."

"Right?"

"Things are off-balance in our world," Nathan said quietly. "The real world. The magical world. And I knew the minute I saw you that I had to keep you safe because you might be able to help set things right."

"Why? Why me? This doesn't make any sense."

He carefully stripped my shirt off, exposing my bra underneath. Nathan averted his eyes, but his pulse hopped in his throat, and his knuckles whitened on the fabric of my shirt. "I told you I don't have an answer to that, but let's just say, I'm not entirely convinced you're human." He moved to the black pants next and unzipped them.

Again, I gasped at the influx of cool air against my skin. "Not human?" I managed.

I could barely think thanks to exhaustion, and Nathan's gentle touches weren't helping. They distracted me in a different way.

"Has anything strange happened to you?" Nathan asked. "Anything you couldn't explain? Accidents or windfalls?"

I considered telling him about the random events I'd passed off as bad luck or clumsiness in my life. The explosions, or moving mannequins, or cars crashing or... there were so many random events. And then there was the tarot card I'd found. Not the one the Hierophant Society had sent me, but the other one. The one with the number on the back that no longer existed.

Nathan stripped off my pants completely then stepped back. His gaze traveled over my body, head-to-toe, and he cleared his throat. "You need to shower," he said.

"No," I replied. "I really don't. You've already showered me in enough bullshit to last me a lifetime." As sexy as he was, he wasn't giving me the answers I wanted. He wasn't acting normally, even for a psycho magic dude. "Cover me with a blanket and leave me alone."

Nathan's nostrils flared. He did as I'd asked, though, tucking the blanket around me gently, up to my chin.

He bent close to switch off the bedside lamp. "Sleep well," he said, his lips close to my ear, sending a shiver through me again. "Tomorrow we'll start fresh."

16

Braddock arrived at 6:00 a.m. the following morning and hauled my ass out of bed. I was permitted a shower, a quick meal in that private room, and then forced down flights of stairs and into the basement. This time, I noticed the off-shooting passages, the strange discoloration of walls that were actually doors, as we descended.

"Meet me in this room at 5:00 p.m. sharp," Braddock said, opening the door for me. "I mean it, Miss Crowley. Not a second later."

"I heard you." I tried not to be irritable about it, but I couldn't keep the nip from my tone. It was clear that Braddock didn't like me. Didn't want me around. I got it. I didn't belong, but that didn't mean I had to like her shitty attitude.

I stepped into the hall of admission and the door snapped shut behind me.

"Hey, wait," I said, turning back to it. "What about lunch?"

"Thinking of your stomach, already, Miss Crowley? Did they not feed you this morning?"

Scholar Harwa sat behind his grand desk with its hieroglyphs and depictions. He rested one meaty red-raw hand on a stack of books, his black claws shifting as he tapped his fingers impatiently.

A flash of last night came back to me, and fear wormed into my belly.

I'd seen the precursor to what vampires could do.

"You've encountered more of my kind," Harwa said, croaking it out. "I'm surprised you lived to tell the tale."

"Why don't you look like a human?" I asked.

Harwa raised what I assumed was an eyebrow. It was really just a meaty patch of flesh above his eye.

"Oh, I see. You mean, why do I not wear the guise of a human instead of looking like this?" He gestured to himself. "This is my true form. It takes significant energy to maintain the appearance of a human, energy I no longer have at five hundred years of age."

My jaw dropped.

"And I have no reason to hide. I am in the employ of the Academy of Scribes, and everyone who attends the academy or is part of the Hierophant Society which is connected to this portal, knows what I am. Why hide my true nature? Far less duplicitous. Would you feel more comfortable if I was a doddering old man? Or perhaps someone who looked a little more like Nathan Sword."

I colored. "I don't care what you look like."

"I am so utterly relieved."

So, vampires were good at sarcasm. Cool.

"Come here, child." He beckoned.

"Call me Evie."

"Very well, Evie. Come here, please."

I approached the desk, taking breaths to keep my panic at

bay. Scholar Harwa wouldn't hurt me, if only because he was forced not to.

"Correct," Harwa said. "Only because of that. You smell quite delicious, if I'm honest."

"Thanks?"

"You're welcome. Twenty-one is a good year, is it not?" Harwa sniffed and shifted the stack of books toward me. "A good vintage, I mean."

"Funny."

"Yes, blood comedy is a gift of mine. Now." Harwa clapped his hands and his claws clicked gently. "Your first class this morning will be with Scholar Jezebel, who will be introducing you to the finer details of magical race, class, and proficiency. Introduction to magic is the name of the course. I have taken the liberty of having a timetable drawn up for you, and this is your map. You are to stick to the areas I have highlighted in green. Those highlighted in red will lead to a swift death for you."

"So, like the third-floor corridor in Harry Potter?" I asked, raising an eyebrow.

"Who is Harry Potter and why does he contain a third-floor corridor? The mind boggles. Humans will remain a mystery to me."

"I know you can read my thoughts."

"Yes, but it's rather like reading a book that was written in no particular order with some words misspelled and others written backward."

"Thanks."

"Once again, you are welcome." Harwa tapped the map with his claw. "The red corridors are off-bounds because they're frequented by a particular society's students. A society which mostly consists of half-breed vampires, shifters, and darker entities. They do not look upon interference kindly."

"Which society is that?" I asked.

Harwa hesitated, his dark red eyes wandering to the door I'd come through. "The Hanged Man Society."

"Oh."

"Now, you will find everything you need to know on these two information sheets," Harwa said. "I'm sure your stomach will lead you to the cafeteria when it's time for lunch, but if you happen to get lost, I've marked that particular area in blue on the map."

"Thank you."

"Just doing my duty, Evie."

"Still," I replied. "Thank you. Weirdly enough, I feel like you're the only, uh, person I've had a real conversation with since I've been here."

"Oh, dear. I pity you."

"I'll just fuck off then, shall I?" I grabbed my books, schedule, and map and headed for the door. Or portal as Harwa had called it.

"Evie," he croaked.

I turned my head.

"Once you step through that door, I will be unable to protect you. Neither will Mr. Sword, or Miss Braddock, or any of the others in this society. It is no man's land for a reason. Stick to the green areas on the map if you value your life."

"I will," I said, and then, with a sweaty palm, I grasped the door handle and let myself into the Academy of Scribes.

17

Holy crap on a cracker.

I stood on the third floor, behind a wooden balustrade, looking down into a glistening wood-floored atrium filled with light and sound and people. Or creatures. A mixture of both. A few of them hung out next to a fountain, laughing and chatting. Others walked by below, heading toward classes, I assumed. There were animals too, mixed in among the other students, and a few very obvious vampires. None of them used phones, because, of course, phones wouldn't work down here.

The light that filled the atrium came from the crystal roof itself, which glowed but provided no view. It was simply white, shining as if the sun was just on the other side.

I took a breath, but it did nothing to still my heart.

If I'd thought things were weird yesterday, it was nothing compared to this. There were a *lot* of people down here. It was an underground university, brimming with students. How the hell did they keep it hidden?

Scholar Harwa had said that all the societies around the

city were connected to this Academy. And then there had to be other cities of supernatural creatures, of sorcerers and vampires and heaven alone knew what else.

I swallowed.

Take deep breaths. This is fine.

"First class," I muttered. "Look for your first class." I clasped the books to my chest and scrambled the schedule off the top of them.

8:00 a.m.—Introduction to Magic, Hall 3A

OK, simple enough. Hall 3A. I grabbed the map off the top of it and squinted at the intersecting hallways of green and red and yellow and this was so friggin' complicated. And I had ten minutes until my first class.

I hurried down the steps to my left, the soles of my heeled boots clopping against the wood. I reached the bottom floor and stopped to scan the map again, trying not to pay too much attention to the groups of people nearest me.

"—that?"

"Weird."

"She doesn't smell normal."

Great. Now they can smell that I don't fit in.

I exhaled, lifted my chin, and started walking. Heads turned, people watched me as I navigated along the corridors. Most people wore regular clothing, jeans and shirts, or dresses or whatever, but there were a few people with hoods and cloaks, others who peered at me from within the cowls of hoodies.

You're fine.

This was what I'd always wanted, right? To go to college? To have a normal life.

Yeah, because vampires and magic are normal.

A young woman with face tattoos and two nose rings leaned against the wall, arms folded, studying me as I passed by. She smirked, but didn't say anything.

3A. Focus on getting to class.

I checked my map and took the hall toward my class. The corridors here were just as confusing as the ones upstairs had been. The floors were stone, the sconces on the walls holding flickering torches. The aesthetic reminded me of a castle library.

Finally, I found the heavy wooden door with a golden "3A" printed on the front. I opened it and entered a broad auditorium with a series of raised stone daises and wooden desks sweeping upward. The teacher, or scholar, sat atop another of those desks with hieroglyphics and ancient Egyptian symbols.

Most of the desks were already full, and I suffered the stares from more humans and creatures as I made my way up to the back of the class and found an empty desk. I loaded my books on top of it then leaned on them.

Chatter filled the class, people leaning between desks, talking; I observed, drinking in the atmosphere, the strangeness.

There were vampires here too, young men and women probably around my age, a few with eye colors that didn't make sense. A group of people *glimmered* at the other end of the room, drawing attention but keeping to themselves, they had hair colored in bright greens and golds.

The door to the classroom opened, and a hooded figure entered. The only empty seats were next to mine, and I gritted my teeth.

I didn't much like the idea of this dementor-looking mother fucker sitting next to me, but I didn't have a choice.

He walked up the steps and took a seat to my right, the soft scent of spicy cologne drifting over to me. The hands poking out of the ends of his sleeves were pale and strong. A man's hands. Then why wear the robe?

I lifted my gaze, and a shock passed through me. As much as I'd been studying him, he'd been doing the same to me. My heart skipped a beat.

The eyes peering out at me from within the hood glowed red ever so slightly, but the tip of the nose was human, the jawline strong. He tugged the hood closer to his face and turned away.

"Good morning, class," Scholar Jezebel said. "I'm glad you all made it on time this morning. I know some of our first years struggle to find their way around the Academy." Jezebel was curvy, with dark flowing locks and a million watt smile. "As you might know from your schedules, I'm Scholar Jezebel, and I will be introducing you to magical classes, races, and proficiencies."

One of the glimmering dudes near the front of the glass groaned and rolled his eyes.

"I know that most of you have a solid understanding of this information thanks to your past education, but it's in the interest of all societies and magical peoples to have a base understanding of this course material. Understanding leads to acceptance, and acceptance helps our different races to work together." Jezebel's smile brightened further, and she lifted her arms, feathered wings spread from her back, spanning well past her arms, so that they nearly brushed the sides of the room. Each feather was cream and tipped gold, as if it had been dipped in ink, and Jezebel's head glowed ever so slightly.

I gasped, and, thankfully, wasn't the only one.

"I am a child of Horus," she said. "Humans would call me an angel, but you will learn that that's not exactly true. Though, I'll admit I take that compliment every time." The wings folded and disappeared as quickly as they had come.

After last night, I'd figured that it was magic that had made me sick. But I felt no twinge of a headache now, no nausea or dizziness. Then did I have an actual disease? Or...?

"Open your books to page 10, please," Jezebel said, "and we'll get started."

I took a breath and opened the textbook that had been assigned for this class. *Magical Classes and Races: An Introduction.*

Page 10 was the start of a new chapter.

An image of the pharaonic figure fighting a snake dominated the first page—the picture itself embossed on the cream paper in bronze ink.

"We'll start with an introduction to the duality," Scholar Jezebel said, circling the desk and taking a seat atop it, her ankles crossed. She was beautiful, dark skin glowing faintly, her gaze almost regal. "As most of you will know, the duality are the two creative forces that govern our world. The forces of order and chaos, Atum and Apep. From these forces spring all races."

I had heard pretty much the same from Scholar Harwa upstairs, but I paid rapt attention nevertheless. I'd always been jealous of girls who'd gone to college, and this was my chance. Kind of. Maybe. I couldn't be the only college student who'd been abducted and forced to learn things that were way out of their depth, right?

That's not funny at all.

"The basic races are simple, the humanoid sorcerers, the

children of Anat or the fae, the sons of Sekhmet or vampires as they're commonly called, and shifters under the guidance of various gods and goddesses."

"What about half-breeds?" The glimmering guy in the corner, green-haired, gorgeous, and painfully arrogant, lazed in his chair, eyeing Scholar Jezebel.

Jezebel gave him a withering look, and he straightened incrementally. "I'll be guiding the class today, Leaf. Feel free to apply to become a scholar once you've graduated, but until then, keep your questions until I ask for them."

He averted his eyes at the embarrassment while others in the class chuckled.

"Shifters governed by the gods and goddesses have specific skill sets. As a child of Horus, I'm able to bring peace when it's required. Good for negotiations or dealing with difficult students."

Another smattering of appreciative laughter.

I was so out of my depth here. Holy crap.

And what had she called vampires? The sons of Sekhmet? Did that mean they were all male?

"Humanoid sorcerers, those closest to the pharaonic line, have various magical abilities or classes, governed by the creative duality." Jezebel paused, sweeping her gaze over the classroom, and the students stiffened—a ripple that spread through the room. "Hybrids," she said, "are the mingling of races. This mixture has granted them unique powers and weaknesses."

Hybrids. Half-breeds? Why had everyone gone quiet at the mention of that?

"I want you all to study the first chapter now. We'll have an open discussion ten minutes before the end of the lecture regarding the strengths, weaknesses, and intrigues of each race, as well as their basis."

I bowed my head, casting a glance off to the side. The red-eyed, hooded guy stared at me from underneath his hood.

Great. Trust me to sit next to the creepy stalker of the class.

I turned my attention back to the book and paged through it, opting to check out the pictures first.

Sorcerers were on the first page, the depiction of a pharaoh holding a staff aloft, the end glowing with power, light arcing from his shoulders upward.

The sons of Sekhmet, or vampires, looked as gross on the page as they did in real life. A man, his right half smiling, handsome, and human, his left half red, raw, twisted, fingers ending in talons that grasped the top of a woman's decapitated head.

They really went in with these pictures. Damn.

The fae, or children of Anat, were represented by a gorgeous, naked woman, floating atop water among reeds, hair spread around her head, and her fingertips sprouting vines.

Each turn of the page brought a new picture, a new type of being that shouldn't have been possible. I couldn't help smiling.

The children of Horus were described as peace-bringers and eagle-shifters, the image showing another woman, much like Scholar Jezebel, wings spread to the side, gazing toward the sky.

I turned the page and nearly lost my breath.

Hybrid Vampire

A mingling of the sons of Sekhmet and humanoid sorcerers.

Considered unnatural by many, though fast gaining prominence in the societies as they are useful fighters, albeit as weak to alcohol as other vampires. The only cure for alcoholic affliction is to sup upon blood.

My gaze traveled to the picture beneath it.

A man, strong jawline, completely naked, sparking red magic, his eyes glowing with malevolence and his lips parted to reveal black fangs.

The dizziness that had been absent this morning, blessedly absent, slammed into me. I clutched the sides of my desk, the room tipping left to right, left to right, swirling in and out of focus in my peripheral vision. I couldn't look away from the image of the hybrid vampire.

It moved, out of time with my dizziness, seeming to beckon. To threaten me. Its eyes bore through mine, challenging, and blood dripped down its chin, running onto the perfectly sculpted pectorals and abs.

Flashes of hot and cold ran through me. A continuous stream of sensory input, and I squeezed my eyes shut.

Don't pass out. You're not going to pass out. Not here.

The world tipped upside down, and I landed against something warm and hard. Strong arms encircled me, an even stronger chest pressing against my back, holding me upright.

The picture! He's got me.

"—collapsed."

"Miss Crowley?" The voice was female. "Miss Crowley, can you hear me?"

I opened my eyes.

Scholar Jezebel's concerned face waxed into view. "Miss Crowley?"

"Evie," I managed.

"Evie," she said. "You fainted. Did you have breakfast this morning?"

I nodded and the back of my head brushed against something. Someone. I turned my head, panic crawling up my throat, the spicy scent of cologne invading my nostrils. It was him. The hooded guy who'd glared at me from the desk over.

Except he was no longer hooded. His skin was pale as a sheet, hair black, eyes glowing red. His nose was crooked, as if it'd been broken more than once, his lips soft, redder than they should have been.

"—the infirmary. Have a nurse make sure you're fine," Jezebel was saying.

Another wave of dizziness wound through me at the sight of my "rescuer."

"Mr. Davis can escort you," Scholar Jezebel finished.

"No," I said quickly, slipping away from him. He'd been holding me. Cradling me. "I can make it on my own."

"I won't have you fainting in the halls of the Academy, Miss Crowley."

"I can make it on my own," I repeated then scrambled for the door. The farther I got from the guy, the hybrid, that's what he had to be, the easier it was to breathe.

I slipped out of the classroom and shut the thick wooden door behind me, my heart pounding.

What the hell have I gotten myself into?

18

I'D CULTIVATED a list of poor decisions over the course of my life, and there was some stiff competition for the top spot, but this had to take the cake.

Running out of the classroom without my map of the Academy? Yeah, now I was lost and potentially wandering down one of those halls marked as red by Scholar Harwa. Unfortunately, the realization had only come to me five turns and as many corridors away from the classroom.

I'd been so set on putting as much distance between myself and the hybrid vampire. I hadn't seen his teeth, but the picture had told me everything I needed to know. Kind of. For now.

The dizziness couldn't be coincidental, right?

But then, why had I grown dizzy on the night I'd run from Nathan? And why when the other vampires attacked? They didn't seem to connect.

Frustration bubbled through me. When was I going to make sense of all of this?

I took a breath, inhaling the scent of old wood and stone, a mustiness that wasn't entirely unpleasant. Torches flickered along the walls, casting long shadows, and the halls were silent. Everyone was in class.

What if I'm in one of the red halls?

The thought brought on goosebumps, and I turned in a full circle, searching for figures in the shadows.

This was ridiculous. I'd spent the last couple of months walking home from a dangerous bar in a dangerous neighborhood in the middle of the night. I was used to being aware, full of crap, maybe even a little kick-ass.

Yeah, that was fine when you didn't know vampires existed.

An image of Vera with black claws digging into her flesh, her eyes wide moments before she lost her life, drifted up to greet me.

"Stop," I murmured and tugged my tank top straight. I set off down the hall, taking deep breaths and listening hard for any sounds of movement.

The best option now was to navigate back to the classroom and get my stuff so I could go to my next class or get some lunch or whatever was next. The dizziness was gone now, anyway.

Until you see that guy again.

Worse, he'd been sinfully attractive. Like how I imagined Count Dracula would've looked. How I'd envisioned vampires looked before I'd met Scholar Harwa or known they were real.

What was with this week? I'd met two guys who looked as if they could've stepped off the cover of a magazine and both of them were suspicious or downright terrifying. Was I being punished for something?

I took two rights and left, hoping that my memory didn't

fail me. But the halls grew more narrow, the darkness more intense, the torches along the walls spaced out sparsely.

"No way," I muttered.

But another three turns brought me to the darkest hall yet. My skin crawled, and I had no doubt that this was one of the halls Harwa had marked in red. Enemy territory? A place that was dangerous for humans like me.

Stay calm. Just breathe.

The air here was close, almost humid, the musty smell worse than before, smelling more and more like dirt and fungus. Like I was buried underground, in a grave, rather than walking through a building.

How deep underground was I? I hadn't taken any stairs other than the ones from the entrance hall earlier.

I rounded another corner and entered a hall with a single torch. It sputtered, letting out a fizz or crackle every now and again. I walked past it carefully, my feet almost leading themselves, and stopped in front of a thick wooden door, its brass doorknob tarnished. The room beyond it was dark.

Where am I?

There was nothing good on the other side of this door, right? It certainly didn't lead back to the classroom as I hadn't been through a door since I'd left it.

So why did I want to open?

My fingers itched toward the doorknob, my pulse pattering against the inside of my throat.

It was just a random door, for fuck's sake. It was no big deal. It wasn't like I—

"You shouldn't be here." The voice was deep, almost throaty, and came from directly behind me.

I spun on the spot and nearly fell into the hooded figure now blocking my only way out. It was *him.* The hybrid.

His red eyes glared at me from inside the hood. He reached up and lowered it carefully. "You shouldn't be here."

"You said that already." My eyes watered and the dizziness threatened but then receded.

What the hell?

"It bore repeating," he replied.

"What are you doing here?" I asked. "Are you following me or something?" A wave of fear, quashed only by sheer force of will. "Because that's psycho, dude."

"Scholar Jezebel asked me to make sure you didn't get lost," he said. "You left these behind." He lifted a backpack that wasn't mine, unzipped it, and revealed my books, schedule, and map inside. "It's not safe for you down here."

"Is that a threat?" I lifted my chin.

I didn't know why, but he got my back up. It wasn't the same as Nathan. Nathan was plain arrogant. There was something that was *wrong* about this guy. So wrong it was verging on *right.* And I didn't like that one iota.

"Of course not," he said, then licked his lips gently. Those too red lips. Those black, fanged teeth whenever he talked. "Why would I threaten you?"

"You just told me it's dangerous down here, right? And you're blocking my path."

He stepped back, shrugging, allowing me passage but just barely. He was much taller, and lean, but filling up half the passageway so I'd have to brush by him.

Right. Now, I had to figure out which way to brush past him. Face to face? Awkward. Butt to face?

"I can escort you to the infirmary if you're still feeling ill," he said. "But that's as far as I'm willing to take you."

"Such a gentleman." I opted for face-to-face and tried brushing past him. My breasts pressed against his chest, and that spicy cologne nearly overwhelmed me. I stopped, blinking, my eyes watering again.

"I'm not a gentleman." He growled softly. "I thought the picture in that textbook told you as much."

He had noticed. Me staring. Me nearly passing out.

We stared at each other for a long moment, our bodies touching, his breathing even, but his pupils dilating as they roved over my face and lingered on my neck. My heart went crazy, my skin prickling all over.

What are you doing? Move.

His hands pressed to my shoulders, a gentle pressure, and his eyelids fluttered. His palms glided down to my upper arms, and he grasped them. He lifted me effortlessly and set me down ahead of him in the corridor.

My vision swam again. I stumbled, trying to catch myself on the smooth stone walls.

His arm looped around my middle, and he lifted me, setting me upright again.

"You're so fucking annoying," he growled in my ear. "You shouldn't be here if you can't even look after yourself. Weak."

"Let go of me," I snapped.

He did, and I stumbled and nearly fell again. This time, he caught me by the back of my shirt, inches from the ground.

"Why would they allow you in?" he asked. "Why you? Are they insane?"

"That's none of your business." The dizziness had slowly started subsiding, so I shook him off and pressed my hand to the wall, breathing until my heart rate calmed and my vision returned to normal. "I'll take my books now. And my map. Thank you."

He grunted and brought the stuff out, shoving it into my arms haphazardly. "Maybe invest in a bookbag?"

"Maybe invest in minding your own business."

"Whatever."

"The comeback of the century," I said, setting off so I could get distance between us. The thoughts and reactions I'd had to him weren't natural. Were vampires as seductive as they'd been made out to be in human literature? Because if so, at least I had an excuse for needing to change my friggin' underwear.

This guy was a dick.

Well, nobody could claim I didn't have a type, at least.

I whipped out my map and studied it. It didn't help. I had no reference point for where I might be.

A pale finger pressed to the map over an intersection of those red-marked hallways. "You're here." He slid the fingertip farther away, toward the atrium. "You want to get here."

I gritted my teeth. "Thanks," I muttered.

"Just trying to get this over with."

"What? What over with?"

"Following you around and making sure you don't get skewered by the big bads," he replied. "Torture, basically. I've never wanted a pet human, but here we are."

"What's your problem?" I turned on him, enduring another skip in my pulse.

He stared down at me haughtily. "I think that's obvious."

I rolled my eyes, turned away, and started walking, following the paths back toward the blue area. The hybrid vampire haunted my steps, keeping back, but was there every time I turned around, his hood back up and his eyes glaring at me from underneath it, bright red and glowing hatefully.

Finally, the halls grew less musty, lighter, and the sounds of chatter and laughter grew. I'd made it back to relative safety, if I set aside the hybrid vampire tail.

I turned to tell him to get lost, but he was already gone. And I was back to square one with no clue why I was here or what Nathan and the Hierophant Society wanted of me.

19

*T*AROT, *in and of itself, was taken from Egypt and brought into Europe. Though there's some dispute as to its origin among humankind, the supernatural know not only the true origins but the true power of the decks.*

The foundation of Tarot Societies became a necessity after the First Changing, in which all contact with the Duality ceased. Or was lost. Scholars are still uncertain as to which occurred, but the consensus remains that those supernatural creatures who were left without guidance immediately sought it.

The principles of supernatural society as we know it would not have come to be if not for the founding of these Societies. Originally, each of the societies were in possession of a single major arcana card from the tarot deck the {redacted} used to convene with the Duality directly. Those cards were lost or sold during the Second Changing, whereafter a new form of communication rose.

Namely, the creation of several slightly less powerful tarot decks, Pharaonic Decks, each connected to an equally powerful {redacted} (pg. 145, Magical Powers and their Control, Hanrecker & Shrall, 1945). The purpose of which was to convene with the lesser Gods and Goddesses rather than the Duality themselves. A degree of sepa-ration was deemed best.

A simpler description for newer scholars would be as follows.

First Dynasty (3100 BC): {redacted} {redacted} maintain contact with the Duality, Gods and Goddesses without the need for tarot cards.

The First Changing (30 BC): {redacted} {redacted} lose the ability to contact the Duality directly. The Life Deck is created in accor-dance with the Keeper's wishes, as recorded in the Book of Life. {redacted} {redacted} {redacted} genocide.

The Second Changing (1600 AD): The Life Deck is lost, the Keeper retreats to his annals, the Pharaonic Decks are created.

I placed my finger on the page in *An Introduction to the Historical Realities of Magic and its Origins* and exhaled, slowly. What in the hell had I just read?

There was so much more to this "world" than I'd antici-pated. My childish imaginings of what a hidden magical society would be like had been so simple in comparison to this.

And what was with the "redacted" part? Why would they have allowed redactions in a textbook that was being used by students?

"Breathe," I whispered, and took several deep and even breaths.

It didn't help that I was hangry.

The last time I'd eaten had been downstairs at the Academy for lunch, and that had been one of the weirdest experiences of my life. Watching half-vampires, who made me dizzy, and real vampires, drinking blood by the glass? Yeah, weird.

Needless to say, I hadn't had much of an appetite, and now it was a quarter past seven, and I was up in my prison cell.

I scanned the page of recommended reading one last time before grabbing a bookmark from the bedside table and inserting it between the pages. I was the type of girl who could not bring myself to fold the corner of a page. It was sacrilege.

I bounced off the bed and strode over to the door, my socked feet slipping across the boards a little. I tried the door knob but it was locked. Braddock had turned the key earlier.

"Hey!" I yelled. "Hey, I'm starving in here! Hello?"

No answer.

I gritted my teeth.

I'd grown increasingly frustrated as time passed. I was both enamored by this new world and furious at being trapped in it. Ironic for a girl who'd so badly wanted to fit in somewhere. Now, I was being forced to fit, and I wasn't sure if I was the square peg or the round hole.

"Ew," I muttered. "Round hole? Really?"

I was all set to pace back to the bed in a rage, but the latch on the door clicked.

I froze, gazing at it, my hand reaching and—

Nathan opened the door. He wore a shirt, sleeves rolled up, the first few buttons undone to reveal tan skin beneath, and his sparkling blue eyes held me in place for a moment. "Dinner," he said, directing my attention toward the tray in his hand, complete with a domed silver cover.

I backed up a few paces. "Thanks. What is it?"

"I don't know," he said. "Something the chef cooked up." He walked it over to the desk against the wall and set it down.

"Have you been demoted?" I returned to the bed, putting distance between us.

His blond eyebrows dipped inward.

"I mean, surely an important guy like you shouldn't be running errands like this," I said, gesturing to the tray. "Don't you have a servant to do this kind of thing for you?"

"I'm sensing disdain."

"You would be correct," I replied.

Nathan sighed, undoing another button at the top of his shirt and drawing my attention to his Adam's apple. "The funny thing about being wealthy is that all those who aren't assume they'd do anything differently if they were in my position. The majority of people would buy a mansion, a sports car, new clothes, and have people do all the boring daily activities for them, regardless of their opinions or moral compunctions."

"You're wrong," I said, lifting my head. "You can't generalize like that. Not everyone's going to become some weird overlord just because they have money."

"Noble," he said. "But mainly naive. I would envy you, but I'm going to have to strip you of that naivete quickly." He shut the door and locked it from the inside.

"Whoa. Maybe don't talk about stripping me and then lock the door right afterward? That's a good way to get punched in the gonads."

Nathan looked on the brink of an eye roll, but stopped himself. "What's your schedule like tomorrow?"

"I've got a spa appointment at three, why do you ask?" I fluttered my eyelashes at him.

Nathan drew closer to me, stopping a few feet off, as if

he'd hit an invisible wall and couldn't go any further. "I need you to train with me," he said.

"Train?"

"Hand-to-hand combat, basic self-defense," he replied. "I don't want a repeat of the last mission."

"Then don't take me with you." I'd had nightmares about Vera, and I couldn't help the guilt that had set in after what'd happened. "Leave me here. Or let me go."

"I'm never letting you go."

Shivers broke out all over my body, and not the bad kind either. I broke eye contact, refusing to acknowledge the power he had over me, even with just a few words. This had to be a sorcerer thing, right? There was no real connection between us?

I'd spent years believing that I wasn't fit to be a part of the real world, that at any moment, people would discover my terrible secret. Anyway, the thought of being involved with a guy had always terrified me for that reason.

What happened when they found out?

Not happening.

"Fine," I said, "I'll learn the self-defense. Can I have my dinner in peace now, please?"

"There's one other thing," he said. "We're going on a mission next week, so I'll expect you to take this training seriously."

"What mission? Has this got to do with that, uh, Kasha woman and the tarot deck you were talking about?" I desperately wanted to pry the information out of him. He'd been anything but forthcoming.

"Unfortunately not," he said. "She's disappeared, and the

Upside Down Club with its lead has become too dangerous for the Hierophant Society, at least for now."

"So then where are we going?"

"We'll be approaching another contact. J.P. has managed to secure a meeting with the Serpentine Prince," Nathan said.

The name gave me the chills. "The Serpentine Prince?"

"He's fae. Hence the need for self-defense training."

"Why? What's wrong with the fae?"

"Born of Anat, the Goddess of desire and fertility, bringer of war. They are walking dichotomies, both beautiful and violent. Manipulative," he said. "Always keep your guard up with fae."

"I wonder if they keep prisoners." I thumbed my chin, eyeing him.

"No. They do not. Feel lucky this was the society you wandered into." Nathan smile was wry, yet still sexy. Bastard. "I'll leave you to eat and get some sleep." He exited, leaving his cologne on the air.

I waited until he locked the door again before approaching the tray. Since I'd been here, I'd been treated surprisingly well, barring the whole vampire attack and physical restrictions. I'd been given tank tops, jeans, and boots in my exact size and style, as well as great food, books, and a massive bedroom with a view of the gardens below. Granted, that view was obscured by bars, but still.

I still couldn't fathom why, other than Nathan's insistence that I had to be on missions. That I was "important." The phrase made my skin crawl.

Any second they'd find out that I was the real monster. Metaphorically, of course.

I shook off the negative thoughts and lifted the cover off

the tray. A chicken burger and fries, ketchup on the side, and a bottle of water. Not exactly the most "nutritious" food, but my stomach grumbled. The food here was way better than at home. And I'd consider it fuel for my investigations.

Nathan wanted the tarot deck, and as I'd just learned from the book, the current decks were a means of connecting with Gods and Goddesses.

What did Nathan Sword want with the Gods?

DARKNESS.

And then, a speck of light at the end of a tunnel. Sound. Breathing. My breathing.

I flexed my hands, lifted them in front of my face. They were visible only because of that glimmer of something in the distance.

Where am I?

The hall. The Academy of Scribes.

The answers had come from nowhere and everywhere, whispered into my mind. A shiver traveled down my spine, the hair rising on the back of my neck.

Why am I here?

Walk.

Again, the whisper into my mind.

I put one foot in front of the other and found that I was barefoot, the stone cold and clammy against my soles. A smell of mustiness assaulted my nostrils.

This doesn't feel right.

Walk.

I did as the voiceless whisper told me and approached the

glimmer in the distance. The glimmer became four slashes of light in the darkness, creating a rectangle.

A door.

Open it.

I reached it, my pulse pounding in my throat, and stopped. It was *the door*. The same one I'd found in the narrow hallway earlier in the day.

Which day? What?

My fingers reached for the doorknob and rested against them. The light pulsed golden and grew.

Open it.

I tightened my grip, willing myself to do as the voice had told me. What was on the other side? What would I find? What if—?

Too late.

What? What do you mean too—

My body was flung backward, my fingers ripped free of the doorknob, and I landed heavily. My skull cracked against the stone, and the image of the door faded from view.

20

The following day...

I YAWNED as I made my way back up the stairs that led toward the mansion. So far, I'd had breakfast, two classes, and no dizzy spells even though the devilishly attractive half-vampire who had tailed me had been in both those classes. Now, I got to have fun getting beat up by Nathan himself.

What was he called? Not the General but the Steward, whatever that meant. Regardless, he'd given me the freedom to make my way down to the Academy by myself today. No Braddock to babysit me. A relief.

And now, I got the opportunity to muddle my way through the mansion, using a second map I'd been given, to find him in the courtyard for training.

I exited onto the mansion's first floor and brought my map out of my backpack—another new addition I'd found waiting at the foot of my bed this morning. Creepy as hell that someone had come in and put it there.

"OK," I muttered, and opened the map—it was printed out like a tourist's map of the city, which was equal parts amusing and insulting. "OK, let's see." I drew a line along the map from my current position toward the courtyard. It wasn't too far away, but, apparently, the entrance closest to me was situated behind a tapestry.

It should've seemed crazy to me, but after the past few days. Nothing was crazy anymore.

I took the rights and lefts required and arrived in front of a tapestry depicting a battle. Warriors in Ancient Egyptian battle garb road on the backs of chariots, holding spears aloft as other soldiers ran from them in terror.

I shuddered and shifted the side of the tapestry away from the wall. A dark passage beyond.

"Here goes nothing," I muttered, and entered it.

The passage smelled of nothing, and I frowned. Musty smell? Had I dreamed something about hallways and odors?

I shook my head and continued. The sound of metal against metal drew me onward, toward a door at the end of the passage. It bore a small viewing window and was made of thick wood.

And the view was spectacular.

A broad circle of packed ground expanding outward with benches for spectators around the rim. It reminded me of a gladiator ring without the stands. The sky was blue above, and I nearly pressed the door open just to get a hint of sun on my cheeks. It had been so damn long.

Movement stalled me before I got the chance.

Two figures stood in the center of the pit. No spectators watched them.

One was Nathan, his chest exposed, sweat dripping down his tan, lithe body. He grasped a khopesh in one hand, bronze and glinting in the sunlight, and his eyes glowed that unnatural blue as he stared at the man opposite him.

The sparring partner wore a full suit, still neatly buttoned, his blonde hair slicked back on the sides. He was tall, with steel gray eyes, and he turned a small blade over and over in one hand, flicking it almost lazily.

It's the ritualist.

The memory of that night came back full force, and I sucked in breaths to calm myself. No dizziness, yet.

This was the guy who had been converting people into society members with magic.

"—weakened by her presence, Brother," the gray-eyed man said, smiling lazily. "Breaking a sweat during a sparring match?"

"You have no idea what you're talking about, Killian." Nathan took up an offensive posture and began circling, he held his khopesh aloft and angled toward his brother.

"You should refer to me as your General," Killian replied easily, not bothering to turn as Nathan circled him. "Father would not be happy if he heard about your insubordination."

"Father was the one who gave me this task. He trusted me!"

"Well, it was about time you did something of use, wasn't it?" Killian asked easily. "Rather than lazing upstairs and doing the finances."

"Not everything needs to be answered with violence."

"Yes, you prefer subterfuge," Killian said. "Don't you?

Pattering through the dark like a little rat. Remind me how your last mission went, Brother? I believe I lost a valuable Alpha because of your actions with this *girl* of yours."

Nathan launched into an attack, making no noise but the shuffle of his feet in the sand, and Killian moved.

It wasn't that he *actually* moved. It was like one second he was there, the next, he was behind Nathan. Killian looped an arm around his brother's neck and pulled it tight, lifting the blade toward his throat.

Nathan rammed his head backward into his brother's face. The resulting crack made me wince.

Killian released him calmly and withdrew a handkerchief from the top pocket of his suit jacket. How the hell was he wearing a suit in this humidity, anyway? Heedless of the heat or the split along the bridge of his nose, Killian smiled. He dabbed the blood away.

"Feisty this morning," he said. "All those muscles and nowhere to use them, eh?"

"You have no idea what's coming," Nathan replied.

"Failure. I have no doubt about it, Brother. Every task you have been assigned, you've failed. I will relish the day when father banishes you altogether. Perhaps, he'll put you down in the Academy. You can serve lunch in the cafeteria."

Nathan lunged again, a volley of sword attacks, flame leaping from his blade's edge. Killian dodged effortlessly, toying with his prey.

"Oh, little brother. Would that you had been a miscarriage."

"Fuck you," Nathan spat.

"I'm sure you'll get plenty of that from your new toy."

The men separated again, glaring at each other.

"You don't talk about her like that," Nathan said.

"Or what? What on earth are *you* going to do about it?" Killian asked. "You're so obsessed with your special little prize. Your boring little... what is she, human? Or something twisted and desirable? You always had a perverse streak."

Nathan didn't reply, and my heart beat against the inside of my throat, my hands pressed to either side of the door, eyes glued to them.

"What if," Killian said, "I talk to Father about her? What then?"

"He assigned the task to me." Nathan was on the brink of losing control. His lips had peeled back over his teeth.

"What if I pay her a visit tonight?"

"I'll kill you if you touch her," Nathan replied. "I'll fucking kill you."

I hadn't heard Nathan curse this much since he'd abducted me.

"That's quaint. But I think I'll make a point of it. You know, I have a certain charm when it comes to damsels in distress. I'm sure she'd be interested to know why you have her here."

"You can't do that."

"I do what I want," Killian said, "when I want. That's why Father chose me. I'm willing to make decisions you worry over, little boy." He swept his blade out to the side, one hand behind his back, closed into a fist.

Again, Nathan assumed the sparring position, Khopesh held above his head, angled toward his brother, those blue flames licking its length.

I sucked in a breath and exhaled.

The door in front of me opened, as if my breath had the strength of a gale force wind. What the hell?

I didn't have time to contemplate it. The brothers turned toward me.

Nathan's broad, sweat-streaked shoulders were tense, and Killian's focused expression transformed. A smile parted his lips.

"Speak of the devil, and she will appear." Killian did a mock bow. "Hello, little devil. Come play with us."

"Get out of here," Nathan growled at his brother. "Now."

Killian maintained eye contact with me. Like his brother, he was handsome, even with the broken nose, the blood dripping toward his top lip. But he was cold as ice. The gray eyes like steel and full of malice. At least Nathan had a few soft edges to him.

Great, I really am developing Stockholm Syndrome.

Killian lifted his arm and checked the heavy golden watch on it. "Lucky for both of you, I have an appointment. Next time, Nathan, you will consult me before you go on any missions with my soldiers." There was a finality to his tone. He turned and strode from the fighting pit, exiting through another side door on the other end of the space.

I entered the pit. "Thanksgiving must be a hoot in your family."

Nathan spun toward me, anger twisting his features. "You should be in workout clothes. Why are you wearing jeans?"

"I came from class. I didn't want to be late. Sorry? Hey, look, dude, you're the one who's forcing me to do this—"

"For your own good. Now, shut up and do exactly as I say."

21

I'D SPENT the last few months *walking* to work after my bike had been stolen, so I'd had my fair share of cardio, but nothing could prepare me for this.

I collapsed onto all fours on the ground, breathing hard, my lungs burning like I'd run a marathon, my muscles weak.

"Get up," Nathan said. "Come on, you need to be stronger than this, Evie."

Since when does he call me that?

"I'm trying!"

"You're failing."

"Look," I said, sitting back on my ass, trying not to lie down and lose the last shreds of my dignity. "I'm not cut out for this stuff, OK? I never promised I'd be good at it, but I'm trying." My tank top was wet against my chest, my bra creating an obvious and embarrassing outline underneath it. I'd already stripped off my boots and socks. "We shouldn't be out here, exercising at this time of the morning under the friggin' sun, anyway."

"I need you to be strong," Nathan said, and grabbed me by

the arms. He lifted me to my feet, effortlessly, his gaze capturing mine. "I won't let you get hurt."

"Then don't take me with you."

Nathan hesitated, his lips parting. He was still half-naked and was nearly as sweaty as I was. OK, that was a lie. He was *nowhere near* as sweaty as I was, but I had to kid myself to feel better about my abysmal performance.

"You have the muscle tone of a ten-year-old child," he said. "You need to be better than this."

"Shut up. You're not my real dad." The joke fell flat against the pit's packed dirt floor.

"Focus, Evie."

I swallowed, blinking sweat out of my eyes and reaching up to re-tie my purple locks into a high ponytail. "I'm focused."

"I've taught you three things this morning so far," he said. "What are they? Show me?"

"If I'm approached by an attacker," I repeated, "I do this." I shifted forward and jabbed my palm toward Nathan's throat. I stopped just before I hit him.

"Your stance is wrong. Center your weight, prepare yourself. Stay focused on the target. Push through their throat. Picture your weight moving through your body and out through your hand. Force them back." He demonstrated again, and I tried to emulate him.

"Better," he said. "You don't look like you're about to fall over now."

"I'll take it."

"The second thing?"

"The second thing is if someone throws a punch at me," I said.

"Show me."

I swallowed. Nathan faked a punch toward me, and I shifted, pressing his right arm to one side with my right, then lifting my left arm and fake-punching the side of his neck. He'd made me do this about fifty times already. I'd lost count. And then he'd set me on a dummy and made me practice punching for what had felt like an eternity before bringing me back to the center again to execute the move.

"OK," he said. "And the third thing?"

I froze, a coldness settling over me. "If I'm attacked by a vampire, I run."

"Fast," he said. "Fast and around as many corners as you can. You run, OK?"

"But what if I get dizzy?"

Nathan didn't comment. He gestured for me to come closer.

"Nathan, what if I get dizzy? You've got to tell me what's going on. I deserve answers!"

"If you get dizzy, I'll take care of you," he said irritably.

"What if you're not around? Isn't that what all of this is for?"

Nathan barked a laugh. "No. This is for if I'm occupied with an enemy when you're attacked. I won't allow you to go anywhere alone, Evie."

"You can't. Why?" The word echoed in the pit. "Why are you doing this? I deserve to know! You can't keep—"

Nathan grabbed me and spun me around, slipping one arm around my throat as Killian had done to him. His biceps pressed against my airway, but he didn't cut off my breathing. His chest, hot and hard, the planes of muscle slick with sweat, pressed against my back. My ass rubbed against the front of his track pants.

I swallowed. "I deserve to know," I continued, but it came out as a squeak, "why this is all happening."

"The next thing I'm going to teach you," he said, "is how to break an attacker's grip once they have you like this."

I could barely concentrate on what he was saying. I wasn't exactly a horndog when it came to guys, I'd always been more focused on my own stuff—reading, being alone, punching drunk assholes who tried to pinch my ass while I was working a shift. Nathan was beyond distracting, and the pressure of his body against mine was intense.

"Are you listening to me?" he asked, breathing the words into my ear.

"Uh-huh," I managed, still in a half-squeak. "Totally listening right now."

"I need you ready for the Serpentine Prince," he said. "I don't know what they might throw at us." Every word was spoken softly into my ear, like the gentlest of caresses.

You've got to be kidding me with this.

Nathan's grip had loosened a little. His other hand had found its way to my hip, his fingers digging into me, biting into the flesh just above the line of my jeans. Was he toying with me?

Don't trust him. He won't tell you anything.

"I'm going to need you tonight," he said quietly.

My eyes threatened to roll back into my head. I blinked repeatedly, bringing myself back from the brink of obscenity. "For what? I thought the mission was next week." I was proud of how relatively even that came out.

"We've got to prepare. There are things you need to know.

Answers I'm going to give you," he said softly. "Consider it a concession that I'm telling you this now." His hand wandered upward toward my waist, under my shirt.

I couldn't breathe, couldn't think of anything other than his hand against my skin, scorching me with intent.

"But before that happens," he whispered, "I need you to concentrate on what we're doing now."

"Oh, trust me, I'm concentrating on it." I couldn't be this weak. He was not to be trusted. Men who couldn't be trusted went on the "no-sex" list by default.

Except he's protected you. Put your safety first. Put you up in your room like you're Beauty and he's the Beast.

My breaths came in quicker and quicker gasps as his fingers roamed upward another inch. Did he realize what he was doing?

"Focus on your training," Nathan said, "and everything else will fall into place."

"Am I interrupting something?" The British-accented voice came from across the pit. Zoey Braddock, her red hair tied back into a neat bun, stood there wearing yoga pants and a tank top, a pair of sparring gloves hanging from her right hand. "This is a public area."

"We're training," I squeaked.

Nathan, whether it was in defiance or not, left his hand just below my breast, touching my skin. "But we're finished now," he said. "You can have the pit to yourself, Miss Braddock."

"Good." Zoey inserted a pair of wireless earphones into her ears and turned her back on us, walking toward the dummies on the far side of the ring.

I escaped Nathan's grip, blushing bright red, and backed

up a few steps. I opened my mouth to, what, accuse him of turning me on? I wasn't sure.

"Tonight, in my office, at 10:00 p.m.," he said. "Don't be late. And then he turned and walked off toward the benches next to the far exit.

I watched him until I noticed Zoey staring at me, one eyebrow raised. Finally, I turned tail and fled back into the mansion, my mind on a cold shower and a serious reevaluation of my values.

22

I USED my map of the mansion to navigate up too many flights of stairs past windows with views that didn't quite seem right, until I stopped in front of Nathan's door. I'd found a dress in my closet this evening, placed there with an instruction for me to wear it tonight. A private dinner with Mr. Sword.

It was a slinky black number, cut low in the front, tugging on every curve of my body, and definitely *not* what I was used to. But even I had to admit, my purple hair went wicked with black.

I'd been under the impression that this was a debriefing. That the other team of soldiers, J.P. and the rest, would be here.

You're fine. Just don't sleep with your captor.

I'd spent an unhealthy portion of my classes fantasizing about Nathan's body pressed against mine, his hand creeping up my skin toward my bra.

That had to have been nothing. Except even I wasn't enough of a dumbass to think it had been *nothing*. Either

Nathan wanted me or he was using sex as a weapon to make me pliable.

I knocked on the door.

"Enter." His voice sent a hot flush over my skin. He sounded tense, his voice deep, cracking a little.

I opened the office door and stepped inside.

The study had been transformed. The bookcases and their books were still there, but the desk was gone and had been replaced by a small table bearing two trays with silver dome covers. An ice bucket, two champagne flutes, and champagne. A single red flower poking from a crystal vase.

Candles flickered from the four corners of the room.

"Uh." Because I was kind of at a loss here. This was so obviously not a debriefing.

"You'll have to excuse the ambience," Nathan said, standing behind the table, one hand on a chair. "When I informed the chief maid about my intentions to have dinner with you, she took it the wrong way."

Ah, so he hadn't done all this. It was a big romantic accident.

Sure, it is.

"Please, shut the door and come in, Evie. There's a lot we need to talk about."

"I'll say," I muttered, but did as he asked.

I remained on my side of the room, studying him carefully. Don't trust him. Something's not right. I'd always trusted my gut in the past. Why not now?

"Take a seat," Nathan said.

"You hiding chloroform behind your back?" I asked, only half-joking. "Because you've already captured me, you know."

Nathan gave the tiniest smile, and it made me realize how

little he did that. He was always so serious. Maybe it had to do with his family? Killian?

"And even if I wanted to knock you out," Nathan said, drawing the chair back for me and gesturing to it, "I would use much more efficient methods than a rag and some chloroform."

"Well, that's comforting," I replied, and finally came forward. I sat down, and he lingered behind my chair.

Nathan brushed the tips of his fingers over one of my shoulders. "You look stunning," he whispered, a strange catch in his voice.

I glanced up and caught a hint of anger in his face before he hid it from me.

Yeah, definitely don't get with this guy. Definitely not.

Nathan walked to his side of the table and sat down. He removed the cover on his plate and set it aside, revealing filet mignon with a red wine sauce and roasted vegetables.

I took my cover off, half-expecting a salad, and found the same. "This smells amazing," I said and lifted my knife and fork. I cut off a piece of steak and tried it. Perfectly done, still warm, the red wine sauce accenting the flavors well. "Your indentured servants sure know how to cook."

"You still have a problem with that?" he asked. "They have good homes."

"I assume they're paid well."

"They're paid enough," Nathan snapped, then broke eye contact with me. "Anyway, I didn't bring you here to talk to you about servants and wages."

"Right. What did you bring me here for?" I asked, after I had finished my bite. The anger coming from him this evening was renewed. Before, he'd been almost toying with me, now he seemed genuinely upset about something.

"To tell you about the society and your place in it."

I fell silent for a second, then lifted my knife and tapped the side of the champagne bottle in the ice bucket. "I'm going to need a drink for this, I'll bet."

Nathan gave me another of those angry glares before snatching the champagne up, popping the cork as if he'd done it every day since he'd turned twenty-one, and pouring some of it into my glass.

"You're not going to have any?" I asked.

He didn't answer.

"Suit yourself." I tipped my glass against his empty one then took a drink. I had always had issues with authority, and when someone was angry with me for no good reason? I wasn't the type to cower. I kind of wanted to make it worse.

It was a self-destructive *bad* part of myself that I struggled to deal with.

I could tell my behavior was getting to Nathan.

"All right. Lay it on me," I said. "I'm the new Dumbledore, right?"

"Can you be serious for one fucking minute?" Nathan growled it out.

I whistled under my breath. "You've been cursing a lot today. You're going to have to put a few quarters in the swear jar."

"Evie. You're trying my patience."

"How does it feel?" I asked over the rim of my champagne glass. "To have your patience tested? At least you're not a prisoner, right? At least you're not—"

Nathan reached over, grabbed the champagne glass and

threw it aside. It shattered against one of the bookcases, and I winced.

"Hey, what did you—"

Nathan reached across the table and caught my wrist. "Don't play with me," he said. "Don't fucking play with me."

I wrenched free of him and got up. "What is your problem? Why do you have to be such an abusive asshat? I feel like I'm dating you at this point with your manipulative behavior. I've asked you for the truth how many times and all you've done is make things worse." I rounded the table and headed for the door. "So you can keep your answers. I'm leaving. I'm leaving."

"Evie, wait." Nathan tipped his chair over in his haste to follow me. He grasped me by the shoulders, turned me around, and pinned me against the door, and pressed his body against mine.

My eyes widened at the feeling of heat between us, and the press of his erection against my midriff. He was hard? After throwing a champagne glass across the room? After yelling?

"Get off me," I said coldly.

Nathan groaned and pressed his head to the door beside my head. "I feel like I'm going crazy," he breathed. "Evie, I'm sorry."

"Sorry. For what?"

"The glass. Threatening you. I'm sorry."

I didn't say anything.

"The longer I'm around you, the worse things become. I'm supposed to be protecting you, but all I can think of is all the things I would do to your body if I got the chance. I can't keep my thoughts straight. I can't."

If he'd told me this before he'd thrown the champagne

glass, I'd have been all for it. But my gut had been right. I wasn't about to embark on an affair with a sorcerer who couldn't control his temper.

Nathan pushed away from me, walked across the room, and stood staring at the books, his arms behind his back, hands clasping each other.

A silence grew between us.

"The societies were founded by the families. I am part of one of the founding families. A descendant," Nathan said, after several minutes of quiet. "My forefather possessed the Hierophant card from a tarot deck that we once used to contact the Duality. Apep and Atum. Chaos and Order, the energies that are responsible for everything in our world." He turned toward me, his eyes unnaturally blue as they were when he was filled with magic. "The gift of these tarot cards was immeasurable. The ability to commune with the very energy that created us? It was rumored to be like ascending, just talking to them."

I didn't move, but stood with my back to the door, my hand now on the handle, watching him.

"The deck was special. It could only be used if every card of the major arcana was brought together. When they were, you could contact the Duality. You could do it no matter your power. The purpose was to ensure that everything here, on earth, was continuing in their image. That they were worshipped, that their children, the creators of the various races and classes, were happy with our progress."

"But most of the cards are lost," I said. "Read it in one of my textbooks. After something called the Changing?"

"The Second Changing," Nathan said. "The point is, I want those cards back. Our family wants to ensure that we are doing the will of the Gods and Goddesses justice, and we want to stop the Council from exerting force upon the societies. Things are getting bad in our world, Evie. The Council has too much power and without a means of contacting the Gods or Goddesses..."

"So, that's what the Kasha woman had? The tarot cards?"

"It's more complicated than that," Nathan said.

"Of course, it is."

"After the Second Changing, less powerful decks were made, those were used to reach the Keeper of the Book of Life. They could be used by Tellers," Nathan said. "A Teller like Kasha Ramone."

"So, she has one of these *lesser* decks?" I asked.

"A few cards from one of the Pharaonic Decks, yes. And a complete deck will help us figure out the location of the Book of Life," he replied. "And the Keeper. The Keeper will help us commune with the Gods and Goddesses again and tell them what the Council's doing."

"OK, so you need some tarot cards to get to the Keeper of a Book of Life, so you can stop the Council from doing what exactly?" I asked.

"They imprison hybrids, like half-vampires, usually without much proof that they've done anything illegal. They perform private executions. They hire mercenaries to infiltrate societies and execute their heads if those societies don't bend to their will. This is not what the Duality, the Gods and Goddesses, would have wanted. There's no peace. It's like we're living under a dictatorship, do you understand?"

I chewed on the inside of my cheek.

"I can show you." He removed his phone from his pocket and unlocked the screen. "See this? This is the Society App.

The Council uses it to push bounties out, to tell us who has done the wrong thing, to inform us if any new laws are being passed." He showed me the screen. "This is the most wanted list, see? Every single being is a hybrid or a vampire. And their charges are all fake."

He scrolled through the list of names and faces.

"They'll be executed for crimes against the Council and the supernatural community."

"What do you expect me to do about this?" A part of me genuinely wanted to help, but it felt huge and confusing.

A tarot deck. A Book of Life. A Keeper. Gods and Goddesses.

"It's going to be a long journey, but I need your help in finding one of the lesser decks. A Pharaonic Deck. It's the reason we're going to the Serpentine Prince. He's rumored to have once had one in his possession before the Council began confiscating them."

"Why me?" It was the question I'd asked on repeat since the start of this fucked up journey. "Like J.P. said, what's so special about me?"

"You're not fully human," Nathan said. "You can sense when things are off-balance, it seems, within magic itself. I need you around as a lodestone. Someone who can guide me when things go awry."

"But why?" I asked. "Why would I be able to sense anything to do with magic?"

"I'm not sure. But I'm willing to bet we'll figure that out once we find the Keeper. The rumor is the Book of Life has all the answers to every question, and the Keeper has knowledge that fills in any gaps that might remain." His expression was pleading. "Just trust me, I need you by my side. If I hadn't realized that you had this rare ability to sense when things aren't right, I would have let you go. I would have wiped your mind. This is for the safety of us all. Of all magical beings. Don't you understand, Evie? You're not human. You're one of us."

My knees weakened at the prospect.

One of us. You belong. One of us.

Nathan reached me and grasped me around the waist, lifting me again. "I'm here, don't worry. I'm here. I'll help you figure out what's going on, but you have to help me. Every time you feel dizzy, you've got to tell me because it means something bad is coming."

But I felt that way during the ritual downstairs. I felt it in this mansion.

"I'm not like you," I said. "You have no idea who I am." I tried pushing out of his arms, but I was too weak.

"Just trust me. I will protect you. To the ends of the earth, I will protect you." He pressed a kiss to my forehead before stepping away. "All you have to do is tell me when you feel ill. Tell me when and how strong it is, OK?"

"I still don't understand."

"If I knew more, I would tell you, Evie. That's the honest truth."

I met his gaze, searching those too-blue eyes for a lie. If it was in there, I couldn't find it.

23

I COULDN'T SLEEP.

Not only had I discovered that I was "not human", but I lay in bed, the key to the door on my side of the room for once. Nathan and Braddock were trusting me not to run. Why? Because I was one of them now?

How long had I wanted to hear those words? How long had I wanted to be a part of something that was more than just me?

Ever since the incident, I'd been on my own, rejected, wanting to fit in but waiting for people to find out the truth about me. How long until Nathan, Braddock, and the rest of the Hierophant Society realized what a fuck up I was?

Think of other things. You're not human. Not human?

Because I got queasy around magic? Or an overflow of magic? Or something wrong with magic? An imbalance, Nathan had said, but then he hadn't said much of anything.

I couldn't just sit in bed going over this again and again in my mind.

I didn't want to be in this room, but I was in too deep to

try making a break for it. I wanted the truth. Why had weird stuff happened around me all my life? Why did I get sick around certain people, scenarios, or types of magic?

I craved information.

And there was a wealth of it under my feet. An entire Academy. And if my map was correct, a library full of books about magical creatures and races. The one we'd used in class had some information but nothing beyond the basics according to Scholar Jezebel.

I got out of bed, wearing the cotton PJ shorts and shirt that had been provided for me, and slipped on my socks and boots. It was a weird look, but I didn't care. Nobody would see me, hopefully.

A quick rifle through my backpack later, and I had the map of both the mansion and the academy out. I navigated my way out of my room and down the stairs, taking several turns until I found the entrance to the stairs that led down into the basement.

It was eerily quiet on the way down, especially once the electric lights ceased and the flickering torches began. I tried not to pay attention to the creeping sensation that I was being watched from the doors I passed on my way down.

Finally, I reached the entrance area where Scholar Harwa usually sat.

I pressed my hand to the door, expecting him to be in there, but found the desk empty, the four walls staring at me in silent judgment.

"OK," I whispered. "Light. I need light."

As much as I wanted to believe I was capable of it, I doubted I'd be able to navigate through the Academy without it. There were no lamps in the entrance hall, and a tug on the torches flickering in their brackets proved fruitless.

I exited into the Academy and found the atrium full of light. The glass ceiling still glowed as brightly as it had this morning, and the effect was a little mind-bending. Full daylight at night. A grouping of lanterns, unlit, along with a small stand holding what looked like a long-necked lighter, waited beside the balustrade.

Did they put these out for students who had to study late at night? A thrill chased through my veins. What if I ran into other creatures? People?

Was it weird to want to make friends with people who likely thought I was something I wasn't. A sorceress.

I lit the lantern, shakily, then descended the steps. The light from the atrium didn't reach the long stone halls beyond, and my insides twisted with nerves. There were torches flickering along the walls here or there, but it was mostly dark the further in I traveled.

"The library," I whispered, and took out my map. The library appeared to be a floor lower than this one, so I navigated through the passages that were marked green on my map until I found the entrance to the library.

The vast wooden doors stood open, providing me with a view of bookcases in perfectly neat rows, aching underneath the weight of the knowledge they held. It was spectacular, lit by guarded lanterns to prevent a fire, I guessed. Interestingly enough, the floor wasn't stone, but entirely carpeted in beige. It was a weird mix of modern day and magic that I couldn't quite get used to.

I entered, glancing toward the empty librarian's counter, and proceeded past it and deeper into the space. I squeezed past bookshelves, allowing myself to become lost. The smells, the atmosphere! I shut my eyes for a second and just enjoyed it. Wood and pages, the quiet that came with it was almost sacred.

Of all my favorite places in the city, the library had been it. A place where I could spend hours reading without judgment.

A noise brought my back to the present with a bump.

Someone else was here. I'd distinctly heard a shifting of something. Someone walking? Quietly. Like they hadn't wanted to be noticed.

I walked to the end of the row of bookcases and looked around. No one. But there was a cubby with seats and desks nearby.

I read the key on the side of the bookcase. I was in the Magical Tinctures section, apparently. I walked all the way down the row and up the aisles, reading the various signs until I found the correct section. Magical Races.

There had to be information about what I was in one of these books. I walked along the row, neatly sorted in alphabetical order, and read the titles at random.

A Dissection of Injustice: Magical Races and Their Effect on Society.

Racism and Supernatural Creatures: A Study Aimed at Combating Ignorance in the Modern Day Magic-Wielder.

The Big Book of Magical Races: Volume 1.

I paused and reread that title. Could this be the book I wanted? It was massive, the spine made of leather and striped horizontally with gold leaf. I tugged it out, making a note of where I'd found it, then navigated to a nearby cubby.

"Holy crap this thing is huge." I heaved the book onto the table with a thunk that echoed. Finally, I drew back one of the antique chairs and lowered myself into it. "What are you?" That was whispered to myself.

Nathan said I was magical, but not too magical. Human but not really. So what the hell was I?

I opened the book and started paging. The edges of those pages were well-worn, as if many fingers had turned them before me. I kind of liked that feeling. Had there ever been another curious student, wondering about their origins, who had paged through these books?

The first few chapters contained a much more detailed discussion of the basic races we'd gone through recently.

Notably, the half-vampires weren't in this book. Perhaps, they were in Volume 2?

I found all new creatures, though.

Lion shifters. Fae of every variety, some of which had special powers specific to their area of origin. Vampires, who were officially called the Sons of Sekhmet. The Daughters of Sekhmet were separated out, interestingly, as if they were different from their brethren.

Each of the races had a handy breakdown at the end of the chapter.

Sons of Sekhmet

Called vampires by most modern day supernatural beings, thanks to the increasing popularity of human literature among the youth in particular, the Sons of Sekhmet are much more powerful than the name "vampire" would suggest. They require blood and flesh to survive, but may take this blood and flesh from any creature, rather than just a human being. Though, after council rulings regarding their eating habits and the need for peace among supernatural societies and sects, most "vampires" opt to feed on humans.

Strengths

~ Heightened strength.

~ Able to change from humanoid to their true form.

~ Drinking blood or eating flesh increases their strength tenfold.

Weaknesses

~ Weakness to sunlight (but will not burst into flames as is written in most human fiction).

~ Extreme weakness to alcohol springing from their origin. Able to drink blood to cure this affliction to some extent.

Origin

Sekhmet, the lion-headed Goddess, Warrior Goddess, bringer of despair to the enemies of Re. She descended upon Egypt upon Re's wishes, wreaking havoc, drinking the blood of humanity and thus creating the Sons and Daughters of Sekhmet. Re stopped the bloodshed by tricking her into drinking copious amounts of ochre-dyed beer, thus ending her reign of terror.

"Holy shit, that's cool," I whispered.

Every description was eye-opening, but I skimmed some of them, the ones that I surely wasn't a part of.

Extremes

Not much known about these beings except that they are incredibly dangerous.

Strengths

~ Unknown magic source. Deadly.

Weaknesses

~ Unknown

Origin

Unknown

Unlike the other pages, there was no image of an extreme. There was no image at all. Was I a part of this group? This *deadly* group?

Fear clawed at my throat.

I exhaled and continued my search.

Children of the Fae

Not to be confused with the children of our Goddess, Anat. These are the hybrid children of humans who have fallen in love with the fae. A dangerous coupling that can produce anything from incredibly powerful fae-hybrids to sickly half-fae who can pass as humans and who have very few powers of note.

Strengths

~ Depends largely on the strength of the fae who sired the child.

~ Usually does not present magical ability until later on in life.

Weaknesses

~ Often sickly

Origin

Intercourse between the children of Anat and human beings. A dangerous coupling because of the illnesses that might spring forth from such couplings.

Another possibility, right? Was I somehow the child of a fae? But no, that would have to mean that my father had been one, and I had never noticed anything like this.

Stop it. Don't think of them. Don't think of them.

I blocked out the memories and turned the page.

Feathers of Ma'at

Not much is known about the Feathers of Ma'at. Long since vanished. An ancient prophetic group who may or may not have had a part to play in the founding of common society.

Strengths

~ Unknown

Weaknesses

~ Unknown

Origin

Sons and Daughters of the Goddess, Ma'at.

Maybe this one?

My head spun with the possibilities. Was I really one of these people? I longed to check this book out and take it up to my room with me, to spend the rest of the evening reading in bed, but the librarian wasn't here, and I wasn't about to rob a magical library. I'd probably burst into flames or something for removing a book without permission.

My fingers danced toward the edge of the page.

A footstep sounded behind me, barely audible, and I froze.

I turned my head and found a hooded figure, all in black, watching me from behind the nearest bookcase. Red eyes burned, glowing malevolently in the darkness. We stared at each other for two heartbeats. No words. No recognition. Just the sense that I was about to die.

Vertigo threatened.

I left the book open on the table and darted up from my chair, toppling it behind me. I sprinted between the bookcases, my boots thumping on the carpet, casting frantic glances over my shoulder.

The figure followed. Almost gliding over the carpet, the long robes it wore hiding its body from view. What was underneath? Could it be a half-vampire? A real vampire? It wasn't allowed to hurt me here, right?

Half-vampires locked up for targeting other creatures? Locked up for minimal offenses? Vampires can feed on anything and anyone.

I ran into the adjacent hall.

A cold wave of horror came next. I had forgotten both my maps in the library. Both of them! But that *thing* was still behind me, gliding along, soundless, following, red eyes burning bright.

"Leave me," I squeaked and kept running. "Leave me." I'd forgotten the lantern in the library too.

I ran, heedless of direction, my lungs burning, following the advice Nathan had given me during our training. If it's a vampire, run. And that had been for when he was around. Now, I was down here in the dark, alone.

Was I in one of these forbidden red hallways? The ones that belonged to other societies?

The sense of evil increased, and I didn't dare look back. I was sure that thing was still there, following at its leisure, watching my fear with a great deal of enjoyment.

Just keep going.

I had to believe that I would find my way back to the atrium. I tried remembering the path back, but terror clouded my thoughts.

Left. Right. Left. Down the stairs? No, not down the stairs. Where am I? Where am I?

And then that strong scent of mustiness assaulted my nostrils, the growing mushroomy odor that I associated with the bad parts of the Academy. The dangerous parts. The halls narrowed, the flickering torches grew further apart.

I can't keep going. I have to fight. Or something. I have to!

I turned, planting my feet and putting my fists up. "Leave me alone!" I thundered.

But the words echoed against stone. The thing that had followed was gone. No red blazing eyes, no dark robe.

"Am I going mad?" I whispered, shaking and gripping my upper arms. "Am I mad?" I managed to smirk at myself. "Yeah, that's helpful. Talk to yourself, that's reassuring."

Stop.

I sucked in breaths and circled on the spot, trying to

gather my bearings. I took a few steps forward and glanced down a side passage. It was incredibly narrow and ended in a doorway.

I shuddered.

It was the door.

The door I'd encountered the last time. The locked door that I had dreamed about? Had I? I couldn't quite recall, but it felt as if I had been here more than once.

I looked both ways, but I was alone.

I'm down here already. I might as well, right?

Slowly, I started down the narrow passage. The further I went, the narrower it became, my sense of claustrophobia growing. Why would they have designed a passage like this? And what was behind that door?

I reached it, finally. The door was outlined in flickering light. So, there was a torch inside. But what else was—

"—choices."

I blinked. What the hell? I know that voice!

"Resistance is futile. You're aware of that, so I don't understand why you won't cooperate," Nathan said, within the room.

My pulse fluttered. What was he doing down here? In this particular room? If I hadn't known that electronics didn't work here, I would have been sure that he was having a phone conversation with someone.

"I could call others to do this instead of me," he said, followed by a grunt. "You realize it would be much worse then. Cooperate with me. You know I'm going to need more than just one tiny sliver of information."

My mind reeled. Who was he talking to? I reached for the doorknob.

A strong, pale hand grasped hold of my arm, and a palm clamped over my mouth. An iron grip on both. I was drawn against a strong chest, and warm breath whistled against my ear. "Don't," the deep, growling voice said, "open that door. Don't make a sound."

"I will return," Nathan was saying in the room. "And you will—"

I lost the last portion of the sentence. I zoomed backward, carried by whoever had me, swooping along the hall, my feet lifted off the ground. My capturer dragged me out of that hall, down another, up a flight of stairs, and away, until we arrived back in the atrium of all places.

Finally, he released me.

I stumbled forward, turned, and brought my fists up. "Back off," I shouted.

"Quiet." It was a guy wearing a hoodie and a pair of tight-fitting black jeans that showed a little too much of everything, muscles and all. Not that I cared at this point. Red eyes blazed at me from underneath that hood. He reached up and lowered it.

It was him! The guy who sat next to me in most of my classes. The hybrid-vampire who had followed me on my first day at the Academy.

"What's your problem?" I snapped. "Why did you chase me out of the library? Why didn't you say something, huh?"

He stared at me, tilting his head to one side. He licked his too-red lips, exposing his black teeth and fangs beneath. "The library? I wasn't in the library tonight."

Then who the fuck chased me down here?

"And you shouldn't be down any of those halls," he said.

"There are powers at work here that are beyond your control or reasoning."

"Whatever, dude. Why does everyone here talk like they're a prophet or something."

"Sorry, dude," he said, lisping a little around his fangs. "Guess I'll lower my IQ for your benefit. Does that work?"

"Why, because speaking colloquially makes a person dumb? Great opinion, bro."

"That's not what I said."

"That's what you insinuated."

"Do you have to be so argumentative?" the hybrid-vampire asked. "I didn't mean it like that, for fuck's sake."

"Whatever. Just stay away from me."

"Sure."

"Whatever."

"Bye." He folded his arms, staring at me, one eyebrow raised. Man, he was good-looking. And for whatever reason, he didn't make me dizzy anymore. Not in the "something's wrong" kind of way. Or maybe I was just sick?

That spicy cologne smell drifted over, and I wriggled my nose. "What's your name, anyway?" I asked.

"Oh, we're talking now?"

"Sure. Why not?"

He harrumphed. "Tyson," he replied.

"Wow. Super powerful vampire name."

"I'm not a vampire," he said, still with that slight lisp that was actually kind of cute. "Don't you pay attention in class?"

I shrugged. "Look, Tyson, I don't know why you're following me, but I'm not interested in buying whatever it is you're selling, OK?"

He stared at me for a moment then turned and walked off.

"Hey! I was still talking to you."

Tyson paused, looking back at me, his strong jawline accented perfectly by the light from the ceiling. "Wait here. I'll be right back."

I rolled my eyes and considered disobeying him, but he streaked off, gliding soundlessly as my pursuer had.

My pursuer. What had that been about? Surely they could have killed me at a moment's notice. Why had they stopped following me?

Tyson returned before I'd come to any conclusions. He carried the book I'd been reading as well as my maps. "You mentioned the library," he said. "I figured you ran out again without taking your stuff."

"Thanks," I said, and accepted the book and maps from him. My fingers brushed his, and my heart turned over. I cleared my throat. "Uh, but I didn't exactly check this book out of the library, you know."

"I did it for you," Tyson said. "Just return it in a week. There's a self-service section at the counter for late-night checkouts, by the way. For future reference." He tucked his hands into his pockets. "And maybe don't, uh, go wandering late at night. Humans aren't safe here. Not down there, anyway."

"Why, what's down there?"

Tyson hesitated. "We call it No Man's Land," he said. "Or No Creature's Land. Pick your poison. It's a part of the Academy dungeons and it doesn't have an affiliation with the Academy itself or the societies. People use it to do illegal shit, most of the time."

"Illegal shit," I whispered.

What was Nathan doing down there?

"Yeah, so, like I said, not a safe place for humans."

"I'm not human," I replied. "Apparently. I don't know. That's what I've heard."

He stepped closer to me. "May I?"

"May you what?"

"Of course," he said. "You don't know. My mistake. May I sniff you?"

"That's the weirdest thing anyone's asked me, and there's been a lot of fuckery over the past week. Why do you want to sniff me, pray tell?"

"It's a vampire thing," he said, "that was passed onto me by my progenitor. I can smell what type of being you are. Kind of."

"Oh, for real? Heck yeah, you can sniff me!" Anything to clear things up.

"And there's the weirdest thing anyone's said to me, maybe ever," Tyson said and actually grinned. He had a nice smile, black fangs included.

"OK, so how do we do this?" I asked nervously. "Where do you smell me?"

"The neck is good." He lifted two pale fingers. "May I demonstrate?"

"Yeah, sure."

He pressed them to my throat, right over my pulse. "There would be good."

I tried not to react to his touch, but it was electric. Different. "OK, sure. Go ahead."

"If you could just tilt your head, just so." He shifted my head, exposing my neck.

Are you mad? He could be about to bite you? He could—

Tyson held my head carefully in one hand, resting the

other lightly on my collar bone, his thumb in the hollow of my throat. His red eyes searched my face. "You're sure?"

"You're not going to, you know?"

"No," he said.

"Then I'm sure. I want to know." Why do I trust him?

Tyson brought his nose down to my throat and pressed the cold tip to my skin. Goosebumps erupted on my skin, and I let out the tiniest of sighs. Still embarrassing, but whatever.

He inhaled, softly, his grasp gentle as silk. Finally, he released me, returning my head to its normal position and stepping back. His eyes glowed brighter than before. "I can't place it," he said, "your smell. But you're right, it's not quite human. There's something else mixed in with it. Something dark."

"Dark!"

"Dark is not necessarily a bad thing," he said, flashing me another black-toothed grin.

But it was as if he'd realized my worst fears. Dark. Evil. Bad.

"You're upset," he said. "Did I hurt you?"

"No," I replied. "But I should go to bed. Thanks for your help. Goodnight, Tyson."

"Sleep well."

I walked toward the staircase, pausing to look back only once I'd reached the top of the third flight. He was gone, the atrium empty, and questions multiplied in my mind.

Why had Nathan been in that room in a corridor that was "no man's land?"

24

A WEEK of classes and training hadn't helped dispel my concerns. I kept my distance from Nathan unless I had to train with him, and even then, the heat of our chemistry had fizzled. There was something about a dude who thought it was OK to throw things when he got mad that just didn't do it for me.

Maybe because it reminded me of drunk guys in the Devil's Share? Or maybe because it was a fucking huge red flag.

Either way, I kept my distance.

The night had arrived. It was time for us to visit the Serpentine Prince. I stood in my bedroom, glaring at my reflection in the mirror.

A gorgeous, sheer dress with lace covering for my breasts, ass, and pussy lay on the bed. I had refused to put it on. I didn't know what Nathan was playing at, but I'd be going in leather pants and a tank top.

A knock came at the door, and it opened before I could answer.

Nathan entered the room. He paused, frowning. "Why didn't you wear the dress?"

"Because I'm not a prize pony you're going to trot out in front of some horned up fae prince," I said. "And because I have autonomy over my body as a woman."

"We don't have time for this. Come."

I considered denying him, but we'd worked on this for the past week, and I had to hope that this Serpentine Prince might let something slip that would help me work out what I was. And the prospect of stopping a genocide by contacting the deities seemed good too.

Nathan held my gaze for a second, daring me to say something, before turning and striding from the room.

I followed him, but we didn't head downstairs to the Academy or one of the debriefing rooms beneath the mansion. Instead, we took a path upward, upward, upward, until we reached a ladder against the wall that led up to a trapdoor.

Good thing I didn't wear the dress.

Nathan went ahead of me, climbing the rungs with ease. He unlocked the trapdoor with an ornate key then popped it open with his shoulder and climbed inside.

I followed him and we entered an attic. A large empty space filled with moonlight from the windows at either end. Wood-floored. A circle had been drawn in the center of the room and had been marked with symbols in chalk, a flame, a feather, a crystal, a flowing waterfall.

"What is this?" I asked.

"This is how we reach the Serpentine Prince," he said.

"What, you can't just magic us there?" I asked.

"I'm not that kind of sorcerer," he said.

"Then what kind are you?"

Nathan huffed out a breath, irritably.

So far, I'd learned that magic could either influence a person physically or mentally, and most sorcerers could only do one or the other in the various classes: Destruction, Illusion, Defense, or Malleation.

"I'm an illusion sorcerer," he said. "Mental illusion."

I sucked in a breath. "Wait, what? I thought you were destructive. With the fire?"

"Illusion," he corrected stiffly.

So the flames he'd threatened me with hadn't been real. The night I'd run across the yard outside, where the wall had seemed to grow further and further away, that hadn't been real. Neither had the image of Nathan stepping out of the air. They had all been lies.

What about you is real, Nathan Sword?

"Shall we?" Nathan asked, gesturing to the circle. He walked to a set of supplies that had been left on the outskirts.

"What do I do?"

"Stand in the center."

I did as he'd asked, setting my jaw, determined. I would find a way past Nathan's tricks and lies and get to the bottom of this, one way or another. I had kept my knowledge of the door to myself. The last thing I needed was Nathan flinging things across the room when he found out.

If he could be duplicitous then so would I, if only to find out what he was up to. *Don't trust him.* That had been repeating for the past week now, and I got the feeling it had nothing to do with the abduction. It was a deeper sense. A wrongness.

Nathan lit incense, then came over and anointed my head with a strong-smelling oil, doing the same with his own head.

"What's that?"

"Snake oil."

I snorted at the irony, then recoiled. "Wait, literally?"

"Yes."

"That's vile."

He ignored me and lifted what looked like a wand from the stash of items then walked around the circle, murmuring under his breath, pausing to salute at each of the drawings. Finally, he stepped into the circle and pointed the wand directly at the center.

"Four corners protect, united, bring us to our destination," he grunted.

A flash of light filled my vision, blinding me. It cleared, and we stood in the circle, except the floor was no longer grass. It was tall grass, rustling softly. The sky was a gorgeous shade of blue, the perfect, sunny day, and the air smelled of flowers, grass, and fruit.

A path led through the grass, into an apple orchard nearby.

"Watch out for snakes," Nathan said, tucking the wand back into his pocket. "It took me a long time to convince the Serpentine Prince to allow me into his realm. If you get injured here, I will bear the brunt of the punishment for your death."

"OK?" I followed Nathan exactly, watching my step, searching the grass for long bodies. "Wait, if you took ages to arrange this meeting, then why did you have that thing in the attic."

"The circle can be used to visit other parts of the fae

realm," he replied. "You just require the correct oil. J.P. managed to secure the correct oil for me, thankfully."

"So, really, he arranged the meeting and the oil, not you."

"Quiet," Nathan said.

I ground my teeth, a headache developing in the center of my forehead. No dizziness, though.

We reached the entrance to the apple orchard, and Nathan stopped. "I'm going to repeat this for a final time," he said. "You are not to talk to the Serpentine Prince unless I say you can. You will do as I say or you will die in this realm. Nothing here is safe. Remember that."

"Roger that, Captain."

"And don't eat the apples."

"I didn't plan on it," I said.

We entered the orchard, walking between the trees, the trees silent, and then it occurred to me. There was no noise. Not a rustle of wind, not a chirp of birds, just the rustling of the grass. But if there was no wind, then where did the rustling come from?

I stared at the grass and swallowed, hard. The grass was *crawling* with snakes over every kind. I forced my gaze upward to the trees, but that was no better. Each apple we passed was brilliant, red, ripe and juicy, the size of a grown man's fist. They hung suspended, looking ready to be plucked.

Garden of Eden?

We walked for five minutes before arriving at a clearing between the trees. A tree throne, seemingly grown into that shape, branches twisting to form a seat, dominated the space, but was empty, a single apple resting on the seat.

Nathan stopped, put out a hand, and waited.

The rustling continued, but the snakes didn't leave the grass nor did they hiss or approach us.

"What now?" I whispered.

"Do you feel ill?" he asked. "Dizzy at all?"

"No."

"Then be quiet."

Asshole.

"What's this?" The hiss was gentle, erotic and right next to my ear.

I jumped and stumbled forward, grabbing hold of Nathan's forearm out of instinct.

"What in the name of Anat have you brought me, Sword?" The man, no, the fae, who had spoken glimmered bronze and gold, the skin of his chest covered in scales, though he had the shape of a man.

He was painfully beautiful. More beautiful than handsome, and he circled us, slithering on a snake's tail that started just below his midriff.

"Oh dear," he hissed, a forked tongue poking out from between his human teeth. "Oh dear me, such a gorgeous thing you've brought me. Is she a gift?"

"In your dreams, asshole," I said.

"Shut up." Nathan grunted.

"A beautiful voice to match the face. But it seems my natural guise is upsetting her," he said with a hiss of laughter. "Would you prefer this?" He clicked his fingers, and the snake's tail vanished, replaced by two strong, muscular legs, and, uh, well, a very well-endowed region in between them.

I averted my eyes. I wasn't a prude or anything, but that was a lot of schlong for a first meeting.

"Apparently not," he laughed again, and clicked his fingers

a second time. I peeked and found the tail was back in action. "Sword, I have always considered you to be the predictable type. This is an interesting development."

"She's with me, Seth," Nathan replied.

"Seth? Since when are we on a first name basis?"

"The Serpentine Prince then," Nathan said. "Whatever suits you best."

"Interesting again." The prince lifted the apple from his throne, tilting his head to study me, that disturbing forked tongue darting out from between his lips. "Interesting." He took a bite of the apple, juices spilling down his chin. "How rude of me," he said and held the apple out toward me. "Are you hungry?"

"No, thank you," I said.

"Polite for a human," he said. "Though, my experiences have been limited to playthings. There's nothing polite about screams of pleasure mingled with pain." His shimmering skin was fascinating to behold, and he didn't make me dizzy. A good thing, I assumed. "Oh, don't worry, dear, I don't take them without their consent. Everything is very contractual."

He called me a human. Everyone assumes that. Am I?

I was so tired of this confusion.

"We came to talk to you about an important matter," Nathan said irritably.

The Serpentine Prince cast a green-eyed gaze toward him, his pupils morphing to slits. He crossed the distance between himself and Nathan within milliseconds. "Don't forget where you are, sorcerer."

"I haven't," Nathan said, lips thin. But he didn't snap or get angry.

Just how powerful was this Serpentine Prince. There was

still not a lick of wind nor a sound. The only movement from the snakes in the grass. And the position of the sun hadn't changed. There were no shadows, and, it occurred to me only now, no heat. It was as if we'd entered a picture. A three dimensional picture.

The prince swept toward me, his tail whipping through the grass, and drew himself up straight. He towered over me. "What is it you have come for, little plaything?" He pressed his fingers into my hair and lifted a few purple strands. He inhaled them gently. "I expect you came to be charmed or enchanted. Your imaginings of the fae are likely more wholesome than the truth."

"I'm not your plaything," I said and took a step back, the heels of my boots near the long grass.

"Careful, dear. My friends are listening."

I glanced back and found several hooded snakes had risen from the grass. I stumbled forward, and the prince caught me, pressing his hands to my shoulders. They were cool and soft.

"She's delightful, Sword. What a treat." He slithered to his throne, clicked his fingers, and became "man" again. Naked-ass man. Flowers grew at his feet, and the tree throne bent toward his will, growing steps for him to ascend. He sat down atop it, wide-legged, with everything on display.

I kept my eyes on his keen face, high cheekbones, bronze hair. His nose was thin but straight, and the longer I looked, the more the features of a snake stood out to me.

"I came to talk with you about a deck," Nathan said, skipping past the prince's words. "I believe that you once were in possession of one of a Pharaonic Deck. Is that correct?"

The Serpentine Prince's features shifted, became more snake-like, the pupils becoming slits again. He studied Nathan in silence, the fingers on his left hand tapping gently on the arm of his throne.

"Is that true?" Nathan asked.

"It took you such a great cost to acquire this meeting with me, did it not?" the prince asked. "Such a great cost."

"Yes," Nathan replied but shrugged. "I will do what it takes."

"What cost?" I asked. "What cost?"

"Oh dear, she doesn't know," the Serpentine Prince said. "Shall we show her."

"I came to talk about the deck." Nathan's voice became strained.

"All that pain for a question. You're aware, you simply could've had your man speak to one of my inferiors. I would've been happy to send the answer along via more regular channels."

"I wanted to do this in private," Nathan said.

"Why's that?" the prince asked slyly.

"You know why."

The prince glanced at me. "Why, Sword, did you want to meet in person?"

"You know why!" Nathan grunted. "The Council will not approve of me searching for a deck."

"Just as they would not approve of me owning one," the prince said, then lifted a finger and pointed it at me lazily. "Who is she? She doesn't smell quite human enough. Is she with the Council? I assure you, I will do much worse to you than the plaything you delivered to me for a chance to talk face-to-face."

"Plaything?" I turned to Nathan. "What is he talking about?"

"It doesn't matter. Now, be quiet!"

I stepped away from him, putting distance between us, and the dizziness returned. I grasped my head, stumbling.

"What's wrong with her?" the prince asked.

"Nothing," Nathan said. "Tell me about the deck."

"Leave her here with me, and I will tell you what you want to know."

"You've already taken your pound of flesh!" Nathan said. "You don't need her."

"But she would be such a lovely addition to my collection." His voice grew closer, accompanied by gentle footsteps in the grass. Fingers gripped my chin and twisted. I stared up into those green eyes with their slit pupils, the face glimmering like a starburst. "You know, dear," he said, "you can trust me more than him, and that's quite a statement to make."

"Let go of her. She's mine."

I pulled out of the Serpentine Prince's grasp, glaring watery-eyed at Nathan. "I'm nobody's property."

"She's too lovely, almost. There must be something wrong with her," the Serpentine Prince said.

"We came to talk about the deck."

Finally, the prince sighed and walked back to his chair, dropping the half-eaten apple to the ground. It dissolved along the way, turning to nothingness by the time it should've struck the ground. "I'm afraid I can't help you. I no longer have a Pharaonic Deck."

"Where is it?"

The Serpentine Prince sat down on his throne again.

I straightened, though the dizziness resumed.

"Where is it?" Nathan repeated.

But the prince would say no more. He flicked his fingers

toward us and snakes emerged from the grass, circling our ankles, chasing us backward, guiding us along the path and away from the prince.

"You, dear, may come back any time. I would love to have you in my court one day," the prince called after me.

25

We arrived back in the attic of the mansion in a flash of light.

"Fuck!" Nathan roared, and threw the wand across the room. It turned end over end and cracked against the far window. "Fucking idiot!"

I stepped out of the circle, rubbing my arms.

"He's a liar! That mother fucker is lying. He's got the deck, he just won't tell me about it. He knows what I'll do to get it from him."

I was already cold all over from the rage. I lifted my chin. "What would you do to get it, Nathan?" I asked, my voice shaking a little. "What *did* you do to get us a meeting with him?"

Nathan rounded on me, blue glowing from his eyes. "You! You just couldn't keep quiet, could you? He would've ignored you if you had kept your tongue in your fucking mouth, but you can't just SHUT UP!"

I backed away from him, glancing toward the distant outline of the trapdoor.

"This would've gone without a hitch if not for your insolence." He bore down on me, and an image appeared before my eyes, a dark mass of flesh rising from the ground, masking him from view. It unfolded into a walking mass of tendrils, dripping viscera, and sludged toward me.

Terror gripped my heart.

I opened my mouth to scream, but it wouldn't work. The dizziness that had come in the fae realm, or whatever that orchard had been, returned. I stumbled, squeezing my eyes shut and opening them again, but the thing was still there.

Not real.

The thought came like a bullet out of the blue. A voice that sounded like my own, but more confident. A version of Evie who had her shit together.

This is not real.

I backed up, shaking my head, stumbling over the latch of the trapdoor.

Think! He is an illusion sorcerer. Mental illusion. This is fake.

It made sense to me, perfect sense, but it didn't banish the horrifying vision before me. It did, however, make it a hell of a lot easier to control my fear. It wasn't the hulking viscera monster that I had to fear, it was the man who had created it.

Nathan wanted to, what, scare me into submission? Punish me for having "failed" him with the Serpentine Prince.

Run.

I bent and found the smooth bronze circle that was the trapdoor latch. I pulled the door open, then dropped down and shimmied out of the attic, backward, my feet finding the rungs. The viscera monster squelched and groaned, bending toward me, but I ignored it, set my jaw, and took the ladder two rungs at a time. I landed safely on the floor and looked up at the hole.

Nathan stood above me, glaring down, his skin even paler than usual, his eyes no longer glowing blue but seeming almost dull.

"Evie," he croaked. "You shouldn't have done that."

"Fuck you." I took off running down the hall. This asshole had to be crazy if he thought I was about to hang around and have a calm conversation with him about his abusive and frankly psychopathic tendency.

All that glitters isn't gold, as Shakespeare wrote.

I darted down the hall, and Nathan thumped down from the attic behind me. "Evie, get back here!" he shouted. "Evie!"

But I didn't care what he had to say.

Too much had happened tonight. Shoot, even over the past few days. Nathan was exactly what he'd seemed when I'd first met him. Arrogant, selfish, maybe even a little evil, and he was definitely hiding something.

I took the stairs downward, rushing past windows and paintings. The halls were quiet at this time of night, and I didn't have my map of the mansion, but I had spent the last few weeks exploring, ever since my bedroom door had been left unlocked.

I was fairly confident I could navigate my way back to my room.

Plaything. The Serpentine Prince had said he used humans as playthings, and that Nathan had paid the price of flesh to meet with him. That he had given him a plaything.

My stomach turned at the prospect, and what I had to do next became clear.

"Evie!" Nathan's yells and footsteps followed, gaining, but not fast enough.

I darted down stairs, leaping, pushing myself harder, my lungs burning.

You can do this. Don't stop.

But he was too close.

Going back to my room to get a map of the Academy would take too much time. I had to stay ahead of him if I planned on doing this. But how?

I spotted a tapestry up ahead and made a snap decision. Please, please, please.

I whipped the tapestry back and found a small cubby beyond, leading into a hall. I darted into it and let the tapestry fall, then held it carefully, ensuring that it didn't move even a little.

Thank God.

I didn't want to think about what would've happened if I had pulled the tapestry back and there had been nothing but a wall behind it.

Nathan's thundering footfalls drew nearer. "Evie! Stop! You've got nowhere to go!"

I held my breath.

The sounds of Nathan's pursuit drew level with the tapestry, then passed by. He thought I was still ahead, running toward my bedroom. That was the first place he'd check, so it had to be the last place I went.

Quietly, I slipped out of my hiding spot and turned the corner. Empty. Blessedly empty. Nathan was ahead of me now, and I doubted he would figure out I'd tricked him until he got to my room.

The awesome thing about narcissistic dudes? They always

thought they were smarter than everyone else. He wouldn't for a second consider that I wouldn't keep running.

I set off, taking stairs downward. I didn't know the mansion off by heart, but down was the way to go. The Academy was beneath my feet somewhere, and I simply had to reach it. The lower I went, the more familiar the halls became, until I was positive I had entered the one that held the small room where I'd eaten breakfast the past couple of weeks.

My feet whispered across the carpeting, and I wound down the stairs, fear clogging my throat, my ears perked.

The door that led down to the Academy was shut tight. I opened it, and the familiar smell of old stone and deep places reached my nostrils.

Home.

An absurd thought given the circumstances.

Into the bowels I went.

26

I wasn't sure why, or how, or if maybe this was my hidden, and possibly useless, magical power, but I'd found the strange door. The one I'd dreamed about. The door behind which I'd heard Nathan talking. Threatening someone.

Truth.

That was what I wanted.

I'd figured what I wanted was to fit in with these people, but if fitting in with the Hierophant Society meant punishing people with horrifying visions when they did something "wrong" or any of the horrible behaviors that Nathan had elicited… I didn't want to belong anymore.

Because being a part of that would mean I was just as bad as *her*.

Mother.

"Stop," I whispered to myself.

Now was not the time for a trip down memory lane.

I stood at the intersection between the long hallway and the narrow one that led to the door, my hands tucked into my leather jacket. It was cold down here tonight, though I wasn't sure why. A gentle drip had started nearby.

I shivered, glancing left and right.

Nathan had no idea I'd found this door. I'd never told him. This would be the last place he'd look, and this might be the place that held the answers I needed, the truth about the society and hopefully myself.

The thought of going along with what Nathan wanted and trying to find the Keeper of the book to get answers revolted me now. He had ulterior motives, of that I was positive.

No use hanging around. Do it.

This time, it was the confident sounding version of me who said it.

Hurry up, now, come on. Before you get in more trouble.

I swallowed and walked down the narrow passageway, pulse pounding in my ears. The door was still wreathed in flickering light.

Do it. Do it.

A vague memory of falling or being pushed backward rose from the annals of my thoughts. I grasped hold of the door-knob and turned it. The door opened inward, unlocked.

I entered what was, in essence, a prison cell.

A man hung against the wall, his head dropping against his naked chest. He was muscular, a beast of a dude, a smattering of hair traveling down his navel toward the torn jeans he wore. He was streaked with grime and dried blood. His hair was matted, perhaps shoulder-length.

I stood, utterly stunned, my hand on the door handle, not daring to breathe.

Nathan did this.

The room was empty except for a table containing items I

didn't care to identify. There was a single torch flickering on the stone wall.

Do something. The confident voice.

I moved forward, and the man shifted, the chains holding him up rattling against the wall. His ankles had been tied together. The chains that held his arms traveled toward a ring and pulley system to a wooden lever on the opposite wall.

I rushed toward it, my boots scuffing against the stone, and tugged on the lever. I let the man down slowly, and his head snapped up instantly, his eyes, flashing burnished gold, found me.

"You," he growled. "Evie."

I sucked in a breath and nearly released the lever. His body jerked toward the floor an inch, and I caught the lever again in time. I finished lowering him to the ground. He knelt, his arms at his sides, watching me.

"Evie," he repeated.

And his face, beneath a grizzly beard, was familiar. He looked kind of like a beat up Jason Momoa without the tattoos. And he was achingly familiar. Like I'd met him somewhere before, but just couldn't quite place it.

"You know me," I whispered. "How?"

"Not now," he croaked. "Get me free, quickly, before he comes back. I'll explain everything once we're out of here."

"Who? Nathan? He has no idea I'm down here."

"Not Nathan. He was here a moment ago. He'll be back any second. Key on the table."

I glanced toward the table of objects, strange items that looked devilish to me. I went to it, searching frantically for the key. The table had drawers, and I opened them, barely breathing now.

A prisoner. Here. In the Academy? Did anyone know about this? What about the half-vampire, Tyson?

"Wait," I said, as I rifled through the drawers, "if Nathan's not coming, then who—"

A cold hand caught my wrist and spun me around.

Killian Sword, his steel gray gaze biting into mine, caught my other wrist. He squeezed tightly, a grimaced twisting his face. "Look what we have here. A little girl who's wandered into the spider's nest. What on earth do you think you're doing here?"

The prisoner's head hung again, but he cast golden-eyed glances toward us, measuring, perhaps weighing his options?

I sucked in breaths. "Mr. Sword," I said, because who knew what a megalomaniac like Killian would like to be called? My only experience with this guy had been the way he'd treated Nathan on the practice pit. "How are you today?"

"How sweet of you to ask," he said, squeezing my wrists so hard it felt as if he'd break my bones.

My eyes watered, but I refused to make a noise.

"I was doing wonderfully until you intruded upon my session with Mr. King."

King? Where do I know that name from? King? It was so familiar.

"I'm sorry," I said, drawing my head up and meeting him stare for stare. Fake it until you make it, baby. "But I'm here on Nathan's instruction. You see, we've just been to see the Serpentine Prince."

Killian's eyes narrowed. "The Serpentine Prince."

"Correct," I said. "In his orchard, full of snakes." I sighed, acting as if I wasn't the least bit concerned about the ache of his fingers cutting into my flesh. "Needless to say, it wasn't the best experience."

"No? Your mission wasn't a success?" Killian asked, a little too happy at the prospect of Nathan's failure.

"How about you stop trying to break my arms," I said, "and I'll tell you what happened."

Killian considered it. "Why were you rifling through the desk."

"I'm just here on Nathan's orders," I said, betting on the fact that he hadn't heard me talking to this King guy. Man, why was that so familiar? "He asked me to fetch a key or something? He said it would be in the desk."

"Why would Nathan ask you to fetch the key?" Killian still hadn't released me.

"I don't know, why don't you ask him? I was just doing what he asked. He was really upset about the prince. He said something about another meeting. One that wasn't planned. He mentioned that he had enough snake oil to get back through the portal with more than one person."

Killian finally released me. "More than one person?"

I rubbed my wrists, pretending to be irritable at the inconvenience rather than utterly fucking terrified. "Yeah. I think… Ugh, I really shouldn't say, Mr. Sword. Nathan's going to be so pissed if I tell you."

"Spit it out, girl."

I chewed my bottom lip like I had the power to consider it. "Nathan mentioned taking J.P., Braddock, and Sylvian through the portal," I said at last. "I don't think he wants you to know, but I'm not sure why."

"Where did he set up the portal?" Killian asked, a muscle in his jaw ticking.

I have him. He's buying it.

I was banking on the fact that Killian was the "General." Killian had been very clear. Nathan was not to do anything with his "soldiers" without permission. That had to be why we'd gone on the mission to see the Serpentine Prince alone.

"Tell me!" Killian commanded.

"It's in the attic," I said. "Nathan said it was one that everyone used to reach the fae world."

"Idiot! He should never have— No matter. Come with me. You're going to take me to him, right now," Killian said and grasped my upper arm.

I wrenched free of him, sneaking a glance at the prisoner, praying that he would read the unspoken message. I'll be back for you. I will be back.

Not that I could fucking do anything except get a bad case of vertigo and potentially trip over the table of torture devices.

"I can walk without you squeezing on my limbs, thank you, Mr. Sword."

Killian inhaled sharply, nostrils flaring. "Very well. Lead the way."

We exited the prison cell, Killian shutting the door and locking it behind us. I took up a position in front of Killian, accompanied by his mouth-breathing down my neck, and squeezed down the narrow passage toward the exit.

I had a choice there. Make a run for it left or right and hope he didn't catch me, or go along with the ruse and try to find another method of escape. I couldn't go back up to the mansion.

Scholar Harwa had mentioned that the home bases of the

other societies were all connected to the Academy. Maybe I could find an entrance to one?

"Evie?" Nathan's voice echoed down the adjacent passage. "Evie?"

Well, shit.

This was bad.

I reached the end of the tunnel just as Nathan appeared in its mouth.

"Evie!"

"Nathan, what's this I hear about taking my soldiers to the Serpentine Prince?" Killian snapped it out immediately.

Nathan opened his mouth to reply, and time slowed to a stop. Not metaphorically, literally.

A golden light hazed into view in front of me, accompanied by the gentlest of noises, a brushing of wind against trees? A single golden feather drifted down from the ceiling above, and I put out my palm.

That confident voice, that I had been so sure belonged to me, whispered in my ear, powerful and warm. A woman's voice, accented, definitely not American.

Now is your first great choice. The woman's voice. Warmth surrounded me. ***You must choose the way of justice, fairness, of goodness of the spirit, little feather.***

I stared at the gorgeous golden feather in my hand, weightless, perfect, and looked first at Nathan and then at Killian.

Choose?

Choose them or run? Run and go where? Do what? I had nowhere else to be. Nowhere to belong.

Choose the way of justice, fairness, of goodness of the spirit.

The feather in my hand dissolved, and the light vanished, time rushed back into being.

Nathan's open mouth began to move, to say things to Killian that would expose my lies.

Here goes nothing.

I centered my weight and punched the flat of my palm upward toward Nathan's throat, as he had taught me in the training pit. Except this time, I didn't stop myself from hitting him. I struck his throat, hard.

His eyes widened, hands came up, but I didn't stick around for the fallout. I turned the corner and ran for my life.

27

"BITCH!" Killian yowled, and the rush of footsteps started.

They were after me. Or Killian was at least. Of course, they were after me. What had I expected, that they would stand there, shell-shocked that the purple-haired chick had thrown a throat punch?

Had I made the right choice? It felt like it, though I didn't see how ramming my palm into Nathan's Adam's apple counted as fair or in keeping with having a goodness of spirit. He'd made a pretty ungodly noise when my hand had made contact with his flesh.

Shut up and run. That was normal Evie talking. Not the confident Evie voice with the weird accent. I was pretty much sure it wasn't even my voice but another woman's.

So, I'd have to add insanity to the list of problems I'd cultivated over the years.

Insane, freakish, purple-haired, too horny, bad with men, terrible past. Oh boy.

I pumped my arms back and forth, but my legs were weak

after the chase in the mansion, and I had *no idea* where I was headed.

These passages, the musty, mushroom-smelling ones, were completely unfamiliar to me. Darker than the others, the torch brackets even further apart, and they were growing narrower by the second, harder to move in.

I glanced over my shoulder and caught sight of Killian rounding the corner after me, wearing that ridiculously crease-free suit and looking well-put together even as he chased me. A grin parted his lips. Pure hatred and enjoying it.

I made the right decision.

Nathan was bad. And I had been a part of that badness. I had gone with him to see the Serpentine Prince. I had decided to help him find the tarot deck that would help him communicate with the Gods and find the Keeper.

I sucked in breaths and turned another corner. My only hope was that I'd find a hidey hole as I had with the tapestry upstairs, but there was nothing here.

Another corner and another. My energy flagged.

Don't give up. Come on. Just keep moving.

"You can't run much further, little girl," Killian called after me. "You can't run much further." His chuckle echoed through the halls.

Please. Give me a way out. Anything. Anywhere! Please. I made the right choice, didn't I? I did the right thing!

I turned the corner and skidded to a halt. Dead-end.

"No," I whimpered.

Killian's laughter grew louder. He was just around the corner. Just there. He would kill me, for sure, or they would imprison me again in that mansion. They would never let me out. They would—

A soft, cool hand closed over my mouth, a strong arm wrapped around my waist, and I was pulled backward into the shadows, up against the stone wall that was my demise. A hard body behind me, muscles taut, and the scent of spicy cologne.

"Don't make a noise," Tyson whispered into my ear. Tyson, the half-vampire who had pulled me away from the door and Nathan's voice the last time. "I'm hiding you from his view, but if you make any noise, he will hear you, OK? So don't move. Don't even breathe too loudly."

He removed his hand from my mouth slowly, but held me around the waist against the wall. I didn't move, just as he'd said, and stared directly ahead.

It felt ridiculous.

Surely, Killian would round the corner and find us standing there, him holding me around the waist. What if Tyson was working with them? What if this were just him delivering me to the Sword brothers?

It was too late to back out, now. I had to trust Tyson on this. What other choice did I have?

Killian strode around the corner, holding a ball of flame in one hand. It was the natural color of fire, nothing like the blue flame illusion that Nathan had used. Something told me it was real.

Destruction sorcerer? Physical destruction?

He stopped, holding the flame aloft, a frown creasing his brow.

"Where are you, little girl?" he called, softly. "I know you're around here somewhere." He walked down the narrow passage toward us, stopping just short of the wall.

He lifted the flame higher, to help him see? Or in preparation to attack us?

I held my breath, my lungs aching.

Please, let this work.

Killian remained still, staring at the wall, his brow creased for ages. Finally, he walked off and rounded the corner again.

I let out the breath, slowly.

"Wait," Tyson breathed into my ear. "Just wait."

We waited.

Killian reappeared for a moment, checking back down the passage, then left, his footsteps retreating down the hallway.

I remained frozen for another several minutes, Tyson's arm around my waist a comfort, though I barely knew him.

"I think he's gone," the half-vampire said at last. "Finally. Wait here and let me make sure the coast is clear." Tyson released me, and I slumped. He took a step then paused. "Are you OK? Do you need my help to stand?"

I shook my head, pressing my hand against the wall. The stone was rough and a little clammy.

Tyson nodded and walked toward the intersection. He wore his favorite hoodie and jeans, and looked both ways before returning to me.

"He's gone. For now," Tyson said then folded his arms. "I take it you're not best buddies with the Sword boys anymore?"

"That sounds like a terrible euphemism," I said between deep breaths. I had to get my heart rate back down. I was exhausted, out of shape, my legs practically strawberry jelly at this point. "I think I need to sit down."

"I don't think sitting here is a good idea," Tyson said. "I can take you somewhere safe, but I've got to know if you—" He cut off, listening hard, then shook his head. "I have to know if you're with the Hierophant Society or not."

"With them?" I whispered, sinking to my knees and then sitting down, unceremoniously on my butt. "I was never *with* them. They sent me a tarot card, and I was curious. Then they fucking abducted me and told me I'm some special part-human and that they needed my help. I was never with them."

Tyson looked down on me, his red eyes blazing. "You seemed pretty comfortable with them before. Happy to study at the Academy with them backing you, right?"

"Yeah, well, that was me making the best out of a bad situation. That was before I saw… Tyson, they're keeping a man in that room. Remember that room that you pulled me away from? That one that I was trying to get into?"

He nodded, an incremental tip of his head.

"They're keeping a prisoner in there. His name is King or something. I have to go back and free him. I have to help him." I tried to struggle to my feet but collapsed backward.

Tyson dropped onto his haunches in front of me. "Wait," he replied. "You can't do anything like this. Live to fight another day, right?"

"Will you help me get that guy out of there? It's wrong. It's evil." Evil like you. I shook the thought away. Regular me talking, not the other voice.

"I've been trying to free him for months," he said.

"Wait, what? You knew?" I tried to grab the front of his hoodie, but my fingers wouldn't work as well as normal. My hand flopped down. "Why am I so tired? Wait, you knew. You knew and you didn't help him?"

"I've been trying to get to him," Tyson said, glancing over his shoulder. "But there hasn't been an opportunity. I can explain this to you in more detail, but not here. Come with me." He put out a hand.

"With you?" How did I know he wasn't another Nathan? Or that he was to be trusted at all?

I didn't.

I put my hand in his anyway. "OK."

28

"I've got to warn you before we go up there," Tyson said, as we entered a second atrium I hadn't known existed. This one's glass roof was exactly the same, except red light filtered down from above, rather than the white that had glistened from the roof of the atrium outside the Hierophant Society's entrance.

"Warn me? I thought you said this would be safe." I hugged my arms. I was tired, so achingly tired, that it took ages for the words to form. It was like my brain was coated in a layer of molasses.

Was it the feather thing that had happened? The golden light and the voice and that decision I'd made?

It had been important, and I still wasn't entirely sure it had been the right one, but for the certainty that what Nathan and Killian were doing was wrong.

"You will be safe. From the Sword family. As long as they don't know you're here," Tyson said. "But the people in my society won't trust you at first. They know about you."

"Know about me?"

"Everybody's heard about the human pet the Swords have adopted. My society knows that you aren't exactly human, but they're not sure where your allegiances lie."

"Wherever people aren't being imprisoned or treated unfairly," I said. "That's where my allegiance lies."

"Look, that's satisfying for me to hear, but just be warned. Things might not go the way we expect at first. They won't hurt you, but they won't trust you either."

"That's fine," I said. "I'm not that big on trust at the moment anyway." Life so far had consisted of one terrible event after the other, and the past few weeks in this new magical world hadn't been an improvement. All I wanted was freedom and answers. Was that so much to ask?

"I'm going to try to convince them that you're OK. On our side."

"I'm not on anyone's side," I replied. "I don't even know what the sides are. I don't even know why there are sides."

"Man, they really kept you in the dark."

I nodded, my head moving way too slowly.

"Either way," Tyson said, taking a breath. "You have a choice. You can come up there with me and be safe, but they probably won't trust you at first. Or you can go."

"Go where?"

"I don't know? Back where you came from? Home?"

"I don't have a home." Except for the Academy. Apart from the odd stare or whisper, the dizzy sensations and that horrible door, this place had been more comforting than the Hierophant Society. Was it possible I could take up a job in the cafeteria or something?

"Your choice."

This time, there was no feather or golden light. The time to choose had passed, it seemed. "I'm coming with you."

"OK," Tyson said, gesturing toward the stairs. "After you."

I grasped hold of the balustrade and we made our way up. I stumbled a few times, and Tyson caught me by the waist, keeping me upright, overwhelming me with the kindness of his touch, the scent of his skin.

"I could fall asleep standing, swear to God," I whispered.

Tyson didn't comment, but on the first floor landing, he bent and swept his other arm under the crook of my knees. He carried me up the steps until we reached a door. That door led into a connecting room, similar to the one Scholar Harwa used, but here, the drawings on the wall depicting the Duality, Deities, and the Societies were darker, twisted.

Should I be worried? Probably.

Tyson carried me up several flights of stairs, similar to the ones under the Hierophant Society then stopped beneath a trap door. He set me down.

"Can you stand? It will give them a better impression if you stand."

"I can stand."

Tyson reached up and clasped the handle of the trap door. He paused again. "The leader of our society is Dale King," he said.

"King," I whispered. "But the guy down there—"

"Yeah. That's Mr. King's son."

I sucked in a breath. "But that's not allowed is it?"

"No, it's not. But we'll discuss that with Mr. King. Look, you should know he's pretty upset about losing his son. So take his anger lightly, OK? He's nicer than he seems."

"Nicer?"

Tyson thunked the trapdoor open with his shoulder.

"Wait," I whispered. "I don't even know what your society is called."

Tyson grabbed me by the waist, lifting me easily. "We're the Hanged Man Society," he said. "The misfits, hybrids, shifters, vampires in hiding." And he tossed me bodily into the room above.

I landed in a heap, but I wasn't hurt, and the floor was kind of nice. Wooden and hard, maybe a little sticky, but nice after everything I'd experienced over the past couple of weeks.

The noise of Tyson climbing into the room followed. "Are you OK?" he asked, brushing my hair off my cheek.

"Yeah. Just tired."

"Can you sit up?"

"Not without help."

He carefully dragged me over to a wall and propped me upright. The room had plaster walls with wooden floors and decor that was well-worn but homey. Nothing like the opulence of the Garden District mansion housing the Hierophant Society.

And, apart from all of that, there was another person in the room with us.

"What's this?" A man with burning red eyes stood near a door at the opposite end of the room. "You're bringing prey into our midst."

"Get a hold of yourself, Walker. You're not out roaming the wilds anymore."

The man hissed, exposing blackened teeth and fangs. Another hybrid. One who wasn't as polite as Tyson nor anywhere near as handsome. Middle-aged, bald, lean.

"Well, she's a stranger, and Mr. King ain't going to like that."

"No shit," Tyson said. "Mind getting him for me? This is kind of important."

Walker's gaze narrowed and he gave me a proper onceover, then started. "No way. Is that—?"

"Yeah."

"You're in deep doo-doo, bro."

"Get King."

The hybrid laughed all the way out of the door and into the hall beyond. Also wooden-floored by the sounds of it.

"Where are we?" I asked. "I mean, in the city? Are we still in New Orleans?"

"Yeah," he replied. "In the French Quarter."

"Oh. Oh." The French Quarter where the Upside Down Club had been. I hadn't realized that one of the other society's headquarters was in the area.

Ugh. Don't try to think too much. It hurt my head.

I shut my eyes for a second. The curt snap of a door and irritable voices woke me what felt like milliseconds later.

"What is the meaning of this?" A tall man wearing a thick, dark beard strode into the room. His skin was a deep tan, his eyes burnished gold, and his long, thick brown locks flowed toward his shoulders. Another Jason Momoa, except this one was older, with gray hairs intermingled in the brown, plenty of demonic looking tattoos, and a broken nose.

"Hi," I managed.

Refreshingly, no one told me to shut up.

"I hear you're looking for some non-human baggage. I thought I'd sign up."

Walker, who had returned with the new guy, sniggered and turned his head as if he didn't want to be seen laughing.

"This is King," Tyson said, returning to my side.

I tried to scuffle to my feet, and Tyson helped me.

"Nice to meet you, King. I wish I had known you and this society existed before ten minutes ago," I said.

King stared at me, his beard shifting as he pressed his lips together and released them. "You know my name, young lady," he said, "do me the honor of telling me yours."

"Evie Crowley," I replied. "I'm the purple-haired assassin who's come to murder you. That was a joke. A bad joke. I'm sorry, my brain is basically cotton candy at this point."

"She's got news," Tyson said, "about Ari."

The relative calm King had displayed vanished. "Tyson," he growled. "Tyson, I warned you about doing anything before we were ready. I warned you."

Tyson put up his hands. "I haven't done anything. She was the one who did it. She didn't know."

"How could she not have known?" Walker snapped. "She's basically been sucking Sword dick for the past couple of weeks."

"Hey!" I clicked my fingers at him. "Hey, Mister. I don't suck dick. Dick sucks me." I blinked. "Wait, that didn't make sense."

"Is she OK?" Walker asked, tilting his head. "Like?"

"No, she's not OK." Tyson launched into the tale of how he'd found me and what I'd told him, briefly, and King listened with a great deal of impatience. "I brought her back here because she has no idea what's going on. No idea."

I braced myself against the wall.

"She's a threat. For all we know, she could be working with them," Walker said. "We should throw her out. Or at least lock her up until we can question her."

"If we lock her up, we're no better than them," Tyson said.

"Excuse. Me." I pushed off the wall and stumbled into the middle of the room, raising a finger. "Excuse. Me. I am not. Going to be treated like a child. This is the last time I'm going to ask this. Like. Ever. What in the fuck is going on around here?"

The three men stared at me, eyebrows raised, two pairs of red eyes, one pair of gold, equally wide.

My finger drooped, and the floor tilted toward my face. "Oh, sh—"

Blackness.

29

*T*IME *TO WAKE UP,* **little Feather.**

The words were soft and warm, like an embrace, and they came from everywhere. Within the darkness of my mind and outside of it.

I took a deep breath and opened my eyes.

Worn wooden beams above, and soft lamplight from my right. I turned my head and found an electric light on the bedside table. The windows just past it, were boarded up, though they had a set of white curtains accented with yellow flowers.

I pushed up in the bed, glancing down at my wrists and then ankles. No restraints. Given the shitshow of the past couple of weeks, that was a pleasant surprise. The room was tiny compared to the one I'd had at the Hierophant Society, but it was quaint. Almost cozy.

The rough brick walls, the wooden flooring, the comfy bed with its wire frame. The boarded up windows, though, that might be a problem. The door was closed too. Was it locked?

I forced myself out of bed and found that I was still in my leather jacket, tank top, and leather pants. Another pleasant surprise.

Nobody had changed me like a fucking infant in my sleep. Or right in front of me. It felt weird to have my privacy respected.

I walked across the room and placed a hand on the door-knob, I turned it, and the door opened.

A man, lazing in a chair across from my doorway, straightened. He wore jeans, a ripped up t-shirt, and was exceptionally hairy. "Hungry?" he asked.

His eyes were normal colored but that didn't mean much around here.

"Uh, I guess? I don't know. Where's Tyson?"

"With Mr. King in the study. He'll want to talk to you."

"OK," I said. "And you are?"

"Wolf shifter," he replied.

"No, I mean, what's your name?"

"Ned."

"I'm Evie."

He got out of his chair and shuffled off. I waited out in the hallway, patiently, listening to the sounds that drifted down the hall from an open window. Jazz music, laughter, drunk people talking. Yeah, the French Quarter at night. If I hadn't been sure, the pungent odor of urine would've convinced me.

It was the type of smell you got used to after a while. A mixture of scents and sounds that was uniquely NOLA.

Ned returned and handed me a protein bar and water. "Chef's gone home for the night," he said. "We don't got nothing but protein bars, raw steak, and blood packs."

"I'll stick with the protein bar, thanks."

Ned shrugged. "Bathroom?"

"I'm OK for now, thanks." I tore the protein bar open with my teeth and ate it greedily.

"You want to talk to King?"

"I should. Probably. Right?"

"I don't know, man, they just told me to watch the door. When they say watch the door, I watch the door."

"That's it? Just watch the door?"

"Yeah, and feed you if you're hungry," Ned said.

"OK. Then could you show me King's, uh, study?"

"He's got an office." Ned beckoned for me to follow and loped off down the hall, bulky and in charge.

I followed. He didn't take me far, just around one corner in the hall and up a single flight of stairs. He knocked on a door then opened it.

"King, she's here to talk to you."

"Great. Thanks, Ned."

Ned stepped aside, and I walked into the office. It held bookcases, filled with thick leather-covered books, many of the spines worn and old, a desk that looked as if it had hosted a lot of drinking parties, and a fan in the corner that ticked and whirred as it cycled the stale air in the room.

Ned shut the door after me.

Tyson sat against one wall in a creaking armchair, his arms folded. King stood, both fists planted on the table, his burnished gold eyes focused on me.

"Hi," I said. "Sorry to barge in like this, but I figured we should talk about stuff. And I wanted to thank you."

King raised his bushy brown eyebrows.

"For not locking me up," I said. "It's a nice change."

Tyson shifted, shooting a look at the leader of the Hanged Man Society.

"I think," King said, after a minute of silence, "that you should start at the beginning."

I didn't owe him anything, but I did owe Tyson my life, and the nod he gave me was all I needed. I wasn't about to trust these guys, but my experience with them so far had already been way better than what I'd had with Nathan.

"OK," I said, and I told him.

Everything from when I'd been kicked out of my apartment to the letter falling into my lap, to meeting Nathan and being held prisoner, up to my discovery of King's son in the prison cell. I left out the boring parts, the embarrassing parts, but told the truth.

"You're not lying," King said.

"Of course not," I replied. "But how can you tell?"

"I'm a lion shifter. That's one of our things. Detecting bull-shit. If you can't trust your pride, what's the point of having one?"

"Now, that's a credo I can get behind," I said, offering him a grin.

Mr. King didn't smile back, but he didn't look as angry as he had last night either.

"What happened after you found Ari in that cell?" King asked.

My eyes widened, and I sucked in a breath.

"What?" Tyson asked, sitting dead still but alert.

"Ari. Did you say Ari?" I asked.

"Yes. You know my son?" Mr. King asked.

"No. At least, I don't think so. I've had this tarot card for months now," I said. "I found it in my apartment one morning. It had a guy's name and number on the back. Ari King. That was the name."

"Do you still have the card?" Mr. King asked.

"Nathan took it and all my things," I said. "The only thing I kept were my clothes and my kicks."

"Darn." Mr. King thumped his fist to the desk. "Darn. Months ago? That's when you found that card?"

"Yes."

"Darn. Ari always was stubborn," Mr. King said.

I opened my mouth and shut it again. I had waited so long to understand what was happening to me and now that I was on the brink of fitting the pieces of the puzzle together, I was afraid.

"She doesn't know anything," Tyson said, taking the option away from me.

"Ari was captured by the Hierophant Society two months ago. He left our sanctum here in New Orleans with a plan to travel to the Lower Ninth Ward," Mr. King said after a beat. "He wanted to find the person who was causing a disturbance."

"Disturbance?"

"Ari has a gift for sensing when things aren't right," Mr. King said. "On a magical level. He's a shifter like me, but he's got a special gift. Mental defense. He can protect from mental attacks, detect danger, and imbalance. And the fact was, he'd come across Intel that the Hierophant Society and several clusters of Extremes were looking for *something* in the Lower Ninth Ward."

"Something?"

"You," Mr. King said.

Tyson got up, walked to a chair nearby and dragged it over. "You should sit," he said, leveling me with a stare.

"What about you?" I asked. "Do you know all this stuff?"

"I mean, I didn't until a few hours ago. Trust me. Sit down."

I had trusted him this far. I gave him one last look, taking in the pale skin, the strong jawline, rose red lips and dark hair. Like an evil prince out of a fairytale. Finally, I sat down.

"What do you mean, they were looking for me?" I asked Mr. King. "Why?"

"You are part of a race that's been lost since the First Changing," Mr. King said, "and a part of the reason the Council has decided to recall all the Pharaonic Decks. You're a Feather of Ma'at. A justice bringer. An auditor. A supernatural being who was once capable of not only convening with Ma'at the Goddess of justice who weighs the hearts of women and men against her feather to determine their worthiness, but who could convene with the Duality. In short, you are a descendant, perhaps the only one, of a group of people who were meant to maintain balance here on Earth. To ensure that everything was kept in the Duality's image. That men and women were just in their use of their powers."

It was a lot.

A lot more than I had anticipated.

And a lie. It had to be.

"I can't be *that*. I can't be this justice-bringing, fair, good person. I'm not a good person. I have… there are things in my past. There are things that are just bad. Evil. I might be evil."

"Regardless of what you think, you *are* a Feather. The illness you get when things are off-balance proves that. And that's why Sword wanted you. They're up to something, and it's going to be bad if they get what they want. The Hierophant Society has acted according to its own wishes, outside the bounds of law that govern the Tarot Societies, and the Council does nothing to stop them. We don't know why, but going against Bernard Sword, the leader of the Hierophant Society is akin to a death wish, especially for our kind."

"Your kind?"

"Shifters, vampires, and especially, hybrids. The Council would love to wipe us off the face of the planet. Too much trouble to deal with," Tyson said smoothly. "Regulations about what we eat and when, how we interact with others, that kind of thing."

Mr. King nodded. "The so-called peace all the societies live in is a farce and has been for years now, ever since the Council stopped adjudicating and started arresting, trying to control the actions of supernatural beings down to their last meal. They're trying to be sly about it, but the only safety left to us is within societies. Even that's waning. How much longer until the Council has us arrested for illegal activities they don't have the inclination to prove?"

I chewed on the inside of my cheek.

So, Nathan had lied. Of course, he had lied. He had told me I was special and I could "detect bad things" but that he didn't know why.

"Nathan told me that they were trying to combat the atrocities the Council was committing."

"Lies," Tyson said.

"I mean, I get that *now*. The whole kidnapping an entire ass man is kind of a giveaway."

"You said that you went to see the Serpentine Prince, but not why," Mr. King said. "Can you elaborate?"

I had kept Nathan's reasoning to myself during my tale about what I'd experienced, but I let it spill out now. "He's looking for a Pharaonic Deck because he wants to get to the Book of Life and the Keeper. That's what he told me."

"Ah," Mr. King said. "That makes sense. That's why he needs you."

"What do you mean?"

Tyson frowned. "Then they're not as close to the Council as I thought. Why would the Council back the Swords if they knew about what they were planning?"

"Huh?" I looked from Tyson to Mr. King.

"What did Sword tell you about the deck?" Mr. King asked.

"That you can use them to convene with the Keeper?"

"You?" Mr. King asked. "You mean the Feathers of Ma'at."

"Diviners and Tellers."

"Another lie." Mr. King sighed. "The reason Sword was keeping you was because the only individuals who could use the decks were the Feathers. The adjudicators. Diviners use the decks for other purposes, or they collect them for a sense of power. They can't reach the Keeper. Only you can."

"Why does he want to contact the Gods and Goddesses then?" Tyson asked. "It's not because he wants to get on the Council's bad side. There must be another reason. If he really wanted to report them, contacting Ma'at herself would solve that problem."

"When last did you contact any of the gods or goddesses?" I asked.

"Not in recent history," Mr. King said. "To our knowledge. Decks that can reach the Keeper have all been confiscated. The Feathers of Ma'at and their descendants are dead or were killed under suspicious circumstances."

"Oh."

"They have no idea what's going on down here," Tyson said. "No idea what the Council's doing. Vampires and hybrids who aren't officially signed up with an accredited Society are put in camps. There's a new underground of illegal Societies. Hybrids and shifters on the run."

"Why?"

"Why do people do anything?" Mr. King asked. "Power and money."

I grasped my forehead. "So, what do we do?" I asked. "To stop it all?"

Mr. King laughed. "As simple as that?"

"I don't know. If the Swords are doing something bad, we should stop them, right?" And where did that leave me? Was I supposed to judge people? Decide right from wrong? That made my skin crawl.

But you've already done that, little one. That soft, sweet voice.

I tried ignoring the comfort it brought me.

"Sure," Tyson said. "That'll be easy."

"What do we do?" I looked from Mr. King to Tyson. "Surely, we should go get your son? He would know more, right?"

"We can't save him yet," Mr. King said, voice shaking with rage. "Not until we're sure that we won't suffer immediate destruction by the Council's hands."

"But he's suffering!" I hated how that felt. Leaving a man to suffer went against Ma'at, I had to assume. Man, that felt weird to think.

I waited for the voice, but it didn't come. Whatever was

happening, I didn't have a consistent connection that "being." That or I just wasn't consistently crazy yet.

"It can't be that black and white," Tyson said. "We have to be careful."

Mr. King nodded. "If we get our hands on a Pharaonic Deck, we'll have a bargaining chip. A means of getting Ari back and ensuring the safety of the Hanged Man Society after the fact. Then, we'll work against them in secret."

"I don't like it," I said.

"It's cunning," Mr. King conceded. "But what other option is there? Busting in there will lead to Ari's death. The deaths of my entire Society. I won't allow that."

I got the sense that his words were final. He had the Alpha ring to his tone, the same one Vera had had when commanding her four soldiers what felt like a decade ago.

"OK," I said, thinking hard. "I think I know where we need to go. But it won't be easy."

"The Serpentine Prince?" Mr. King asked.

I hesitated then let out a breath. "Yes. I think he's got a deck. And I know what he wants in exchange for it."

30

I STARED at my reflection in the mirror in the bedroom I'd
been assigned. The mirror had been tacked to the inside of the
closet door, and it had a crack running down its length,
marring my reflection. I didn't want to pity myself here, but it
felt fitting.

These people, creatures, whatever you wanted to call
them, expected me to be this "Feather." A justice-bringer. A
person who gave out judgments and made decisions about
what was right or wrong.

How could I do any of that when I was so *wrong* myself?

My purple hair hung limply around my face, wet from the
shower, and there were dark circles under my eyes. I held a
towel to my chest, covering my body.

I squeezed my eyes shut for a second then dropped the
towel and opened them again.

There she is.

An arcing scar just beneath my breast on the left side.
The spot where the knife had connected with my flesh
and scraped across the bones of my ribs. The doctors had

said I was lucky to be alive, not that I remembered much of it.

A Feather.

I scraped my palm over the scar, covering it for a second, imagining that I could scrape it away. Finally, I turned and dressed. My bra, the worn tank top I'd had on when I'd escaped the Hierophant Society, and a pair of leather pants.

I had no money, and from the state of the Hanged Man Society, I doubted they had much either. Suiting up in brand new clothing wasn't going to happen. I had the clothes on my back, the boots on my feet, as I'd had many times in the past.

A knock rattled the door in its frame.

"Yeah?"

The door opened, and Tyson entered. He carried folded clothes in his arm with a sheathed blade atop it.

"What's that?" I asked.

"This?" He lifted the piled. "This is a secret portal to the netherworld."

I snorted despite my melancholy. Finally, *someone* who had a sense of humor.

"Right," I said. "Put it on the bed and I'll jump right in."

"We tried our best to find your size in everything," Tyson said, placing the clothes on the bed. "Leather pants, leather corset, utility belt, that kind of thing. The corset is special."

"Special?"

"It was made by a vampire," he said. "They imbue some of their power into everything they create."

"Oh, OK," I said, and walked over to it. "It's not any, uh, special kind of leather is it?"

"Ask me no questions." He shrugged. "Because I don't have a clue what the answers are." He picked up the sheathed blade and held it out to me. "This is old, but it will work in an emergency."

"I don't know how to use a knife," I said.

"It's pretty simple." Tyson grabbed the hilt of the knife, which was bronze with a hilt that bore the rays of the sun along its side. He withdrew it from its leather sheath and held it aloft. He spun it easily in his hand, flicking it this way and that, and totally showing off. "Use this end on your enemies." He touched the pointy tip, drawing a single drop of red blood from his finger.

I stared at the single droplet on his finger.

He caught my gaze with his and lifted that finger to his lips, licking off the droplet, slowly.

I swallowed. "I meant that I won't use a knife. Sorry that wasn't clear."

"Why is that?"

"Long story," I replied.

"We've got time before we leave." Tyson invited himself to sit down on the pale sheets, specked with their yellow flowers.

It was an obscene sight, this incredibly powerful hybrid, grasping a knife in one hand, lazing on my bed. Though, it was really my bed, was it? I was just here temporarily. Until we fixed things. Or until I figured out what I was going to do about the whole "Feather" issue.

"Talk to me," Tyson said.

I chewed on my bottom lip. I wanted to tell him everything, pour it out and lay myself bare, at least in the metaphorical sense.

Not once in my life had I allowed myself to talk about *it*.

"Are you putting some weird vampire spell on me?" I asked.

"Vampires don't have magic," he said. "Not in the traditional 'sorcerer' sense."

"What about hybrids?"

He smirked. "You were the one who was meant to talk, not me."

Another chewing on my lip.

"Why do you think you're bad?" Tyson asked, his blood-red lips moving over his black teeth, in that pale, strong face, the red eyes somehow noble, gave me all kinds of chills. The forbidden kind. Surely, humans weren't meant to *be* with hybrid vampires.

But you're not human, remember?

"Why do you think you're bad, Evie?" he repeated.

"Just stuff that happened."

"What stuff?"

"I don't talk about it," I replied. "There's no point."

"If we're going on a mission together, I need to know that you'll be able to think clearly, that you won't be acting on emotion," Tyson said, flipping the knife end-over-end and catching it by the hilt. "Emotion is dangerous in tense situations."

I rolled my tongue over the backs of my teeth.

"Come on," Tyson said. "You're talking to a hybrid vampire. What could you have possibly done that was *so bad*? Did you murder someone?"

"No."

"Drain someone of their blood and drink it?"

"No! What the fuck?"

"Exactly." He shrugged. "There's nothing you can say that will shock me. I don't know whether you've realized it yet, but you're surrounded by freaks who have done bad things. So, if you're a freak too, you fit right in."

The trouble was, I didn't want to be "bad." The freak part? I didn't mind being a freak.

"I'm bad too, Evie," he said. "My progenitor impregnated my human mother, then ripped me from her when I was a child. Killed her so that he could raise me in his image. But he hated me, and I hated him. So here I am. Free. You should try freeing yourself from your past too."

Tyson waited a couple of minutes then shrugged, got up and dropped the knife onto the pile of clothing on my bed. "Suit yourself," he said, and made for the door. "Just don't make any decisions based on emotion tomorrow. We need to think and act clearly if we're going to get the cards before Sword does. Mr. King already thinks you shouldn't be a part of the group."

They had to take me because I "knew" the Serpentine Prince. And because he wanted me. I was the prize that could be exchanged for the cards.

I still hadn't worked out how I would get back safely with the cards as opposed to becoming the prince's "toy."

Tyson opened the door.

"She killed my father." The words came out of nowhere. Not technically true. They came out of my mouth, but it felt as if they'd appeared out of the ether.

"Who?" Tyson asked, shutting the door again.

"My mother," I said, after a beat. "My mother murdered my father, and then she tried to do the same to me. With a knife. The cops, uh, the cops shot her when they got to our apartment. I was six."

Tyson nodded.

"And I have been... I have been..." I swallowed and exhaled. "I have been waiting for that part of me to arrive."

"So you think because your mother was a murderer, you're going to be one too? That's what you're worried about?" he asked.

I looked down at the floor. It sounded dumb when he said it.

Tyson approached.

I looked up in time for my vision to be eclipsed by those red lips. For one, heart-stopping moment, I was sure he would kiss me, and I was so not in the mind frame for that. But Tyson merely grasped my shoulders, gently, meeting me stare for stare.

"Take it from someone who had an asshole for a 'father,' " he said. "You're not your parents' mistakes. Just because you have genes from somebody, doesn't mean you're going to wind up being like them. That's not how it works. Life is about choices, and the fact that you're worried about doing the wrong shit? Means you're probably not going to do the wrong shit, even if you had the urge to."

The words were a balm, but I understood that they were a temporary one. Still, it had felt good to get it out, even if it was just a quick sentence.

"Let's make a deal," Tyson said.

"What deal?"

"Totally voluntary, but if you're that afraid of being evil," he said, "I can kill you."

"What?"

"If you do something inherently evil, lose control, become the bad bitch and not in the colloquial cool sense, I can off you," he said, smiling, those black fangs on display.

There would be worse ways to die.

Apparently, the hormones were in full swing today.

"What do you say?" Tyson asked. "If you go bad like an avocado, I'll squash you."

"I'm not sure that's a good metaphor, but OK," I said, and stuck out my hand. "Deal."

He shook it, laughing.

"Is that it?" I asked. "Do we have a blood pact now?"

"Well, no. I didn't want to get too serious. What if you decide to go back on your word? If we do a blood pact, that's unbreakable. I'll have to kill you if you do evil shit. And we'll have to define what evil shit is," he said. "And vampire blood pacts are a little weirder than the stuff you see in human movies."

"Oh yeah?"

"It's more like a blood, sex ritual thing," he said. "I'm assuming we can go with the, uh, handshake for now, yes?"

"Sure," I managed, choking it out.

Tyson left me with another of those devilish grins and made for the exit. He paused in the doorway. "Evie," he said, "I doubt I'll have to kill you. And not just because you're a feather. You act all bad-ass, but you're clearly a square."

"Hey!"

He shut the door behind him, and for the first time in what felt like forever, I smiled. A normal, natural smile.

31

Night fell on the French Quarter, and I navigated the halls of the house, cramped, wooden and creaking, down a set of rickety metal stairs, into the front hall of the Hanged Man Society's headquarters. This place wasn't nearly as confusing as the Hierophant Society house had been. There was no sense of time loss or impossible architecture. It was just a house, a worn one, full of scratches on the furniture, with boarded up windows.

Mr. King stood in front of the door, waiting for his "troops" to gather. I had been instructed to meet downstairs, wearing the protective gear I had been assigned at this specific time. 11:58 p.m. exactly.

Tyson leaned against the wall, wearing a cloak as he had done during class at the Academy, his red eyes burning within the hood.

"Just us?" I asked. "No one else?"

"I won't risk more of my society members on this task," Mr. King said. "The smaller the group, the easier it will be to pull this off.

"Then why not just send me?" I asked.

Tyson made a tiny noise in his throat.

"What?"

"Where we're going, you'll need protection," King said, "and Tyson will be able to provide it."

"Huh? We're not just going upstairs? To the portal?"

"We don't have a portal," King said. "We don't have fae friends to create one, so we're going to a common one that's used by Tyson's kind."

"Half-vampires?" I asked.

"And vampires," Tyson said. "Hence the need for your protection."

"Oh."

"We'll be attending the festivities at the Upside Down Club tonight," King said.

And my heart damn near stopped. "That's the place! The place where we went looking for Fredrick Dorgoste," I said.

Where Vera had been killed because of *me*. Or rather, because Nathan had chosen me over her.

"Correct," King replied.

I had told him every detail of my stay with Nathan, gone over it in exact detail about ten times, so he was well aware of the mission and how it had ended.

"Then, surely we can get to him? He knows the woman who has a deck."

"He's dead," Tyson said. "The vampires at the club killed him after Nathan's group of soldiers tried to break-in. And Kasha Ramone is unreachable at present."

"In hiding," King said, nodding. "I can't sniff her out."

The way he said "sniff" gave me the impression that he was completely capable of sniffing her out, literally.

"Probably fled to the fae realm or another plain of existence," Tyson said.

King clapped his hands together and rubbed. "Are we ready?"

I didn't reply, but my hand strayed to the weapon strapped to my hip. The dagger surely wouldn't do much good against vampires. I wasn't even sure how one killed a vampire. Scholar Harwa had been able to read my thoughts, so the element of surprise was probably out of the question.

"Stay close behind me," King said. "Tyson will bring up the rear." He opened the door and slipped out into the night.

I was instantly assaulted by the smell of the French Quarter. Alcohol, sweaty tourists, an undertone of vomit, all accompanied by the sounds of smooth jazz. It was familiar to me, like coming home, and though it was pungent, it didn't bother me that much.

We strode down the pathway, and slipped between the tourists. They didn't notice us, much as they hadn't when I'd been accompanied by Nathan's soldiers.

"They don't see us," I whispered.

"That's because of me," Tyson replied.

Of course. He had made me invisible to Killian at the Academy. He could do that at any time? While moving?

"What can't you do?" I asked.

"I'm flattered," he said. "There are many things I can't do. Apparently, being accepted by either vampire society or supernatural society is on the list."

"Hybrids are rejected?"

"Thoroughly," he said.

King didn't stop us from talking, and though I was tense, it wasn't anywhere near as bad as it had been with Nathan and the others. Maybe he thought it would help us act natural?

We entered the quieter, darker streets of the French Quarter, moving toward that house with its metal balcony and shuttered windows, its wooden front door, firmly shut. Instead of lingering in the alley, we approached the door outright.

"Act confident," Tyson breathed in my ear, stopping behind me. "Pretend like you belong. Like you're not prey."

Prey. A chill ran down my spine.

"Pretend you're the hunter," he said. "That you're the one who's come to mete out justice and judgment."

Be a Feather. The words came from the warm female voice.

Hello? Is that you? Ma'at? I called out in my mind. No answer.

It seemed she could reach me whenever she wanted, but I was either unable to reach her or she just didn't want to talk to me.

Be a Feather. I repeated the words to myself.

"OK," I said.

Tyson brushed past me, the back of one of his hands briefly touching my knuckles, and my heart turned over. He had promised to kill me if I turned "bad." But that all depended on his definition of bad, didn't it?

He knocked once. A small window in the door opened and two blazing red eyes peered out.

"Back so soon?" The voice was male, full of amusement. "And with friends. A shifter and a human?" A strange lustiness, that I was pretty sure had nothing to do with sex, came over his voice.

"Not human," I said firmly. "But whatever gets you off, I

guess."

A pause and then a rough chuckle.

"Very well." The door latch clacked and opened. The vampire holding it was massive, the top of his head scraping the lintel, his eyes blazing red. He was in human form, even though he surely couldn't avoid notice at that height. He would wind up in a record book if he went out on the street. "You may enter, as long as you understand the rules, Hybrid."

"I accept them and any punishments associated with them."

The doorman gave a nod then gestured with a tiny, mocking bow for us to enter.

Tyson led the way this time, and King took up the rear. The front hall was dark, the floor lined with candles, wax melting directly onto the floorboards. There was no other decor, apart from a few picture frames that had been hung on the walls. The contents of those frames, images of pain or torture, were all upside down.

I didn't bother twisting my head to get a better look at what they depicted. I didn't want to know.

We continued down the hall toward a door. Music thumped from behind it. Not jazz, but deep, rhythmic house music punctuated by unearthly roars. My skin prickled, my hair stood on end.

"Be the hunter," Tyson repeated.

"What punishment was he talking about?" I managed.

"If we fuck up, they do to me what they did to Fredrick Dorgoste."

I tensed and King laid a hand on my shoulder. "Nothing's going to go wrong."

If only I could've taken comfort from his words. This club

reeked of depravity. Of blood lust and evil, and I was here with members of a society that were outcasts. Vampires and half-vampires and shifters. I knew nothing about them, yet I had trusted them.

They could be lying, just like Nathan lied.

Tyson kept his hood up and opened the door that led into the club.

Vampires everywhere, some in human form, some in their true forms, red raw, twisted, with those black talons and teeth. And that wasn't even the worst part of it. The world was upside down, quite literally.

Vampires in their human form, looking like sexier versions of normal people, lay on sofas or danced on the dancefloor to the music. A group of female vampires had a human man on the couch and were doing things to him, both sexual and violent, and he appeared to be *enjoying it.*

The roof was the opposite of the scene below. Furniture had been tacked to it, and vampires in their true form either sat, danced, or hung from it, upside down, like giant bats without wings, blinking and in a trance.

"Rhine," King whispered.

"Rhine?"

"It's a drug that some vampires use. They're resistant to it, take it instead of drinking alcohol because alcohol renders them weak against attack," King breathed. "Rhine is like vampire weed, but to humans or other supernatural creatures, it's more dangerous than heroin."

Another wave of fear coursed over me.

"Rhine lulls you into a sense of security and then slingshots you into a high that makes you believe you can do impossible things."

Tyson moved past vampires on the dancefloor, heading toward another door at the back of the room. The vampires turned as I passed, both male and female, making eye contact, licking their lips, even gesturing suggestively.

"Ignore it," King said.

I gave each of those vampires a haughty stare in return, hoping I was portraying confidence.

We reached the door, and Tyson knocked once, pressed his ear to it, then entered. He shut us in and locked the door right away.

"We're safe for now," he said and removed his hood.

The room reminded me of a dirtier version of the attic above the Hierophant society. A circle had been drawn on the floor, runes marking four corners of it, fire, water, earth, and air. The chalk that had been used wasn't white as it had been in the Hierophant Society's attic, though. It was a deep red inching toward black.

Blood.

I shoved the thought aside.

The music outside the door changed, the beat deep as it had been, but the sounds of a string instrument layered over it, whining and high-pitched.

"Snake oil?" I asked.

"Not necessary for this," Tyson replied. "Consider this an all-purpose portal. It was made with blood, so we can go wherever we want with the right sacrifice."

Another wave of hair rising.

Tyson extended his hand to me. King had already entered the portal and stood there, larger than life.

I bit my lip and took Tyson's hand. I'd come this far, hadn't I?

32

Tyson's words at each of the runes were inaudible. His lips moved, but the sound didn't emerge, or if it did, it fell flat to the ground, and as he mouthed them, each of the runes lit up a vibrant scarlet. The outside line of the portal colored that same red, the circle completing with us inside it.

I kept my arms at my sides even though I was tempted to hug myself.

What are you doing here? How did this happen?

But anything was better than being a prisoner. Anything was better than the Hierophant Society, right?

I hadn't felt nausea once in the past couple of days at the Hanged Man.

Tyson joined me, raising a hand to the sky and sweeping it down. Crimson light flashed and eclipsed my world, and I stumbled. Firm hands caught me, both King and Tyson from either side. King released me, but Tyson's hand lingered. He squinted in the bright sunlight from above.

We were here.

The Serpentine Prince's world. His orchard, in the exact

spot where Nathan and I had arrived the last time. There wasn't a breath of wind, just as it had been before, and the sky was blue and cloudless.

King didn't squint like Tyson did, but he frowned.

Gone was the scent of overripe apples or the gentle rustle of movement in the tall grass either side of the path leading toward the orchard's entrance.

Silence.

And something else.

A smell. Copper. And the tang of smoke on the air.

"Oh no," I breathed.

Nathan. It had to be. Had they come back for the deck? Had they found it?

I set off down the pathway ahead of King and Tyson, and they didn't stop me from taking the lead. I reached the gate to the orchard and opened it, moving between the trees. The apples had fallen from the trees and lay rotting on the ground. To my left, in the grass, scorched earth and the bodies of snakes. Thousands of snakes. Immolated. Their burning carcasses turning the air wretched the further we went.

This is so fucked up.

Tears stung my eyes and a wave of nausea came. I held it back, forcing myself to stare directly ahead at the exit into the clearing. A shape materialized. The throne, except it was no longer a throne. It was a burned husk, charred and ashy, pieces of it drifting away into the wind.

"When?" I asked. "How?"

"It can't have been too long ago. The throne is still burning," King said.

We entered the clearing, and the dizziness came. I grasped my knees. "This is wrong," I said. "This is all wrong."

Snake bodies littered the grass. They had been throne backward, as if from a central explosion, and the ground was scarred with deep gouges.

"Sword didn't do this alone," King said. "He's not powerful enough. A physical illusionist can't mark the ground with magic."

"Then his soldiers. Or the General was here himself."

I breathed slowly, trying to right my senses. I shut my eyes, the silence deafening, until—

"Girl." The croak came from behind the throne. "Girl. Come."

I opened my eyes and stumbled forward, following the sound.

"Evie?" Tyson's voice. "What is it?"

They hadn't heard him talking.

"Girl."

I rounded the throne and stopped, horror clogging my throat. At least it forced the rising bile down.

The Serpentine Prince lay on the ground, bleeding glittering green blood around him. His tail had been cut free, and one of his arms lay a short way off. It appeared as if they had tried to slit his throat.

He breathed through his nostrils, though I didn't understand how, and his green eyes, pupils the slits of snake's, focused on me.

"Girl." His lips didn't move.

"Prince," I said out loud, dropping to my knees because I couldn't keep my balance. "Was it the Swords?"

"Yes." It came as a hiss in my mind.

"I'm sorry. This is all wrong." Even though he took humans

as prisoners. As playthings. This was still *wrong*. I felt it in my gut.

"Do not pity me. I go where no creature can follow. To the stars above to rejoin the creators."

"The deck?"

"They could not get it from me. But you will have it. It is incomplete."

"Why?"

"Some of it was taken. The other cards I retained or recovered. I am too weak to go into detail."

"I understand," I said, my lips barely moving. I couldn't vocalize properly, the dizziness having reached its peak, but he could understand me and that was all that mattered.

"You will find the others." The Serpentine Prince stiffened, his eyes growing wide. "I go where no one can follow. I go where no one—"

"Do you know where the other cards are?" I asked.

"In the long reeds, the marshland, the papyrus, grasped against her bosom." The Prince's body shuddered, and life left his eyes. A green shape rose from his corpse, regal and tall, in the form of a half-man, half-snake, a mist that had no facial features. It rose and the evaporated, and as it did, the prince's body glittered and dissolved, running into the ground, pieces breaking and bleeding.

"Evie." Tyson's hand touched my shoulder. His fingers were cold against my skin. "Evie, can you hear me?"

"Just wait," I mumbled.

"Is she OK?" King asked in my peripheral.

"Have you ever seen anything like that? She was surrounded by light."

King didn't answer verbally.

I kept my dizzied focus on the dissolving green on the ground, the glittery fluid sucking back into the ground. A shape appeared in the center of the mass, revealed slowly by the decay. A green velvet bag, somehow unstained.

I grasped it and lifted it. My fingers fumbled on the velvet ropes. I opened it and extracted the contents. Cards. Tarot cards. I was too tired to count them, but they were gorgeous, drawn in the style of ancient Egypt, hieroglyphs scrawled across them in gold. I held one of them up.

The Devil.

33

"Forty-eight cards." King had placed them on his desk in the office at the Hanged Man Society. Oddly, the cards looked at home against the worn, distressed wood. Maybe that was their nature, though. Or maybe it was the strange attraction I felt when near them. A need to touch them, to keep them safe, like they were living, breathing things.

"Forty-eight," King repeated, "of a Pharaonic Deck. That means we're missing thirty, and about half of those thirty are major arcana."

I sat in the uncomfortable wooden chair in front of his desk, trying not to slump or feel like I'd been called into the principal's office. Tyson hovered nearby, watching in silence.

"Fuck." King palmed his forehead. "An incomplete deck."

"We can still use it," Tyson said, "to trade for Ari."

The right thing to do. Trade the cards for Ari, then work with him to get the full deck back. There was still a gap in my memory when it came to him and the card I had found on my person. Not a part of the Pharaonic Deck, for sure. These cards… I wanted to keep them so badly. I wanted to tuck them back into their velvet pocket and tie it around my wrist, seat the cards against my skin.

They were dangerous, and they needed to be kept from the wrong hands.

And your hands are the right ones? Maybe not, but my gut told me so.

Now, we had to trade them for Ari. Trade them.

It's the right thing to do.

I set my jaw. "Are the major arcana more important than the minor cards?"

"Not technically," King said. "But they're the ones that are used to contact the Keeper of the Book of Life, and that's Nathan Sword's ultimate goal."

"So, we have half a bargaining chip?" I asked.

"Less than that. Fifteen of the major arcana cards are missing. Meaning we have seven total." King took them out and placed them face up on the desk, one by one. "The Devil. The Hierophant. The Priestess. The World. The Sun. Justice."

As the Justice card appeared, showing an image of a woman kneeling winged feathers spread either side, my eyes rolled back in my head and my vision hazed.

Ma'at. The name rolled through my mind.

"Evie."

My eyes snapped open. "Sorry," I said. "I'm listening. It's just these cards are doing stuff to me that I don't quite understand."

"You have a connection with them," King replied. "They're technically yours. Every deck of cards is deeply connected to the Gods and Goddesses, and thus, connected to the Feathers who were meant to mete out justice. That's why you're reacting this way."

My fingers itched to lift one of the cards, and I placed my hands in my lap, balling them into fists. I wanted to dislike the control these cards had over me, but I couldn't. They belonged with me, as surely as my skin belonged on my body.

Ew. Come on. What's wrong with you?

"So, what do we do?" Tyson asked, directing the question toward me more than King. "She's got a connection with them. We could keep the cards and find the others. The Serpentine Prince gave her a clue about the whereabouts of the other cards."

"In the long reeds, the marshland, the papyrus, grasped against her bosom." I repeated it verbatim. "What do you think that means?"

"I have an inkling," King said. "It hearkens back to the creation of the Gods and Goddesses. To Isis, Set, Osiris, Nephthys, and Horus."

I opened my mouth, but the crunch of wood splintering effectively cut off all thought. My eyes widened, and Tyson stiffened. King was already out of his seat. He rushed to the door and wrenched it open.

Shouts came from the lower floor of the house and figures rushed past in the hall, barreling down the stairs. The sound of growling, of screams, and the sizzle of electricity. Things breaking.

"What's going on?" I asked.

"An attack." King shut the door again quietly, turning to Tyson. "Guard her and the cards with your life. Get her out of here if you can, but only when the coast is clear. I'll distract them." Light glowed from his golden eyes, and hair sprouted around his head, a deep golden mane encircling it. His face changed shape, even as golden fur grew on his hands, his nails lengthening into claws. He opened the door and shut it, still transforming.

"Tyson," I said.

"The cards."

I was out of my chair in a flash and at the table. I gathered the cards hastily, placed them in the green velvet bag, and did what I had wanted to do since I'd found them. I tied them to my wrist and slipped the velvet bag against my skin, letting out a sigh.

Tyson watched me wordlessly.

I don't like how I feel. But at the same time, I did.

"Get under the desk," he said. "Hide until I tell you we can move."

I did as he'd said. I wasn't under any illusions here—I would be about as useful in a fight as fried chicken at a vegan convention. I hugged my knees and listened to the horrible sounds from below. A lion's roar. The crunch of flesh and bone, the splatter of something wet. Thumping footsteps on the stairs outside.

Tyson rounded the desk and dropped down in front of me. "They're coming," he said, holding my gaze with his red one. "I can smell them. I can feel them coming. I'm going to try to keep you safe. He licked his lips. I'm going to try."

"I know." My hands moved of their own accord. I pressed them to his cheeks, slid them over the back of his head and drew myself toward him. "Thank you for everything." My lips were inches from his, my heart pounding out a rhythm of desperation.

Tyson stared me directly in the eyes. He drew his tongue over his fangs, slowly, then pressed a single finger to my lips, soft and warm. Then he drew back, stood, and circled the desk.

The door burst open, and I squeezed my eyes shut.

Is this how you'll let it happen? Someone else sacrificing for you, while you cower under a desk?

No.

I scrambled out from my hiding spot and straightened, my hand moving to the dagger on my belt. Tyson faced off against a man I vaguely recognized. One of the acolytes from the ritual I'd witnessed on my first night with the Hierophant Society.

The man shot flame at Tyson, but the hybrid vampire merely stepped out of the flames' path, impossibly fast, blurring out of the way.

I bit my lip and drew my weapon, holding it out, impotently.

Tyson's back was to me. Likely, he thought I was underneath the desk. Another soldier entered the room, followed by another.

"Capture them." The voice was full of heat, anger. Nathan had entered the room. His khopesh was coated in blood and resting easily in his hand. "Hurry."

More men filing into the room. An impossible amount. Too many for Tyson, even, let alone me.

A soldier approached, and my gaze snapped to him. It was J.P., grinning at me, his smile vicious.

"Hello, chickie," he said.

A voice sounded in my mind, *his* voice. "Put down the knife or I'll kill you."

Tears streamed down my face, and I resisted.

"Come on, chickie. Put down the knife. Don't be a fuckin'

dipshit." The voice intensified, the command thrumming through my brain.

My fingers released, achingly slow, and I fought them every step of the way. No! No, no, no.

"I will break your mind, meals on wheels," he said in my head. "Drop the knife and come here. Now."

The knife fell from my fingertips and my feet moved of their own accord. To my unending horror, I moved toward J.P.'s open arms. A screech of protest ripped free from my throat.

Tyson turned and caught my gaze. His eyes widened, and he lifted his hand to the side of his neck where a needle had penetrated his skin. The soldier, the ritualist, standing behind him had injected him with something.

"Fuck," Tyson muttered, then stumbled. He growled and tried moving toward me, but it was as if he was caught in honey. Two steps, struggling, and then he keeled over and hit the deck.

Where are you? I called out to the Goddess who had interjected so many times in the past. Help me!

You chose this path, Feather.

And then a cable tie was zipped into place over my wrists, and I was escorted through the wreckage of the house, past bleeding and burning bodies, out into the night.

<h1 style="text-align:center">34</h1>

They had put me back in the room.

My prison.

The four poster bed, the bookcase, complete with my clothing in the cupboards, or rather the clothing they had chosen for me. The backpack with my books was gone. The maps too. And Tyson was elsewhere. They had him trapped, God alone knew where.

Alone.

I had chosen this. On the night with the feather, the white light, when I had punched Nathan in the throat and run for my life. I had chosen this.

Tyson was the closest person I had to a friend, and they had taken him. And the cards too. The velvet purse that I had tucked against my skin, under the sleeve of my leather jacket, was gone.

The weirdest part was that I could feel them. The cards.

If I closed my eyes and tilted my head back, an outline of gold appeared above my head. Far above. Blinding in its light.

The cards were upstairs. They had them, they had Tyson,

and Ari King too. And the Hanged Man Society was dead because of me.

Pain unfolded in my chest, and I lurched off the bed, my hands still behind my back. I marched to the door, my boots squeaking on the clean floor.

"Mother fuckers!" I yelled and unleashed my fury with a kick to the bottom of the door. "Let me out of here, right now." Another kick.

The door rattled in its frame.

I kicked continuously, well aware that I would never break this door, but I didn't care. My frustrations had reached breaking point. They had killed the Serpentine Prince and destroyed his throne and realm, killed innocents, enslaved a man, tainted what little knowledge of myself I had, and now this.

They had the cards.

The cards that made sense to me and felt right. Good. Pure.

And Tyson was in danger. What about King? Was he alive?

"Let me the fuck out!" I howled and kept kicking.

The lock clicked, and the door opened. I tried to run immediately, lowering my head and charging like a two-legged bull.

Strong arms caught me and walked me backward, and Nathan's familiar scent filled my nostrils—citrus and lies.

"Easy," he said.

I backpedaled, pulling out of his grasp.

He kicked the door shut then turned and locked it again.

I should've been afraid at the implication, but I was just so fucking angry. Fear could wait. "Let me out of here," I said. "Right now."

"Evie, relax." Nathan put up his arms. He wore his usual suit, the top buttons of his shirt undone, his blond hair perfectly parted to one side. I couldn't fathom how I'd found him handsome. He was the purveyor of death and lies. "Just relax. I understand that you *think* you know what's going on, but you don't."

"Where are my cards?" I asked. "Where's Tyson?"

Nathan's eyes flashed that glowing blue. "Don't worry about the hybrid. He's being taken care of."

Nope. Don't like the sound of that. "Let me out."

"I can't do that until you've calmed down, Evie. And as for your cards," he said, "they're not really yours. That is *our* Pharaonic Deck. Mine and yours. My father's. Together, we can restore balance to the world."

"Save it, dipshit. I know the truth about you and your family," I snapped.

"You think you know the truth," Nathan said, "but you're trusting the word of vampires, hybrids and shifters. Don't you see how ridiculous that is? Those are inherently evil creatures. They eat flesh and drink blood for power."

I pressed my lips together.

Don't let him gaslight you.

"Come on, Evie, you're crazy if you think that what they said is the truth. I'm here to protect you. Take care of you."

"The same way you took care of the Serpentine Prince?" I asked.

Nathan stiffened.

"I saw what you and your friends did to him," I said. "I know what happened."

"You don't know anything." He strode forward, bearing down on me, and I backed up, lifting my chin in defiance.

The backs of my legs hit the bed, and he took me by the shoulders.

"They're lying to you, OK? They're the liars, not me."

But my gut said otherwise. And like Ma'at had suggested, I'd made my choice. I had chosen the "inherently evil" creature who had yet to do anything inherently evil around me. Nathan might've had a pretty exterior, but the inside was trash rotting in the sun.

"I've missed you," Nathan said, softening his tone. He drew closer. "I've missed you so much, Evie. I've wanted you for so long." He pressed his lips to mine, and I caught his lower lip between my teeth and bit until I tasted blood.

Nathan yelled and ripped free of me, stepping back, blood dripping down his chin. His eyes glowed blue. "I see your new friends have been educating you."

"Fuck you." I spat blood on the floor. "You don't touch me."

Nathan stared at me for a moment, completely silent. Then he grabbed me by the arm and marched me toward the door.

"Let go of me."

"Shut up," Nathan snapped. "You'd better keep your tongue and your teeth to yourself from now on. You're about to meet my father."

BERNARD SWORD SAT IN A ROOM FULL OF LIGHT AT THE TOP OF the mansion, in one of its two side "towers." He was so high up, it had taken us an hour to get here, using rickety stairs, passing the attic level where Nathan had sprinkled snake oil on the floor.

The patriarch of the Sword family was a perfect mixture of both Killian and Nathan. He had the blond hair, streaked with gray, a regal attitude, broad shoulders and a traditionally handsome face. He also had Killian's steel gray eyes and dead stare.

"Miss Guinevere Crowley," he said. "Are you sure you don't want to take a seat?"

I ignored him, lifting my chin and glaring down my nose like I owned the room, the tower, everything in it.

Killian had already taken a seat in a leather chair to one side and was casually observing, switching his gaze between me and the windowed view of New Orleans. The city was spread out far below, the yard as well, the gate, the exit into the Garden District.

Nathan stood by my side, still grasping my upper arm a little too tightly.

"Come now," Bernard said easily, his voice mellow yet chilling. "Surely Killian hasn't cut out your tongue yet. You haven't, have you, Son?"

"Not yet, Father," Killian said without shifting his gaze from the city below. "Give it time."

"Now, I wouldn't advise that. We do require her knowledge."

"There are far easier ways of obtaining knowledge than talking, Father."

Bernard gave his son an appreciative smile. "Miss Crowley," he said, turning to me again. "My son tells me that you have happened upon an item of great importance. Is that true?"

I kept my teeth together.

"There's no use lying or even withholding information. I already have it in my office. In my possession."

I shut my eyes, but the golden light wasn't in this room. It came from the other side of the mansion, exactly in line with this level. The other tower.

"Shake her, Nathan. It seems she's overcome with grief." That Garden District twang was mocking.

I opened my eyes again. "I won't tell you anything unless you release Tyson and Ari King, and swear to leave the Hanged Man Society alone."

"Isn't she arrogant, Father?" Killian asked lazily. "This is what happens when you leave her to Nathan's devices. You realize he's put her upstairs in the mansion. In a master bedroom. Clearly, his cock has clouded his mind."

"Don't be crass, Killian. Not in the company of a lady."

"She's anything but a lady," Killian replied.

"And proud of it, dickwad." I made eye contact with Killian and refused to shrug away from his gray-eyed gaze.

They would kill me just like they had murdered the members of the Hanged Man Society, but I wasn't afraid. Ever since the cards… What was it about them? Like touching fate itself. Like touching my true purpose.

"I believe she knows where the rest of the cards are," Bernard said, pushing himself back in his chair.

"Let me have her," Killian said.

"No." Nathan's grip tightened on my arm. "She stays with me."

"Judging by the puncture wound on your lip, Brother, she wants nothing to do with you."

Nathan didn't blush but maintained eye contact with

Bernard. "I can get the truth out of her, Father. She won't want her friends to be punished."

"You," Bernard sighed. "You are weak, Nathan. You've shown compassion where there should be none. You've given the reins of our family name over to your brother the minute you disappointed me."

"I found her," Nathan hissed, shaking me. "I found her. I was the one who brought her here."

Brought me? Of course, the card wasn't a coincidence.

"You should have taken her rather than brought her," Bernard said. "Your decisions are as pitiful as your powers. Killian will have her."

Killian sat forward in his chair, expressing a sharkish grin. "You and I are going to have a great deal of fun together, Guinevere."

"It's Evie," I said, the first shred of fear worming through my belly.

35

"Do you know who I am?" Killian walked me down the stairs, his hand on my back, pushing me whenever I was too slow for his liking.

We had entered the atrium of the Academy and descended, him carrying a ball of flame in his hand to light our way. The Academy was deathly silent, and I doubted that screaming for help would get me anywhere.

If it hadn't helped Ari when he'd been captured, how the hell could it possibly help me?

"Do you know who I am?" Killian pushed me forward, and I stumbled down the stairs, barely keeping myself upright.

I slammed myself into the balustrade to stop from falling forward. A burst of pain shot through my ribs, but I ignored it and kept walking. There had to be a way out.

"I asked you a question, Guinevere."

Now that I'd told him I didn't like my full name, he seemed set on using it, just to upset me. Petty asshole.

"You're the Easter Bunny," I said at last. "And you're going to hop me down to a room full of chocolate eggs wrapped in foil."

Another push, but thankfully, we'd reached the ground floor of the atrium, and I didn't fall.

"I will have to remove your tongue if you insist on being petulant."

I didn't say anything and kept walking down the hallway. I could've guessed where we were headed. The dungeon room where they kept Ari, chained to the wall.

"I am the most powerful man to have existed. More powerful than the sorcerers of old," Killian whispered. "Twice as powerful as my father anticipated. Three times stronger than he could imagine in his wildest dreams."

"OK, Kanye," I replied.

He didn't get the joke, and shoved me again, this time into the wall.

Killian grabbed me by my hair and walked me along the path. "There are two things I know how to do," he whispered into my ear. "Rule over the small-minded, and break the weak. You can decide which you'd like to be. I can break you, here, now, shatter your mind into a million pieces, and the beauty of it all is I don't need to use magic to do it. Consider me a purveyor of the forgotten arts of torture."

There was no use replying. I had to let him talk it out while I tried to come up with an escape plan.

Would Tyson and I be trapped in the dungeon together? Ari was he alive? Could we formulate a plan to get out?

Killian continued talking. "You're going to become mine," he said. "By the end of this, you'll be glad to get on your knees for me. I might even let my brother watch since he's so obsessed with you, Guinevere."

My stomach turned, but I kept my expression blank.

Focus on getting out.

I had been down here a few times, but not enough to have learned the pathway to the hidden door off by heart. So far, it seemed that an unknown power was guiding me, insisting that I follow a path and make choices.

I had no idea if this had been the right one.

But I had a way out.

Each time I closed my eyes, the outline of the cards shone far above. If I used them as a guidepost, I'd be able to navigate my way through the dungeons, the Academy, and back up to the tower to get them.

It was a ridiculous thought, wanting to get those cards, but if they were important to the Swords, then they had to be removed from the Hierophant Society. Before it was too late.

We turned several corners before Killian shoved me into the narrow corridor. We moved down it to the door, still wreathed in light.

Killian unlocked it then shoved me inside. I fell onto my knees, the leather saving me from grazes. The least of my worries now.

Ari slumped against the wall, his arms above his head, hanging, but his knees on the cold stone floor. His hair was more matted that it had been, his beard grazing his muscular chest. His jeans, the only clothing he wore, blood-stained now.

"See?" Killian gestured to him. "Isn't he a work of art? I'm going to make you just as priceless."

Killian kicked me in the stomach. I fell over backward, pain bursting through my center and hollowing me out for a second. A second kick landed on my ass, and he shifted me back, using his feet, until I reached the far corner.

My body screamed at the assault, but I set my jaw against the pain.

Killian hovered over me. "You see, Guinevere, I don't have the same compunctions about getting my hands dirty as my dear, sweet brother does. And we're going to make you very, very dirty." He lifted a fist and brought it down on my face.

A resulting crack, and then everything went black.

PAIN. PAIN. PAIN. PAIN. PAIN.

The dull throb that started in my mind and traveled through my body. Every cell, aching worse than the last one. I worked my tongue around my mouth, checking my teeth. Nothing broken. Had he punched me out? Or broken my nose?

Who?

Killian.

I opened my eyes to darkness. And then, a glimmer of light from somewhere nearby. On a table. A candle flickering. The only light in the darkness.

I forced myself to sit upright, and the skin on my wrists grated against the cable tie. I bit back a yelp.

Ari hung against the wall, elevated now, and his eyes were open, burnished gold like his father's and focused on me.

"You should have run," he said slowly, his voice croaking. "He'll come back for you soon."

"How long have you been here?" I asked.

"I don't know. Months?"

It hurt to talk, and my mouth was dry as bone, but I had to do it. "Ari," I said, and his name felt right in the same way the cards felt right. A recognition. As if I knew him.

"Evie," he said.

"How do you know me?"

"I came to you months ago," he said. "I gave you a card. I invited you to run away with me."

"Because of the Swords."

"And the Council of Horus. The Extremes. There isn't a supernatural creature on this Earth and off it who doesn't want a piece of you," he whispered, voice raw. "They captured me. They wiped your memory."

And that was it.

This had happened to me months ago? I had met this man, and I had no recollection of it? I would've felt robbed if not for the fact that I was already tied up and pretty much fucked.

"Did you know about me?" I asked. "About what I was?"

"I knew you were different. That there was something they wanted," Ari replied, still croaking it out. "I didn't want any of this to happen to you. Or me." A weak chuckle.

He was so buff, it was difficult to comprehend that he was "weak" per se, but he stretched out, worn, and the dark circles under his eyes told a tale of weeks spent here.

"How did you do this without going insane?" I asked over the ache in my head. Man, it hurt to talk, but I had to know more. Now that I had discovered some of the truth, I was desperate for everything. To absorb. To know.

So you can judge. Ma'at's voice.

Why do you do that? I shot back. Why ignore me when I need your help?

Another silence.

"The trick is," Ari said, after a long moment, "that I wasn't sane to begin with." He laughed again, a rasping noise deep in his chest.

"We've got to get out of here," I whispered. "Before it's too late."

Ari considered me. "You still have hope?"

"Yeah," I said. "We got our hands on half of the deck. The Pharaonic Deck. That's what they want, you know?"

"I know. I've been asked about it."

I nodded and regretted it. I shut my eyes against the pain. "They have it upstairs. I think they have Tyson up there too or somewhere. I don't know why they didn't bring him down here."

"Because he's more difficult to control. He'll need constant supervision," Ari said. "Whereas I don't."

"Why?"

"Shifter. Lion shifter."

"OK?"

"All you have to do is keep me away from meat, and that's it. Drains me of power."

"Oh."

"Tyson," he said, "they've got to keep him chained at all times and feed him alcohol. If they let him out of their sight for too long, he'll sober and break free. Hybrids are strong. Not as strong as vamps, but strong enough."

I bit down on the inside of my cheek.

There had to be a way out of this. I just couldn't see it yet.

"He'll be back soon," Ari said. "Try to think of something else. Something that's not this. A pleasant memory. If you let the pain get to you, you'll say anything to get it to stop." He hung his head again, effectively ending the conversation. Snores drifted from him moments later.

A pleasant memory? Yeah, I was shit out of luck on that one.

36

Time blurred.

Minutes stretched into hours. Hours into days. Days into weeks.

That was my assumption. Killian came twice a day. Once in the morning, once at night. He spent an hour on Ari, then an hour on me, beating, whipping, twisting fingers, pulling nails, plucking hair, stretching my limbs. My nose had been broken. My eye was puffy and bruised.

How many groupings of visits now?

Two, four, six, eight, ten.

"Five days," I whispered through dry, split lips. "So not weeks. Only days."

Killian had fed Ari nothing but sips of water to keep him alive. I had had tasteless porridge shoved down my throat along with similar sips of water. Ari was never released from the wall. He was forced to relieve himself in a bucket on the floor beside him. My bucket was in the opposite corner of the room.

The same cable tie was around my wrists. That was it. I

was free to walk the room, though I doubted it was a concession. I was too weak to move much.

"Evie." Ari's voice, warm, the only connection to reality I had left. "Evie, how are you today?"

We'd already had one visit from Killian this morning? Maybe it was night? I couldn't tell. There was the candle, four walls, darkness, pain.

"I'm just fucking dandy," I said. "How about you?" My words were molasses slow.

"Fucking dandy," he agreed.

"He can't keep us here forever." A last attempt at defiance.

Ari didn't answer me, but his golden eyes glowed a little by the flickering torchlight. He watched. During the torture, he watched too. He made eye contact with me, even though it clearly hurt him to watch. He became my focus point so that I had something to think about.

I had told him about the lack of pleasant memories. There was a distant one. Something about a cat. And Tyson. Tyson holding me and inhaling my scent.

"Ari," I said. "How much longer?"

"I will never tell them what they want."

"Me neither." I was aware that the sentences didn't make sense. The answers didn't match the question, but Ari had said what I needed to hear.

I would never break.

Killian had started realizing it too. His "work" had grown feverish. Angry. Maybe time was short? Maybe they couldn't figure out what to do with the cards?

The sound of the key scraping in the lock sent panic through my middle. He's not supposed to be back yet! He's not supposed to—!

I shuffled backward on my knees, trying to make myself smaller, like a cockroach. It was difficult to deal with the fear and face it head-on.

The door opened, and Ari and I tensed.

Nathan entered the room. He held a tray with a silver dome.

Can't be. I've gone mad.

But it was Nathan, all right, and he entered the room, glancing back over one shoulder. He shut the door and locked it, eyes only on me. It was as if Ari didn't exist.

"Evie," he said softly. "Evie. Fuck. What has he done to you?"

"What you wanted him to," I muttered.

"Never this. Never." Nathan came over and put the tray down on the dirty stone floor. He extended a hand, and I turned my head. "Come. Please. I've brought you what I can. I wanted to look after you, Evie. I wanted to keep you safe."

"You wanted to keep me prisoner. Use me to get what you want. To reach the Keeper." I still didn't know *why* that was. For the Book of Life, but what was in it?

"No. Not just that. You know I care about you," he said. "Too much." He reached out and touched a hand to my cheek.

I would've spat on him if I'd been able to work up enough fluid in my mouth, but I glanced toward Ari, and the look on his face stopped me.

Those golden eyes were focused on the tray.

Meat. We need meat.

I let Nathan touch my cheek, purposefully forcing my gaze toward the tray.

"Are you hungry?" Nathan asked. "We can keep this our little secret, OK? I'll bring you whatever you want. Whatever you need. I've been talking to my father, convincing him to let me take you under my care again. The longer Killian takes to get results the better for us." He stroked my cheek, and my skin crawled.

"I want steak," I said.

Ari nodded slowly.

"I want protein. Steak. I'm starving. I can't think."

Nathan lifted the tray. "I brought you cake. I thought the sweetness might help you."

Man, it looked good. A slice of chocolate cake? Fuck. Whatever. This guy was an absolute dumbass. Who brought cake to a prisoner? Out of touch.

I turned my head as if the cake was entirely revolting to me. "Steak," I said.

"OK." Nathan leaned in and kissed my forehead. Another spike of revulsion. "OK. I'll be right back." He left, shutting the door behind himself, and Ari's teeth flashed white by the candlelight. Smiling.

<hr>

As promised, Nathan returned a half an hour later. Ari feigned sleep against the wall, even going as far as to snore. That or he was actually asleep out of sheer exhaustion. Sleep was the only thing we could do in here.

And no one was coming for us. No Tyson, none of the Hanged Man Society, no one. The people who might've cared were all dead.

"Here," Nathan said, placing the tray on the ground in front of me. "I'm going to keep Killian busy tonight. Keep him away from you so that you can regain some of your strength. I promise, Evie, it's only a matter of time until my father places you under my care."

I didn't respond.

Nathan lifted the lid off the tray, and revealed a massive steak, T-bone, accompanied by a side of vegetables and a bottle of water. My mouth instantly filled with saliva.

"I can't untie you without alerting him," Nathan said. "So you'll have to…" He mimed bending over, kind of.

I glared at him.

"I don't expect you to forgive me," he said, "but you've got to understand that I didn't mean for things to turn out this way. I was going to protect you, Evie. I will protect you."

He waited for an answer, searching my face, but I remained mute.

"You'll see." Nathan leaned in and kissed my forehead again. I allowed it, only because I needed him to remain on "my side" for the time being.

I had spent so much time worrying about whether I would turn out evil, whether I would wind up like my mother. Now that I'd witnessed evil, I knew I couldn't do this to another person. Hold them against their will, beat them, damage them physically and mentally. Evil had a face, and it wasn't me. It wasn't even my mother, though her acts had been, undoubtedly deranged.

Nathan. Killian. Bernard.

The Swords.

They were evil. And I wouldn't give up until I had stopped whatever sick plans they'd laid in place.

"I'll come back when I can." Nathan rose, gave me one last longing look, then exited the room. The door locked, and I waited, listening for his footsteps.

Gone.

"He sure likes you," Ari said.

I rolled my eyes heavenward. "He's attached himself to me, probably because he hasn't received any love from anyone else."

"Psychoanalysis," Ari said. "I'm impressed."

I rose onto my haunches and straightened, slowly so I wouldn't trip over. My legs shook, but they held my weight. Nothing in my lower half was broken, so that was good.

Ari watched me, his golden eyes dull by the candlelight.

I stumbled over to the table, turned, and held my wrists over the flame. The heat scorched me, but I stuck it out.

"Careful," Ari croaked.

I pulled my wrists apart with all my might and the cable tie, melting against the flame, stretched. I slipped my hands free.

"Oh my God," I whispered. "Oh my fuck, that feels good." I massaged my wrists.

"I can't imagine," Ari replied sardonically.

"Sorry." I walked to the lever and let him down onto the floor, lowering his arms as well. They limped at his sides, and his arms hung.

Quickly, I grabbed the tray and water and brought it over.

"You'll have to feed me," he said. "Too weak. Just the meat. No veg."

"Veg is mine."

"Absolutely."

I lifted the steak, bone and all, and held it to his lips. They parted and he took a ferocious bite. Two chews and a swallow, followed by another bite, and another. I turned the steak so that he'd get every part of it. Once the major chunks were gone, he nibbled the bits of meat seated against the bone.

"That's everything," I said at last. "Do you need more?"

"That will be enough. Water, and then give me a couple of minutes."

I uncapped the water bottle and fed him some of it. Some of it snaked down his chin and onto his pecs, but he didn't care and neither did I.

Finally, Ari sat back and shut his eyes. "A minute."

I spent the minute eating the veg, shoveling it down with the silver fork—there was a metaphor if ever I'd seen one—that Nathan had brought with the meal. The veg was starting to cool, but it was fucking amazing. Roasted to perfection. I dropped the fork with a clatter and drank some of the water.

"OK," I whispered. "Now what?"

"Hoist me up," Ari said, his eyes blazing golden now. "I need tension on the chains to do this."

"Roger that." I returned to the lever on the wall, still weak but feeling a little better for the food in my stomach. I lifted Ari until he told me to stop.

"Stand back. Near the door."

"What are you doing?" I asked.

"Getting the fuck out of here." His eyes erupted with light, and his muscles tensed, straining. His fingers turned into claws, golden fur growing on the backs of his hands and arms. He let out a groaning roar and pulled his right arm forward, flexing his biceps. The chain snapped free of his wrist. He did the same with his left arm, then dropped to the floor.

He fixed those claws on the cuffs around his ankles and tore them off, and when he rose and faced me, the mane of dark hair turned golden, and he had full-on extended canines.

"OK," I said. "Getting the fuck out of here is a great idea. But that definitely made a lot of noise."

Ari ran past me and shouldered the door. It popped off its hinges like they were made of butter.

"Holy."

Ari turned, grabbed me around the waist, threw me over his shoulder, and ran down the passage at full tilt, out into the Academy, and away from the torture chamber.

37

"We have to go back for Tyson," I said. "I think I can find him. I think." They had to be keeping him wherever they were keeping the cards. Over the past five days, what little conversation Ari and I had engaged in had been about escape, the cards, and Tyson's imprisonment.

"Not now." Ari's voice was a deep growl, and it thrummed in my chest as we streaked along the corridors. "The Hanged Man, first. Then Tyson."

He wanted to return to the society headquarters even though I had told him about the damages. About the dangers. "They might be dead," I whispered.

"They might be alive."

Apparently, he was a glass half-full kind of guy, and I couldn't fault him for that. But Tyson needed help, and the cards called to me. A feeling of home I had dreamed of for years but never felt, and it had nothing to do with societies or people.

If I hadn't known better, I'd have thought something was

wrong with me. Actually, I *knew* something was wrong with me.

Ari took corners at top speed, and I joggled up and down on his shoulder like a sack of shit. In keeping with how I felt, right now.

Every ounce of my being screamed that we had to go back for Tyson. Before it was too late. Or before they got the information they wanted out of him: the location of the rest of the cards. But Ari was probably right. We needed to regroup.

If there was a group to regroup with.

Ari reached the trapdoor and climbed up the ladder that led to it, one-armed, the other holding me in place. I marveled at his strength through my fatigue.

He nudged the door open and we emerged into the Hanged Man. The scent of smoke was thick on the air, mingling with the metallic scent of blood. The floor in here was scarred by deep gouges and black trails, and I took even breaths, trying not to panic.

What if they were here? Waiting for us to come back? To make a mistake?

Ari set me down on a floral sofa that wouldn't have looked out of place in somebody's grandma's house. "Stay here," he said. "Yell if someone comes through the trapdoor."

"Got you."

He strode toward the door at the far end of the room and wrenched it open. A man stood on the other side of it, sword in hand. He brought it down with a yell, but Ari dodged smoothly to the side, the sword thunked against the floor, the wielder unable to stop it before it hit home.

Ari grabbed him by the throat.

"Ari? Ari?" The words came out strained against the lion shifter's grip. "You're alive?"

"Walker." Ari dropped the hybrid. "Where is everyone?"

"Holy shit, I can't believe you're alive." Walker ran a hand over his bald pate, red eyes blazing. "This is the best fucking news we've had all week."

"Where's King?" Ari asked. "How many dead?"

"He's upstairs in the office," Walker said. "They're holding a war council to get *you* out of there. Well, you, the Feather, and Tyson."

"Evie," I said. "My name is Evie. Not just the Feather."

Walker shrugged like it didn't make a difference.

Maybe it didn't to him. I wasn't a part of his society. As far as the Hanged Man was concerned, I was a drifter who had taken an unnatural liking for a deck of tarot cards and got dizzy a lot.

"A war council," Ari said, frowning.

"Yeah," Walker replied. "They'll probably want you to join in, but, uh, maybe you should shower or something first? No offense, my guy, but you stink. You too, by the way." That last part was directed at me."

"Thanks." I rolled my eyes at him and nearly passed out. I was so goddamn tired.

I struggled upright and followed Ari out of the room and into what was left of the house. The interior was scorched, the sofas sliced open, their guts spilling out, and there were stains on the floor I didn't want to identify.

We passed a living room on our way to the stairs, and Ari paused for a second, staring inside. Bodies had been lined up, each one covered carefully with a sheet or comforter. There were ten. Ten dead after the attack on the Hanged Man.

All your fault.

We continued up the stairs, Ari's movement slower than before, his strong, tan hand grasping the balustrade for support, even though it wiggled and was missing sections. Finally, we reached the small study.

Ari entered, and the chatter from within cut off instantly.

King stood behind the table, a patch over one eye, blood staining his cheek and shirt. His fists were pressed down on the desk, a map of the Academy between them. He met Ari's gaze, steadily.

The silence expanded, and I took stock of the others in the small room. A woman, gorgeous, tall, with hazel, glimmering eyes and long curly black hair, stared at Ari, and her jaw dropped. Two other hybrids flanked the table, twins with red hair and strong jawlines, tall and lean, just as shocked as the other occupants of the office.

It was as if time had stopped.

And then…

King practically shoved the table aside, marched over to Ari, and enveloped him in a bear hug. "Son," he choked. "Son."

Ari hugged him back.

King placed a kiss on Ari's cheek. "You were sorely missed."

"I can tell," Ari said as they parted. "But I'm here now. Tell me what's going on, and how I can help."

King turned in my direction, and I shook my head. "Tyson's still with them. They kept Ari and me together, but they've got him somewhere there. With the cards, I think. They're going to try to force information out of him. He's the only person who knows apart from me."

"They won't get it out of Tyson," King said. "No chance.

He's young and new, but he has lead in his veins after what he's been through." The leader of the Hanged Man Society returned to the desk. "We were discussing our next move."

"All out war, King?" Ari didn't sound impressed. "We'll only make things worse."

"What?" The word had come from me without a second thought.

Everyone in the room stared.

"I mean, you can't be serious. Make things worse?" I asked. "I don't think things can get any worse at this point. Look at this place. It's a fucking wreck. People are dead because of the Swords and their society. We have to fight."

"We?" The woman arched an eyebrow at me. "Last I checked, you weren't a part of this society. And Ari is second in charge. Our General. If he thinks fighting is a bad idea..."

"Let her talk, Christa," Ari said.

"Neither of you should be talking." King stretched his neck and massaged it. The one eye that was exposed was fatigued, red, a dark circle underneath it. "You need medical attention and rest."

"There's no time for rest," I said, unable to stop myself from talking. "Tyson is trapped. He's being held hostage by them as we speak."

Ari put up a hand, and a ripple spread through the room, pressing into my chest. "King, the war council needs to wait. Give us time to recuperate and then we'll discuss this at length before we make any moves."

I forced my mouth open, trying to press against the Alpha silence that he'd imposed upon me. "At length? Tyson needs our help."

"You don't have any say in this society," Christa snapped. "For all we know, you could be working for them."

"Yeah, sure. That's why I endured fucking days of torture. Because I'm working for them," I growled. "Get fucking real."

"Enough," King said. "Ari is right. You need rest and then we'll decide what to do. The Council of Horus has yet to make a statement about the Hierophant Society's actions, and my sources tell me they likely won't. They're turning a blind eye."

"But the attack was illegal, right?" I asked.

"Correct," King replied. "Spectacularly illegal, as is every other action the Hierophants have taken in recent history. We can't rely on the Council for help, only on ourselves." King raised a palm, putting an end to the discussion. "Rest, now. And heal. We'll discuss our next steps this evening."

38

Hurry up and wait.

That was what it felt like. I had been tended to by Christa, who hadn't said a word but had placed her hands on me and probed me for injuries. A defense sorcerer who was able to heal my physical injuries. I felt like I'd been wrung out afterward, but there wasn't any pain by the time she was done.

I dressed in a tank top and leather pants that had been laid out on the bed for me. Another knife had been left out on the dresser, sheath and all, this one bearing hieroglyphics along its hilt, but I left it where it was. The thought of using it still made my skin crawl.

At 9:00 p.m., I exited my room and marched down the hall and around corners to reach the study. I entered and found the others waiting.

Ari had cleaned up good. Clean shaven, hair neatly trimmed, wearing a white shirt and jeans that hugged the lines of his muscles. I didn't doubt he'd eaten a metric ton of meat this afternoon. His gaze lingered on me after I'd entered.

"That's everyone," King said.

"I don't understand why *she* has to be here." Christa sat in an armchair against the wall, arms and ankles crossed. "She's not a part of the society. None of the decisions we take should be affected by her opinion."

I was tempted to flip her off, but I had matured since last week? Maybe it had something to do with having my nose broken and my eye punched in—healed thanks to Christa's ministrations.

"She's a Feather of Ma'at," King replied. "An adjudicator."

"The Feathers are all dead." That came from one of the twin hybrids. His brother nodded along with him. "At best, she's a poser."

"And if she *is* a Feather," Christa continued, "that means she *can't* join our society anyway."

My heart dropped.

OK, so maybe I'd hoped to fit in with the Hanged Man Society, for real. To have friends and feel that sense of family that the group clearly possessed. Hybrids, vampires, shifters, and even a sorcerer, living together, making decisions for the good of the society.

I kept my face impassive, forcing myself not to show disappointment.

"Things have changed," Ari said, breaking the awkward quiet, "since the Council started changing the rules and playing sides. If a Feather wants to join the Hanged Man, then so be it. And if she doesn't, she gets an opinion, regardless."

"Why?"

"Because she's the only one who can help us make things right." King growled, taking control of the conversation again. "She's the only one who'll be able to commune with the Keeper and get us the help we need to stop the Council's tyranny from spreading. If she chooses to leave, the Hierophant Society, or any of the other societies can capture her and *use her* to get what they want."

I swallowed. Not a great prospect for me.

"So, she needs our protection." Walker leaned against the wall, next to the exit.

"I'm right here, you know," I snapped. "You can talk to me directly."

Walker shrugged in that annoying "don't give a fuck" way that only bald hybrid vampires could pull off.

"Fine. So *you* need our protection."

"And you need my help stopping this Council thing from killing hybrids, vampires and shifters en masse," I said. "Right?"

King nodded. "Which brings us to the purpose of this meeting. War."

"War is a dumbass decision," Walker said. "We already had our asses handed to us by the Hierophant Society."

"Because we were unprepared." Christa lifted a finger and waggled it at him. "Not because we're weak."

"Sure, whatever," Walker shrugged. "You want to die, go ahead and die. I'm pretty comfortable with not stepping on anybody's toes."

"But are you comfortable with having your toes crushed?" Christa asked. "Because that's what's happening. They're going to wipe every one of us off the face of the earth."

"Bruh," Walker said."Bruh. Are you kidding me? You're a sorcerer. You're not the one that the Council wants to wipe away."

"I may as well be. I'm part of this society."

"Quiet," King said, forcing a ripple through the room.

So, there can be more than one Alpha in the same family? Interesting.

"We have a decision to make," King said. "Either we declare war, prepare the forces we have left, and demand the return of the cards and Tyson. Or we remain silent, bide our time, build our forces until such a point as we can recover what we've lost. The first option is riskier. The second is dangerous in its own way. If we take too long, the Hierophant Society wins."

Every head turned toward Ari, the General, who stood with his arms folded, his head tilted as he studied the map of the Academy on the table.

"All out war will achieve nothing," Ari said. "Not when we're weak. It will paint a target on our backs and on Tyson's. They'll kill him the minute they've gotten the information they need out of him. The only positive would be that declaring open war will prevent the Council itself from interfering."

King nodded. "There are by-laws. But it's not worth the risk. We can't survive a war in our current iteration."

"We can't leave him there." I looked from one person to another in the room. "We can't just leave him there. Ari, you know what they're capable of."

His expression hardened. "Yeah."

"So? We can't leave him there. There's got to be a middle ground, right? Can't we steal them back?"

"Steal them?" Christa snorted. "You're talking about sneaking into the Hierophant Society and somehow finding where they're keeping the cards and Tyson, then, what? How do you expect to get him out of there without them knowing?"

"I know where the cards are," I said, firmly. "I can sense

them. I can take you to them directly. And I'm pretty sure they'll be keeping Tyson somewhere close by."

"Why would they do that?" Christa asked. "You can't just assume they would do that."

"I don't know why they would, I just feel like, I don't know. He's somewhere in the mansion itself. He's not in the Academy. He's not in the dungeons."

"The Swords don't like hybrids," King said after a beat. "They don't trust them. Shifters, they understand, even vampires, but hybrids? They'll treat him like he's a ticking time bomb. They'll want him on their turf, not in the no-man's land that is the dungeons of the Academy. And there's another reason."

"What?" Ari frowned at his father.

King lifted his phone and held it aloft, showing off an image of Tyson's face, red eyes gleaming malevolently. "The Council released this to the Society App three hours ago. They've announced that Tyson Davis is wanted for crimes against the Council. For treason. Punishable by death. They'll take him and drown him in alcohol."

"Then we have to go! We can't wait!" The words came out frantic. "We can't just leave him there to die."

Another quiet.

"One life against the lives of many," Walker said. "Doesn't seem worth it. We should wait and gather our forces. I vote for the second option."

"You're insane. You've lost it. This isn't right."

The hybrid twins glanced at each other. "We vote for war," they said in unison. "We can't let a brother die."

"If we fight we all die," Christa said. "I vote we wait."

It was tied.

"War," Ari said, simply.

"We wait," King put in.

The tension in the room snapped.

"That's it?" I asked. "It's tied?"

Ari shook his head. "King's vote is the final say as the leader of the society. His vote counts as two."

"Are you serious? The Swords could hand him over to the Council at any moment. He could die!"

The word rang in the silence.

"My decision is final," King said. "It's not one I take easily, but it's what I will do for the good of our society. The Hanged Man comes first. Tyson would understand that. Sacrifice. He would want this."

I ground my teeth. "And I don't get a say? Because I vote we go now. We get him. I can find the cards."

"We can't risk you either," King said. "If they capture you again, the chances of you escaping are slim to none."

"I've done pretty well the last two times." Granted, I had help.

"My decision is final." King's eyes glowed golden, and another of those Alpha ripples pulsed through the room.

I stormed out into the hall, anger building to a crescendo inside me.

39

Damn the consequences. Damn them to hell, if there was a hell. Fuck it, I was pretty sure I'd been there.

I paced back and forth in my room, switching my attention between the floor and the boarded up windows. The rest of the house was quiet. Either people were sleeping or... I didn't even know at this point what they did with their spare time, and I didn't care either.

Tyson was about to die. He was about to be handed off to the Council of Horus to meet his fate. This faceless Council I had yet to encounter but which gave me all kinds of creeps. And they would let it happen for the good of the many.

What was that saying? "The road to hell is paved with good intentions." This felt very that. And I wasn't going to let that be the case.

The cards belonged with me. And Tyson deserved to live. No person should die because they were different. Because they didn't fit into the perfect mold of what "society" wanted them to be.

The more I thought about it, the more right I felt.

What are you going to do about it?

I stopped pacing and stared at the dagger where I'd left it on my distressed dressing table.

What are you going to do about it?

I opened the closet and retrieved my leather jacket. I slipped it on then walked to the desk.

What will you do to make sure things are right?

My hand closed around the dagger's hilt. I lifted it and slipped it into the belt loop of my pants. It felt like a more momentous decision than any I'd taken in my life, even though there hadn't been any light to accompany it.

I sneaked to my bedroom door and opened it. The chair outside was empty. I wasn't being watched. The soft sounds of discussion came from somewhere nearby.

A second of hesitation, and then I moved off down the hall in the opposite direction, wincing at the creaking of the wood underfoot. Down the stairs, left, past the living room, now empty of the dead, and into another hall. Past rooms with closed doors until I entered the room with the trapdoor.

It was firmly shut, but this entry hall to the Hanged Man Society was blessedly empty. No one to raise the alarm.

I glanced back into the house a final time then opened the trap door and descended into the stone hall below.

NAVIGATING THROUGH THE UNDERGROUND CATACOMBS THAT were the "no man's land" should have been a nightmare. It wasn't.

I reached a crossroads, shut my eyes, and tilted my head back. The outline of the cards shone golden far overhead.

"More toward the right," I murmured, and took the turn.

I had been walking, quickly, for ten minutes, and was finally approaching the portion of the Academy that belonged to the Hierophant Society. Their connecting atrium was silent, though the white light shone from the clear glass roof, mocking.

Red light for the Hanged Man, white for the Hierophant Society, were all the societies separated by color? And if there was a no man's land of dungeons and catacombs, what other underground facilities were there that I didn't know about.

Places to hide? Maybe entire cities crawling with supernatural creatures?

I hurried up the stairs to the Hierophant Society's connecting door, my heart pounding. I was banking on the fact that the Swords likely thought Ari and I were too spent to fight. Or they thought we were in hiding.

The most logical course of action for the Swords would be to focus on getting information from Tyson then finding me so they could use me with the deck to reach the Keeper. They would plan another attack on the Hanged Man Society if they believed I was there.

Why couldn't King see that? Didn't he realize that they were in danger regardless of whether they acted now or later? They would have to move or find a way to stop the Hierophants from attacking them. Or worse, the Council.

There must be things I don't know. I still wasn't acquainted with this world as well as I would have liked.

I slipped into the entry hall where Scholar Harwa had

introduced me to the Academy. My first, brief, education about the Gods and Goddesses. It was empty, as well, thankfully, so I started my ascent.

Ten minutes later, I exited into the quiet first floor of the Hierophants' mansion. I shut my eyes and found the glowing cards again, then set off. Up stairs, down a hall, pausing to listen. Nothing. Quiet. Too quiet? Maybe.

Move.

My legs carried me, guided me past tapestries, into secret hallways, up staircases, until I reached the base of the tower. The cards were directly overhead in the blackness, and I started up the stairs, wooden, spiraling upward. There were no doors or hallways branching off, just a simple upward climb with a terrifying drop off the side to the floor below. Lanterns attached to the wall provided steady light.

A trapdoor, latched from the outside. Interesting. I unhooked the latch then pulled the trap door downward, unfolding the wooden stairway attached to it.

This is it.

I ascended into a room lit by a central chandelier overhead. As with Bernard Sword's office, the room itself was flanked with floor to ceiling glass windows, but thick black curtains were drawn across them, blocking the view. The room contained two things.

A pedestal, upon which sat a glass case and the velvet pouch of tarot cards. The other was a shape on the floor.

Tyson!

He lay there, wrists zip tied behind his back, his ankles bound, eyes closed. He was paler than usual, and his mouth drooped open, breaths escaping him in rough rasps.

"Tyson," I whispered, and ran over to him, immediately. "Tyson?" I dropped to my knees. I took him by the arm and shook him gently. "Can you hear me?"

His eyes opened, the usual crimson dulled to a murky black. He made an indistinct noise in his throat.

"What have they done to you?"

Alcohol.

That was what Ari had told me. Vampires and hybrids were sensitive to light, but it was alcohol that completely disabled them. And I had nothing to sober Tyson up with.

"Think, Evie," I whispered. "What can you—?"

It came in a flash of recognition.

The textbook! That night in the library, I'd read about vampires and their weakness to alcohol, right? And the listed antidote had been—?

"Blood," I whispered.

My pulse raced.

"I'm going to get you out of here," I said and freed my dagger from its sheath. I cut through the zip ties with ease, freeing his hands and feet. They flopped uselessly to the floor.

I lifted my dagger, stared at the blade, then drew it across my wrist in one swift motion, like ripping off a Band-Aid. Pain flared, and I held back a cry. Held back a memory of something much worse, a drifting unhappiness of being unlovable, worthy of death.

"Here," I said and pressed my bleeding wrist toward his mouth. "Drink."

Tyson's black irises moved slowly, downward to my wrist, upward to my face.

"Drink."

A droplet of blood landed on his lips. His tongue moved slowly over it, lapping it up.

My skin contacted his lips, and his tongue washed over the wound, drinking, the color in his irises brightening slowly. His hands moved, no longer limp, and he grasped my wrist, sucking it, his teeth grazing my skin.

I gasped at the sensation, a light pressure, a tickling of his tongue against me, a little pain mingled in. Not entirely unpleasant. No, not unpleasant at all.

Tyson looped his arm around my waist, and dragged me closer, the other hand fixed on my wrist, holding it to his lips. He rolled me onto my back, pressing the weight of his body on top of me, lavishing my wrist with attention, and my eyes rolled back in my head.

Why does this feel so good?

"Oh my God," I whispered, clinging to him as his body tightened on top of me, power returning to his muscles. "Oh my God. Tyson."

He stopped drinking and lifted his head a little. "Evie," he managed then fell to one side. His eyes were brighter, but nowhere near as bright as they usually were. I scrambled up, coloring at my reaction to his body pressed on top of mine, and the fact that he'd just tucked into me like a fucking full-ass meal.

"Are you OK?" I held my wrist. It had stopped bleeding entirely, and the skin was knitting itself closed? What the hell? Was this a vampire thing? A hybrid thing?

"I think I can walk now," he said slowly. "But that's about it."

I helped him sit upright. "We've got to get out of here," I whispered. "Quickly. Before—"

"Before I arrive."

I spun around, horror mounting.

Killian stood at the base of the trapdoor, smiling. "Guinevere," he said. "What an unmitigated pleasure to see you again. And so soon."

40

Killian took two steps into the room and stopped, his hands tucked behind his back. He wore his usual suit, his blond hair slicked back, and his gray eyes hard as flint. A fresh cut ran the length of his cheek, from underneath his eye to the base of his chin.

"As you can see," Killian said, gesturing to his face. "My father has made his displeasure known about your escape. I assure you, Nathan has had a matching punishment."

I kept my mouth shut and rose, putting myself between Killian and Tyson. This was bad. This was really fucking bad.

The knife I'd used to cut myself lay on the floor at Tyson's side, but he wasn't nearly strong enough to do anything with it. If he couldn't even walk yet, how could I possibly expect him to fight? This was on me, and I was about as capable of fighting Killian as a wet noodle.

My injuries might have healed, but I was still weak. And he was a destruction sorcerer. I had felt that firsthand in the dungeons.

Killian smiled, drawing closer by two steps. "What do you

have to say for yourself, Guinevere? You came all this way to save your friend and, I assume, recover the cards. What do you have to say for yourself?" The last sentence came out as a shout.

I jerked back a step then raised my chin. "Fuck you. That's what I've got to say for myself."

Next to me, Tyson struggled to his feet, using the wall as leverage. His eyes burned a dull red and focused on Killian.

"What will you do, hybrid?" Killian asked. "Save her?"

Tyson grunted and pushed off from the wall, moving toward Killian with stumbling steps.

"Tyson, don't," I cried.

Killian removed a blade from under his sleeve and tossed it, almost lazily. It struck home in Tyson's chest, on the left side. The hybrid staggered, looking down at the hilt of the blade poking from his flesh. He collapsed onto his knees, then sideways into the wall, groaning.

"No!" I yelled. "No, you can't do that!" Surely, hybrids can't die? Not like this? Not like this.

Killian removed another knife, aiming it at Tyson's head.

"No!" I threw myself between them again. "No. You will not touch him."

Killian hesitated, that sick grin spreading the wound on his cheek. Blood leaked from it, dripped from his chin onto his white shirt. He threw the knife lazily into the floorboards. "I won't touch him?"

I shook my head, holding my hands out, terror vibrating through me non-stop.

Killian crossed the distance between us in a millisecond. He grabbed me by the throat, squeezing tight, cutting off my air supply, crushing and bruising. He lifted me off the ground, one-handed. "And what will you do, Guinevere, to stop me? There's no one to save you now. Not my little brother, not your hybrid freak friends, no one. I'm going to bend you to my will, break your body and soul, make you beg to die before I finally get what I want out of you. You will pay for the pain you have inflicted upon my family." He tossed me backward, effortlessly, and I landed on the floor, my head bouncing against the boards.

Fresh hot pain throbbed through my skull, and I scrambled upright.

Killian grinned, bent, and plucked the knife from the floor. He took aim, pointing it at Tyson's head. "Did you know," he said. "That you can't kill a hybrid unless you sever their head from their body? I'd be happy to show you."

No.

Killian took a step forward and then froze, his leg in the air.

Time slowed to molasses, and that blinding light returned. A single feather, tipped golden, materialized above my head and drifted downward toward my open palm.

Two paths lay before you, little Feather. Choose wisely. The path of justice, purity, goodness of heart. A woman's soul might weigh as much as a mountain or as little as a grain of sand.

Two images appeared in front of me, surreal, vapor like forms of myself, wreathed in golden light. One of them pushed up from the floor, grabbed the deck of cards from the pedestal and ran for the door, chased by a light-wreathed image of Killian.

The other image grabbed the knife, rose and sprinted toward Killian, ramming the point of the blade directly into his throat, watching as he gurgled blood and died. Gone forever. The wisp of his life waning.

I could choose to run, or I could choose to fight.

I could remain who I was or become something else? Use a knife, as my mother had used, to snuff out the life of another being.

Not evil. I am not like her. I'm not evil.

Killian had shown me that, hadn't he?

The feather drifted toward me, floating lazily in circles.

I examined the room, searching for any other options but these. Anything that would help me save Tyson without having to *do that.*

But Tyson lay bleeding nearby. He had removed the knife from his chest and held it tight, eyes shut.

Time to choose.

Please, help me. What is the right choice? I don't want to do that.

Only you can make this choice, Feather.

The feather drifted down toward my palm and settled, and my time was up. I had seconds before the slowing of time ceased and Killian threw that knife at Tyson's head.

Before the feather had a chance to disappear, I forced myself up, head and body screaming a protest at the sudden movement, and rushed to the dagger I'd dropped earlier. My heartbeat pulsed in my ears. I lifted it and strode toward Killian.

Am I really doing this?

And so, the choice has been made.

The feather evaporated from my left palm just as I reached Killian. Time rushed to catch up, the soft sound of a chime ringing in the air. I brought the knife up, grasping it in both hands.

Killian blinked, his eyes widened at my sudden change in position. "What—?"

I forced the point of the blade into his throat and rammed it through to the back of his neck. The feeling sent my body into shock. The soft thump of the hilt striking his flesh, the gurgle from his throat, the sudden spurt of blood.

He backed up, grasping at the hilt, staring at me in wide-eyed disbelief. He lifted his dagger, aimed it, but didn't loose it. Instead, he keeled over backward and hit the floor. Dead.

I backed up two steps and nearly fell over, gagging and covering my mouth. Bile rose in my throat, but it wasn't anything like the episodes I'd had before. This was because I had killed a man. An evil piece of shit of a man, but still a man. Or sorcerer. Being. Whatever.

"Evie," Tyson called softly. "Evie, come here."

I turned my back on the corpse of our enemy and shuffled toward him, gagging again, swallowing mouthfuls of saliva.

Tyson wasn't bleeding anymore, and Killian's knife lay on the boards. He exhaled, forcing a smile, showing his black fangs and teeth. "You did good," he said.

"You said you would kill me if I ever—you know."

"Yeah," he replied. "I promised, I would. And I'm not killing you, so what does that tell you?"

"That you're too weak to do the job?" I asked.

"True." He chuckled, wincing afterward. "But nah, it's mostly that you're not an evil piece of shit. Listen, I'm not bleeding, but I can't heal properly because of the alcohol they've been feeding me. We've got to get out. Now."

"Can you walk?"

"I don't know if I can," he said, forcing himself to his knees. "But I'm damn well going to." I helped him to his feet, the effort a welcome distraction. "The cards."

I walked to the pedestal and tried to open the case containing the cards, but it was locked. Tyson came over, bringing Killian's blade with him. He smashed it into the glass, and I removed the velvet pouch from among the shattered pieces.

And then we stumbled toward the trapdoor, past Killian, whose blood had already started to pool.

41

The mansion was eerily silent as we descended. No klaxon wail of an alarm, no chatter or rush of footsteps, no yelling or magic thrown our way. The inhabitants, the acolytes, were fast asleep and we walked, slowly, down the stairs and through the hallways together.

Tyson's arm was slung over my shoulder, and I held him around the waist, going at his pace. The cards were tucked into the front pocket of my jeans, not against my skin this time, but so comforting, regardless.

A connection to something better than all of this. I couldn't quite place what it was yet.

And right now, it didn't matter.

Tyson clung to me, and the tension of his body against mine, the heat, drove me onward. We had to get back.

God, I hadn't even thought of how I would explain this to King. He would be mad. Big fucking mad. If this wasn't a reason for the Hierophant Society to declare war, then I didn't know what was. I had murdered their General.

Murdered.

My skin crawled but I kept moving. I'd already made my choice, and it was too late to turn back now. I didn't feel even an ounce of joy over Killian's death, even though he had tortured Ari for months, and me for days.

We exited the mansion and started down the stone steps, past flickering lanterns, down to the entry room. Scholar Harwa's desk was empty as usual, but the door to the atrium was ajar. Had I left it that way?

I was too tired to worry.

We exited onto the top landing and started down the stairs, holding each other, Tyson pausing every once in a while to regain stamina.

"You OK?" I whispered.

"I'm getting there," he said. "I can sleep this off. I just need time."

"Once we get back to the Hanged Man, you'll have plenty of it." That might've been a lie, honestly, and Tyson had to know that, but he didn't refute the claim.

We reached the bottom of the staircase and set off across the tiled floor together.

"You'll have to lead," I whispered. "I'm still learning how to get to the Hanged Man from here." The last time, I'd had the cards to guide me at least.

"That's fine," Tyson said, groaning it out. "It's—" He froze, stiffening, lifting his nose.

"What is it? Tyson?"

A figure stepped forward from the entrance to a shadowy hall nearest to us. Nathan strode forward under the light of the atrium's glass roof, his face a thunderhead.

"Evie." He bore a scar, similar to the one Killian had had,

down his right cheek. It had been left to bleed. "You know I can't let you do this."

"Get out of my way," I hissed.

Nathan balled his hands into fists. "You were supposed to stay," he yelled, the words echoing off the walls. "You were supposed to stay. I told you I would protect you."

"I don't need your protection."

"Killian will punish—"

"Killian's dead," I said roughly. "I killed him." The words hurt, but I threw them out anyway.

Nathan's expression went blank.

Tyson lifted his head, turning it a little to the left. I had no clue what he'd seen or might be planning, but I wanted Nathan to understand that I was serious.

"I killed him," I said. "I drove a dagger through his throat and watched him die." Ugh, don't throw up. Do not throw up. That will so ruin the moment.

"Evie."

"Go check on him. Where you were keeping the cards and Tyson. Find him there if you don't believe me. Your brother is dead, and I will do the same thing to you if you don't let us pass. If you don't leave the Hanged Man alone."

"Idiot. Don't you know what this means?" Nathan asked. "You've declared war."

The rough thump of paws on the floor distracted us all, and I finally followed Tyson's line of sight. A lion padded into view, massive beyond belief, tail flicking from side-to-side. It's shaggy golden mane was radiant by the light of the atrium above. It let out a roar that shook me to the bones.

Nathan stood his ground, hand moving to the hilt of his khopesh.

The lion gave a second roar, placing himself between us and Nathan. And then, it changed. The cracking of bones, retraction of fur, morphing of shape, elongation of the hind legs. A naked man stood in front of us. Ari's strong tan back, a tattoo of a lion etched into his skin.

"Stop." Ari's voice, deep and growling, rang with the Alpha tone.

Nathan glared at him. "You dare command me?"

"I dare," Ari replied. "If you attack members of the Hanged Man Society, you'll be in contravention of the War Act of 1356."

Nathan blinked. So did I. What the fuck was the War Act?

Tyson's eyes widened. Clearly, he knew what was going on.

"Fool," Nathan spat. "Those months spent in the dungeons have affected your mind. Tyson Davis' life is forfeit under the Council's ruling."

"The Amended War Act of 1945 provides that any and all members of opposing sides will, by law, and without interference from the governing Council, engage in either parley or open war until a victor is declared by blood or forfeit." Ari paused. "I submitted my declaration of war to the Council a half an hour ago. It was accepted."

Without interference from the governing Council? They couldn't touch us. The Council of Horus couldn't touch us or take Tyson now that he was back with the Hanged Man.

"As a member of the Hanged Man Society, Tyson is under our protection. So, you have a choice," Ari said in that growling tone. "You can fight me now, hope that you'll win, and take Tyson to the Council, or you can leave and fight another day."

Nathan's jaw worked, but no noise emerged from his lips.

"What's your decision?" Ari asked, tilting his head to one side.

For a man who was naked as the day he was born, he sure had a lot of presence.

"Evie isn't part of your society," Nathan said. "She doesn't belong."

"She's a recruit," Ari replied smoothly. "She belongs with us. Why else would she have risked life and limb to save a member of our society?"

Belongs. She belongs. My throat closed for a second. I had to breathe.

"Will you fight?" The nails on Ari's hands lengthened into claws. "Or will you retreat?"

"You choose them?" Nathan shot that over Ari's shoulder at me. "The psychopaths? The vampires? Blood-suckers? Flesh-eaters? Abominations? Hybrids?"

"The only psychopath here is you," I said, trembling all over. "You're just like your brother."

Nathan recoiled.

Ari growled, fur sprouting from around his throat. I had witnessed how powerful he was. He'd ripped solid metal shackles from around his ankles. He'd torn chains free of stone wall and broken down a door.

And Nathan? He could make illusions and shit, and that was about it. He was far outmatched, even with the khopesh.

"I'll find you, Evie," he said as he retreated toward the stairs. "At the end of all of this, you'll wish you'd chosen me."

42

The following morning...

THERE WASN'T a ceremony or a ritual where a man made me stand butt-naked with a card pressed to my chest. No binding of me to the Hanged Man. I had been officially assigned a room, told that my name would be submitted on the roster of Hanged Man acolytes, and that was it.

I was a part of the society. Most of the members, Christa, the twins, probably Walker too, didn't trust me, but that was fine.

I had a place to stay. A home. And the cards were mine.

But being part of the society came with its downsides, apparently. First, war on the horizon, and second, an ear-ache from the head of the society about my actions.

"I don't doubt that you thought this was the correct decision to make," King said, standing behind his chair in the office. "And as the General, you are in charge of war activities, but you went against a direct order, Son. You understand that means one of two things."

"I understand," Ari said.

I was next to him, my fingers interlaced, the cards under the sleeve of my leather jacket, against my skin.

"Either, you'll have to challenge me for the position of head of the society, or you'll be removed from the society entirely."

"What?" I gasped. "Ari. You can't—"

"Silence," King snapped. "If not for your rash actions, none of this would have happened."

I glared at him angrily. "I saved Tyson. And the cards. And we didn't tell them the riddle. Are you kidding me with this shit."

Ari laid a hand on my shoulder. "Not now, Evie. Wait."

I shrugged him off and rolled my eyes. "Everything around here is ass backward."

"Until you've spoken directly with Ma'at herself, face-to-face," King said, "I won't be accepting that assessment of our current situation. We will abide by the rules set out before us. And rules state that Ari must challenge me or be dismissed. Insubordination has no place in our society." King met his son's gaze stare for stare, an older, grizzlier version versus the younger, buffer one.

I could almost hear the lions growling.

"I challenge you," Ari said at last, the Alpha ring to his voice, "for the position of head of the society."

"I yield to your authority," King replied instantly.

And just like that, the anger and tension in the study dissolved. Ari circled around to meet his father and hugged him.

"I might not agree with the choice you've made," King said, "but I firmly believe that you will lead the society well. I can't do it any longer."

"You'll stay," Ari said. "For us. We could use your wisdom. Your advice. Right, Evie?"

"Right." I wasn't totally sure what had happened, other than the energy shift in the room, and the fact that Ari talked with even more authority now.

"I'll stay as long as this war continues. The society will always be my home," King said and took a seat on the side of the room.

Ari lowered himself into his father's chair, now his, I guessed, and I decided to sit too, just so I wouldn't be the only asshole standing in the place.

"What now?" I asked. "War? What does that mean to supernatural creatures?"

"It means," Ari said, "that we'll be in constant danger unless we're in the Academy. The War Act states that all battles must be taken above ground and not on society grounds. The Council is to act as an adjudicator."

"But they can't be trusted," I said.

"No, they can't. But they're unlikely to break a written law for fear that their popularity with the other societies would slip," Ari replied. "The point is, we've got to prepare to kick some Sword ass, and quickly. And you've got to find the rest of the Pharaonic Deck before they do."

The prospect should have scared me, but it brought a whole boatload of excitement instead. The cards felt like a part of me. "I'm good with that."

"What about the riddle?" King asked.

"Riddle?" Ari raised an eyebrow. It wasn't something we'd discussed during our imprisonment.

"I don't know if it was a riddle, but it was something the Serpentine Prince said to me before he died. In the long reeds, the marshland, the papyrus, grasped against her bosom."

Ari frowned. "No clue."

King shook his head as well.

"We'll have to discuss this with a Scholar." Ari sighed. "That's the only solution. We find the cards, and you'll be able to contact the Keeper and find out how we right the Council's wrongs."

I exhaled. It seemed like an insurmountable task, but I was ready for it.

I had found my place. I would do anything to keep it.

NIGHT TIME DESCENDED UPON THE HOUSE; THE NOISES OF banging and clattering below as the society members fixed the damage the Hierophant Society had caused had stopped hours ago. I sat on my bed with its cutesy yellow flowers, holding a single card from the Pharaonic Deck.

Justice.

She sat on a throne, one hand grasping a sword, the other holding scales, a lion accompanying her, a scarab etched beside her feet.

Justice.

Was this who I was meant to be? I didn't see how I could ever live up to it. This bitch had dark hair, gorgeous tan skin, and a wicked headdress with a cobra on it. Not only that, she was balanced. She understood the difference between right and wrong.

A knock rattled my door, and I frowned. It was past 3:00 a.m.

"Come in," I called, as quietly as I could.

The knob turned, the door opened, and Tyson entered, red eyes back to their usual level of brightness. And man, did he look good. His dark hair was wet as if he'd just gotten out of the shower, and he was topless, his pale torso muscular yet lean. A line of dark hair descended beneath the line of his cotton PJ pants, trailing from his navel.

I swallowed. "You sleep?"

"Hello to you too," Tyson laughed. "Yeah, I sleep. I'm a half-vampire. We have to sleep just like humans do."

"Oh. Bummer."

"Not really. I like sleeping. It's kind of like dying for a while."

"Is that why you came?" I asked, tucking the cards back into their velvet pouch, then placing them on my rickety bedside table. "To talk about death? Shit, you do think I'm evil, don't you? Come to kill me?" I was only half joking.

Tyson worked his tongue over his black teeth and fangs. "Actually, I came to thank you."

I swallowed my snappy retort.

"You didn't have to do what you did," he said. "I was willing to be the sacrifice. That's what the Hanged Man means. Sacrifice."

"Yeah, but if you're going to sacrifice yourself, it's got to be for a good cause. They had the cards. Where's the sense in dying for that?" I rose from the bed, hugging myself because his glare was a little too intense. The memory of his lips against my wrist, drinking my blood, made me blush.

"You started a war by saving me," Tyson continued.

"I guess that makes you Helen of Troy, right?" I joked.

"Let's not get ahead of ourselves here," Tyson said, drawing closer to me, the pressure of his presence growing. He had kept me glued since he'd entered the room. "Paris was in love with Helen of Troy."

"Right," I managed. "Well, the war was bound to happen anyway, right?"

"Are you usually this bad at accepting gratitude?" Tyson asked.

"I don't know. Maybe it's just the talking thing I'm bad at."

"OK." He crossed the distance between us, grabbed me by the waist and held me against his body. He brought his lips down on mine, a hot, breathless crush that sent pleasure spiraling through my stomach and down to the tips of my toes. He parted my lips roughly, massaging my tongue with his, driving my pulse through the roof.

Tyson lifted me off the floor an inch, kissing me, walking me backward until we slammed into the door itself. His hands roved over my throat, down to my breasts, cupping them, pinching my nipples gently against the cotton of my top.

As quickly as it had started, it ended. He set my feet on the ground and stepped back, touching fingers to his lips. "Thank you," he said, "for saving my life."

My knees knocked together, and I walked to my dressing table, grabbing it for support. "Uh, don't mention it."

"Next time I won't say a thing," he replied, with a slow grin, and then he left my bedroom and shut the door.

I threw myself onto the bed and groaned. I had just made

out with a half-vampire and loved every goddamn second of it.

A giggle escaped me, and I clamped a hand over my mouth. Out of all the paths I'd thought my life would take, this was the least expected, and the most welcome. Nothing was simple. And I kind of liked it that way.

The next book in the Tarot Societies series, Two Vampires and a Verdict, is out now. Click here to get it!

HUNGRY FOR MORE PAGE-TURNING URBAN FANTASY?

If you'd like another taste of what's in store for Evie, you can find me on my website at www.caitambrose.com.

Or you can head over to BookBub and follow me there for more updates about books and what's coming next.

GLOSSARY OF TERMS

Alpha—The leader of a group of soldiers, usually a shifter, though it's common for sorcerers or duelists to take on this role. In shifter groups, an Alpha is the leader of the pack. Alphas have the ability to push commands to their subordinates and expect complete obedience.

Duality—Apep and Atum. The original creative forces of chaos and order from which all Gods and Goddesses sprang forth in Egypt—the true location of the cradle of life.

Fae—Sons and daughters of Anat, the fae are natural creatures who take on qualities and powers of the natural world. They can take many forms but are distinct from shifters in that they are not bound by the same rules when shifting, and are not inherently human with an animal soul attached. They are inherently fae and can dwell in the fae realm without punishment.

Feather of Ma'at—Justice bringers. The Feathers of Ma'at were the original adjudicators of the supernatural races before their extinction after the Second Changing.

General—A military leader within a Tarot Society, charged with organizing war or defense, and running the day-to-day operations when it comes to bounty hunting for rogue elements or protecting the society's interests.

Gods and Goddesses—The pantheon of powers that be who helped bring forth the different races, but who have retreated beyond reach for an unknown reason.

Hybrids—Half-vampires, and, most recently, half-shifters and half-fae, who have been cropping up with increased frequency over the past few years.

The Council of Horus—The governing body that ensures all societies abide by the rules laid out by the Council and its predecessors. They communicate with society heads via the Society App.

Khopesh—A double-edged, sickle-shaped sword that originated in Egypt.

Leader—The leader or head of a Tarot Society.

Pharaonic Deck—A deck of tarot cards that can be used to contact the Keeper of the Book of Life and thus the Gods and Goddesses.

Scholar—A professor or teacher at the Academy of Scribes, whose task it is to educate the new acolytes of the Tarot Societies.

Shifter—An animal shifter. A human being tied to the soul of an animal through their connection to its ruling God or Goddess. Shifting between human and animal form uses a great deal of energy to accomplish.

Soldier—Cannon fodder. A moving part in the plans of the society Leader and General.

Sons of Sekhmet—Otherwise known as vampires, they are the descendants of the Goddess Sekhmet whose bloody attack on the people of Ancient Egypt has affected her progeny.

Steward—A member of a society who is responsible for the day-to-day running of the society itself, including financial obligations and payments. A desk job.

Tarot Societies—Societies of supernatural beings, including but not limited to: shifter, sorcerers, fae (on occasion), vampires, hybrids of every kind, and natural witches and wizards. Founded by the original owners of the Life Deck of tarot cards.

The Academy of Scribes—The Academy where supernatural beings go once they are of the correct age to leave their parents' homes, officially apply to a society, and join their peers to learn more about their existence and culture.

The Book of Life—A mysterious book that holds the answers. Or more questions.

The Keeper—The Keeper of the Book of Life. A being who holds answers. Or, once again, more questions. Can only be contacted by a Feather of Ma'at holding all the cards of a Pharaonic Deck.

MAGIC SYSTEM

Magic is split into two main divisions. It can either be **Physical**, meaning it creates a physical effect on the world surrounding it, or it can be **Mental**, meaning it affects the minds targeted by it, whether that's a lot of minds or few.

Mental magic takes a great deal of energy. **Physical magic** also uses energy but is less punishing unless it is used for several actions in a row.

Energy can be regained by consuming food, or by the use of drugs that negatively impact a sorcerer/practitioner's body and mind if used frequently.

	Mental	Physical
Destruction	Destruction of the mind of a target. Complete collapse. Internal organ failure.	Destruction of the external body, of buildings, or things. Can take many forms, burning, breaking, freezing, etc.
Illusion	Creation of images that are in the mind of the target and not externalized. Placing the target in a trance, rendering them unconscious.	Creation of images or illusions that are external to the target. Images or effects that appear real but are not. Illusion can also be used to render people or things invisible, including the caster.
Defense	Defense of mental attacks for self and others. Healing of mental ailments. Cleaning of the mind.	Defense of physical attacks. Summoning of physical shields to protect self or others.
Malleation	Reading minds, controlling minds, the ability to contact Gods and Goddesses with Tarot Decks via the manipulation of one's own mind.	Including controlling objects with the ability to destroy, create, change, rebuild. Changing of natural and artificial objects.

Table 1. The four types of magic classes and their effects when employed mentally or physically.

www.ingramcontent.com/pod-product-compliance
Lightning Source LLC
Chambersburg PA
CBHW021108110726
47900CB00007B/2086